Silverwood

D. E. VOLLRATH

WICKED PIG PUBLISHING

ISBN-10: 0692444335
ISBN-13: 978-0692444337

Cover Design by www.ebooklaunch.com

To Abigail and Madeline,
who would drink books if they could

CHAPTER 1

————

INTO THE CITY

WITH a lurch the small horse-cab crested the hill and came to a halt. Eleanor Wigton climbed down from the cab and reveled for a moment in the fact that she was no longer bouncing up and down on the hard wooden seat. Uncle William had dismounted as well, and was offering the horse a few bites of carrot. It seemed to Eleanor to be a meager reward for the long slog up a steep, rock-strewn cart track.

Before them the hill fell towards a river below. Following the water upstream Eleanor could make out the city of Flosston Moor, centered upon a triangle of land formed where the Silver River emptied itself into the larger Heartwick. From here most of the city was just a brown smudge smeared across the two rivers, but Eleanor could make out the stiff grey ribbons of the bridges that connected the center of the city to the banks.

Running her eyes towards the north-west she could also pick out a black lump lying hard along the bank of the Silver River, surrounded by a swath of green that stood out from the other dark colors of the city. Penwick Academy, where in a few days she would start her second year of studies.

"Can't make out much from here," said her uncle, coming to stand next to her and stare down at the city. "But I think you can see the Lord Steward's tower there," he said, pointing

1

towards the point of the triangle between the rivers.

"Yes," she said absently and continued to stare down at Penwick.

"Getting a little anxious about school?" Uncle William asked, nudging her with his elbow. She smiled at him but didn't respond. She was a little anxious, although not nearly as bad as last year when she had arrived for her first year. Now it was a combination of nerves at beginning new classes mixed with an excitement at seeing the school for the first time since last spring.

"Well, it's not terrible to have some nerves. Keeps you on your toes, you know," her uncle continued. "Second year's a big step up in difficulty and work. The teachers will be expecting you to focus even harder now they know you've got the skills."

"I know," she said, rolling her eyes a little. This was something Uncle William had mentioned perhaps five times a day all summer. He had attended Penwick years ago, and felt this had given him the ability and duty to pass along these nuggets of advice to his niece. And while they could get repetitive, Eleanor couldn't stay annoyed with him too long. They had been very close her whole life, and she took great pride in sharing his quick intellect and sponge-like memory. She loved her parents and her brothers, but none of them understood her desire to spend six years buried under books at Penwick the way Uncle William did. They even looked somewhat alike, with brown eyes, lanky frames, and straight hair that was either blond or brown depending on how you looked at it. The innkeeper last night had

2

mistaken them for father and daughter, and that was not the first time it had happened to them.

"No sense lingering, now. We can get to Mr. Adler's before nightfall," said her uncle, and he swung himself back up onto the buckboard of the cab. Eleanor followed and the horse headed off down the hill. The road here was far less bumpy, thankfully, as the hillsides had all been picked clear for building stones over the years. The path became sturdier and the land to either side looked tidier as they headed down. Plantations of grapes or fruit trees lay on either side of them now, interspersed with smaller farms whose cows watched as they clopped by.

There wasn't much to do but stare out at her surroundings, and Eleanor found her mind wandering. A notch in one of the wheels made a rhythmic clack that eventually wormed its way into her consciousness and called up an old song that her grandfather had taught her. It was a silly rhyming song, and he always made up new verses when Eleanor visited.

> Lady Asmerada was born in a box
> When it was cold she wore no socks
> She always donned the finest clothes
> But had no ears and a long black nose

Besides Lady Asmerada there was Captain Murphy and his floppy ears, Billy Bumphill with very long legs, Misses Grouper and her crooked teeth, and perhaps fifty more verses. She ran through many of them in her head to pass the time, humming the tune with the wheel knocking out the rhythm. Singing the songs relieved the boredom but left her feeling down. Her grandfather

3

had taught her the rhyme about Lady Asmerada just before he died; it was almost six years ago but she still missed visiting him at his cottage by the sea.

She distracted herself from those thoughts by studying the landscape. It was now late afternoon and the larger farms had disappeared. They saw only rows and rows of vegetables, corn, and tomatoes running in between farm houses that were in distinctly better shape than those farther back on the road. They passed through several clusters of buildings formed around little village squares, with pubs, post offices, and a few shops. The road had improved to crushed gravel as well, and the traffic had increased with wagons full of produce rolling towards Flosston Moor. The road was wide enough in parts that her uncle could skitter their little two-wheeled cab around the slower wagons, and as the sun started to dip towards the horizon they found themselves in the outskirts of the city proper.

The roadway abruptly turned to cobblestones and the spaces between buildings disappeared to nothing as they continued on. The thatched roofs they had seen in the morning were absent and red tiles were now the norm. Alleys and streets intersected the main road often. Most of the houses were three stories, with each one sticking out farther into the street than the one below. At times the eaves would brush those of the opposite house and the street turned into a tunnel of wood beams and plaster.

As they neared the center of the city a sign with a scribbled arrow on it pointed out that The Black Square lay ahead. Clattering on behind a string of delivery carts, they emerged after a few blocks into the expanse of the Square itself. In the center of the Square was a fenced-off patch of grass and flowers, above which rose a scarred and broken tumble of stones that appeared to be the skeleton of an old house. The stones at the bottom were stained with black soot and those above had licks of the same soot spattered across them. The ruined house stood as a monument to those lost hundreds of years ago during the Burning, when a squabble among the wizards at the White Tower had plunged the entire city into a inferno that raged for ten days. The heat of the fire was so great that it cracked the foundation stones of the house in the square and many others like it.

Circling the monument they took the western outlet of the square and headed off down Norfolk Road. This was the nicest section of the city they had passed through yet, with the rows of houses and shops standing next to each other like soldiers at attention. The shops sold brass fixtures, optical instruments, and clocks, among other things. The strange smells of the apothecaries mingled with the odors of tobacco and coffee coming from the cafes that had kept their windows propped open on the pleasant summer evening.

A few blocks later her uncle slowed down the horse cab - much to the consternation of the man driving the wagon behind them, judging by his language - as the cobbled street was obstructed by a canvas tent. There was the sound of hammers against stone as well as what looked like steam rising from an opening in the top of the tent. They waited on the cab while a crowd of pedestrians, a few other horse cabs, and several empty wagons squeezed past the tent going in the opposite direction.

There were torches or lamps inside the tent and every now and then someone would move in front of one, and Eleanor would see their silhouette against the side of the tent. It took three or four before she realized they weren't human shapes.

"Dwarves!" she blurted out.

"Of course," said Uncle William. "Probably had some problem with the water system that required them to come above ground. They can't be happy about that."

"I think this is the closest I've ever come to actually seeing one," said Eleanor. The dwarves, many people would tell you, were the real reason that Flosston Moor was the biggest city along the coast. They had lived in a network of caves underneath the city for centuries, creating underground spillways that siphoned off water from the rivers that they then sifted for gold and silver running down from the White Mountains. For nearly the last hundred years, though, they had also been employed by the Lord Steward to build and maintain a water and sewer system for the entire city. It had allowed the city's population to explode without leading to a messy disaster.

The dwarves were notoriously private. They avoided coming above ground at all costs, and disliked interacting with humans. For them to be working at street level, even behind the tent, meant that there must have been a severe problem with the water pipes in this neighborhood. From the conversations of the people waiting to pass by the tent it sounded as if last night the main pipe had exploded, sending a geyser of cold water onto the surrounding buildings.

"That would almost have to be deliberate," said her uncle. "The dwarves are not known to use flimsy material for this kind of work. I can't see how they would have allowed such shoddy workmanship."

Before Eleanor could reply a uniformed Warden came past the tent and started waving them through. The crowd of pedestrians that had built up around them started to surge forward and they clopped along with the other wagons. The fit was so tight Eleanor felt that she could have reached out her hand and touched the tent as they went by. She heard the grunts of the dwarves at work only a few feet away and wondered if she'd ever see one up close.

After making it past the tent they plodded ahead a few more blocks. By now they were only about a quarter of a mile from reaching the great bridge that would take them across to the Point, the triangle of land between the rivers where the Steward's castle loomed over the city. They turned, though, short of the bridge, taking a right onto what was called a street but only deserved to be called an alley. It was just wide enough for the horse cab to fit. There was almost no traffic here and the shops they passed by looked quiet and empty. Just near the end of the block her uncle pulled the cab up in front of a narrow three-story building with a single window on the first floor and a short flight of stone steps leading up to the door. Hung from the inside of the window were two great maps, one appearing to be a street map of Flosston Moor itself, and the other a set of islands that she did not recognize at all. Stenciled onto the glass pane in the door was, "Dominick Adler, Cartographer".

Her uncle jumped down and stepped up to the door, next to which hung a thin rope that emerged from just above. He gave the rope a quick pull and then turned and gave her a reassuring smile. After a moment there was a fumbling sound from inside, and the door cracked open to reveal a small woman who looked to be the age of Eleanor's grandmother. She had on an apron over a pale red dress and wiped her hands on it before she shook hands with Eleanor's uncle.

"Ah, Mr. Wigton, sir. So excellent to see you again," said the old woman.

"You too, of course, Mrs. Hill," her uncle replied, breaking into a smile, "I hope we didn't disturb you at all."

"Don't be silly, young man," she said, matching Uncle Williams smile with one of her own, "we've been looking forward to your visit ever since your wrote. Mr. Adler will be tickled you're here."

Eleanor's uncle waved to her to come down off the cab and she hopped down onto the cobbles and came up the steps.

"This is my niece, Eleanor, Mrs. Hill," said her uncle, "She'll be starting her second year at Penwick in a few days."

"Well, of course," said Mrs. Hill, "it's a pleasure to meet you, young lady."

"You as well," said Eleanor, shaking the hand Mrs. Hill had offered. She immediately had a very warm impression of the old lady, perhaps because the apron and smell of something baking put her in mind of home.

"I hear you're taking the school by storm," said Mrs. Hill, giving her an approving nod. Taking Eleanor's shoulders in her hands she gave her a long look up and down. "Unfortunately, it looks as if no one's bothered to feed you anything. Did you let the poor girl eat at all today, Mr. Wigton?" she said, giving her uncle an exasperated stare.

"Two full meals, Mrs. Hill, I swear," he said, holding his hand over his heart.

"Likely story," she clucked back. Taking Eleanor by the arm she led them into the house, "Now then, sweetheart, I've made up something simple for dinner tonight. I've always found that a big meal after a long journey upsets my stomach a bit."

Mrs. Hill spoke as if they had known each other their whole lives. They walked down a short hallway which led to a staircase next to an open door. The most wonderful smells of baking bread were coming through the doorway.

"Reuben!" Mrs. Hill shouted up the stairs. A muffled "Eh?" came from upstairs. "Reuben, the Wigton's are here. Go outside, take the cab around back and bring up their things." Another muffled reply was followed by some indistinct thumping that seemed to indicate Reuben was moving.

Having settled that, Mrs. Hill steered Eleanor through the door and into a small sitting room. There were two large armchairs arranged on either side of a circular table that held a stack of maps, pencils, and rulers. They were the only disorderly things in the room, which otherwise was very tidy and well-kept.

9

"Mr. Adler won't let me touch his work," said Mrs. Hill, feeling a need to explain how such a mess was allowed in the house, "as he claims there's a system to it." Eleanor snickered a little. She had heard her uncle claim the same thing when anyone attempted to sort through his study.

"Now, if the two of you don't mind, have a seat here. Although after a few days riding in that cab, I won't blame you if you'd rather keep to standing for a while. I've got a few things to finish up in the kitchen. Mr. Adler should be home any moment now, and we'll get you all a nice dinner after that long day." With a great smile she whisked out of the sitting room into an adjacent dining room, and from there disappeared into the back of the house from where the smells of bread kept emanating.

Eleanor decided that keeping her body upright a bit longer was wise, and began scanning the various maps hung on the walls while her uncle hung up their coats on the hooks in the corner. Most of the maps were nautical charts with a host of markings and symbols that Eleanor found unintelligible. Some appeared to be of the area surrounding the mouth of the Heartwick River, which was about a days ride south of Flosston Moor. Others, she guessed, were of areas farther up and down the coast from there. Half appeared to be the work of Mr. Adler himself, while most of the rest were signed by someone named Mortimer Hassleford.

"So, Eleanor," said her uncle, coming up to stand next to her in front of one obtuse chart, "going to consider choosing Navigation as your specialty next year?"

"Hardly, this all seems so cryptic," she said, "And maybe

10

I should get through this year before I start deciding on which Hall I'm going to enter next year."

"Well, never too early to think about what you'd like to do," he said, "If you make such good grades again you'll pretty much be able to choose any Hall you'd like."

"And by 'any' Hall, you mean Numerancy," she said, knowing that her uncle, as much as he tried to stay neutral on the subject, hoped for her to join his old Hall.

"What, did I say that?" he said, trying to look innocent. "But now that you bring it up, it is an excellent Hall and a very interesting topic. A Numerist is a very valuable member of the community."

The rest of his standard speech on the many important contributions a Numerist could make was interrupted by the sound of the front door opening. A moment later a man her uncle's age, but with far more gray hairs evident, came through the door.

"William," he said, taking her uncle's hand, "I'm so happy to have you here. I'm sorry I wasn't here to greet you."

"Not at all, Dominick. Mrs. Hill has, as usual, been an excellent host. We were just admiring your excellent handiwork here."

"You are too kind," said Mr. Adler, making a slight bow. He turned towards Eleanor and she saw a shy intellectual man very similar to her uncle. She could see why they had found each other at school.

"You," he said, smiling, "must be Eleanor. I'm Dominick

11

Adler, and as long as you are here please treat this house like your own. And," he said, giving her uncle a nudge with his elbow, "as I've had the misfortune of knowing your uncle here for many years, please feel free to ask me for as many embarrassing stories about him as possible."

He laughed and some of his shyness melted away. With a light touch he guided Eleanor into the dining room and her uncle followed behind. Sensing that they had settled themselves at the table Mrs. Hill appeared from the kitchen door with a tray of appetizers: fresh apricots and several types of cheese that Eleanor did not recognize, but which tasted fantastic and foreign.

After the long day of traveling Eleanor was content to sit quietly and enjoy Mrs. Hill's superb meal. While she sipped the soup that arrived next, her uncle and Mr. Adler bantered back and forth about a variety of mutual friends, some of whom they had attended Penwick with, and others she had never heard of. They made it to the main course of a simple roast chicken without Eleanor doing much more than mutter a few affirmatives in support of her uncle.

It was a typical meal for her in that way. She had always been quiet, and tended to be an observer, a listener. It was responsible, she knew, for the academic success she had enjoyed last year at Penwick. Sitting and paying attention were bound to help one with the reams of information that had to be memorized and processed at the school. On the other hand, they were not qualities that made someone particularly popular, and Eleanor had remained a bit of a loner throughout her first year. No one had ever been mean to her, that was true, but neither had she become fast friends with many of her first-year classmates, except her roommate Miriam. There were days in which this bothered her more than others, days when she wished she were more rambunctious and outgoing even at the expense of success in class. It wasn't every day, though, and most of the time she was quite content to be "shy Eleanor" and sit observing everything around her.

There were benefits to that attitude and they came into focus now. The two older men were becoming more and more engaged in conversation, and in doing so had become less aware of her presence. This meant that they had turned to topics, and expressed opinions, that otherwise not have been spoken of in front of a twelve year old.

"What's the thought around town about young Henry Norfolk?" her uncle was asking. She recognized the name. Henry Norfolk was the only son of the Lord Steward of Flosston Moor, and as the Lord Steward had recently fallen ill, Henry was likely to become the new Lord Steward sooner rather than later.

"Same as it has been since he was old enough to slip out alone," said Mr. Adler. "He's a drunk and an idiot, and God help us when he takes up residence in the Tower."

"Must be some of his father's people that can keep him from doing anything too stupid, now, can't there?" her uncle asked.

"You'd hope. Except that Henry's always been at odds with the Steward, and it wouldn't surprise me if he sacks the whole

13

staff just because they remind him of the old man. Most of them have not been too kind to him. Don't forget that the Sheriff has personally put Henry behind bars."

"Right, right," said her uncle, with a look on his face that suggested there was a whole lot more to that story. "Still, he must understand that it's in his best interest to keep the city running along smoothly."

"I'd like to think so, William, but he keeps some odd company. Keeps a room down along the wharves, close to all the pubs the sailors frequent. Worse, people tell me he's been spending a lot of time down in the Warren."

"Sorcerers?" her uncle blurted out. Eleanor was surprised as well. There were many neighborhoods in Flosston Moor that students at Penwick were not supposed to visit, but the Warren was at the top of the list. It was a nest of ancient stone buildings south of the school, and as the Headmistress would remind everyone at the opening convocation, a haven of thieves, smugglers, and those who purported to work magic.

"If you'd like to call them that," Mr. Adler was replying. "Most of them today are just charlatans, fakes with quick hands looking for easy marks. I'm not sure what's worse, actually. That Henry is stupid enough to get fooled by some con artist, or that he's doing business with wizards in the White Tower."

Eleanor absorbed the last comment with interest. She and her classmates had often speculated on whether there still were any wizards left in the White Tower. They could see it from the astronomy tower at Penwick. It was this odd, gnarled growth

14

that looked like an old tree trunk rising up out of the Warren. It may have been white once, a long time ago, but now it had the brown and grey look of many of the old buildings in that area of the city. Every now and then someone would claim to have seen a burst of light or a puff of smoke coming out of some hidden window, but none of the students had really ever believed it. Mr. Adler appeared to think that there was someone in there, perhaps helping to lead Henry Norfolk astray.

"Well," said her uncle, "I guess we can hope the old Steward hangs on a while longer, then." Mr. Adler grunted an agreement as he drained his glass, and before he could say anything more definitive Mrs. Hill had bustled into the room with a tray full of desserts.

Eleanor took a piece of lemon cake while her uncle and Mr. Adler helped themselves to pie and more wine. The conversation drifted away from the political and on to odds and ends from around the city. The long day and large meal had started to wear on Eleanor's concentration, so it took her a second to process the fact that someone had spoken her name.

"So Eleanor," said Mr. Adler, "has your uncle been pressing you already about joining the Numerancy Hall?"

She blushed a little at the attention. "Not too badly, sir," she said.

"Let me guess," continued Mr. Adler, sitting up straight and doing a decent impression of her uncle's voice, "Eleanor, Numerancy is a very valuable speciality. You know there is a lot more than simple accounting involved, and Numerancy provides

15

an excellent base upon which you can establish any number of careers."

She laughed in spite of herself, as this was a word-for-word recitation of her uncle's regular speech on the subject. She tried to suppress the giggle, but then Mr. Adler brushed aside the hair on his forehead in a dead-on impersonation of her uncle's habitual move and she could not help herself at all. Her uncle was a good sport about it and joined in with the laugh, telling Mr. Adler that he'd find a way to return the favor some day.

"Well, not today, you won't, William," said Mrs. Hill as she came through the kitchen door once more, "It's high time we get this young lady upstairs. She's probably exhausted and you two are just going to spend the night telling the same ridiculous stories you do every time you see each other."

From the tone of voice it was clear that Mrs. Hill did not intend to be argued with, and Eleanor excused herself as she tried to settle down the last giggle. With Mrs. Hill hustling up the stairs behind her, she found her way to a small guest room where her bag had been set on a luggage rack and the bed turned down. After assuring Mrs. Hill repeatedly that she would be quite all right with the accommodations, Eleanor prepared herself for bed. It had been a long day, and although she was quite tired rest did not come. The anxiety and excitement of heading back to Penwick tomorrow fluttered around in her mind until long after the long summer sunlight had faded into black.

CHAPTER 2

THE CONVOCATION

BREAKFAST was run with an efficiency that made Eleanor suspect Mrs. Hill would have made a fine ship captain. They did not see Mr. Adler, who it seemed had gone back out last night to attend to some business and was therefore sleeping in a little late. This, according to Mrs. Hill, was a common event for him as the ship captains who purchased his works were always in a rush to leave.

"Of course, that has almost nothing to do with changes in tides," Mrs. Hill clucked as she swept around the table. "Most likely they've lost at dice, or started a fight in some tavern, or are anxious to be gone before the moneylenders find out they're in town." Eleanor and her uncle could do little more than nod in agreement and finish their eggs.

"Now, you two take your time doing your shopping. I'll have Reuben bring your cab around once you're ready to head over to the school." Mentioning his name had seemed to alert Mrs. Hill to some other chore that needed his attention, and as she disappeared through the kitchen door they could here her shouting for Reuben out the back door.

"Well, then," said her uncle, "if you're all set, let's get to it." They cleared their dishes onto the tray in the corner, and made their way out the front door into the narrow side street.

17

To their right they could already make out the bustling activity of Norfolk Road at the end of the block.

They approached the busy street and paused for a moment. The push of people and carts in both directions made Norfolk Road seem almost impenetrable from their vantage point. Trying to find a way down the massive avenue without being bumped or nudged would have been like trying to walk through the rain and not get wet. So after a deep breath they plunged in, heading to the right towards the center of the city. They only had a few blocks to go and the natural movement of the crowd carried them along. For a few minutes they were able to find a peaceful spot in the wake of a horse-cart full of barrels but it turned soon afterwards and they were plunged forward again by the waves of people.

Finally her uncle pointed and shouted in her ear, "Over there!", and they did their best to muscle their way to the very side of the street where several shops stood with wrought-iron fences around small patios fended off the surrounding crowds. Making their way through a gate, they found their way into a little pool of calm.

They were in front of Elmer Squint's Stationery. There were not a lot of requirements for Penwick students, but a ready supply of paper and pencils was a necessity. The windows of the shop were stacked with stiff cardboard boxes of paper on top of which sat racks of pencils of various shapes and sizes. Eleanor and her uncle pulled open the door, ringing a small bell, and a dark-haired man with his sleeves rolled up and wearing a long apron appeared out of the back.

"Hello, welcome to Squint's," he said, his tiny body maneuvering around several piles of boxes to reach the space in front of a small counter. "How may I help you today?"

"Eleanor?" said her uncle, giving a nod towards the man, who was wiping little wood shavings off of the back of his hand.

"Right," she said. Eleanor's uncle had a habit of doing this. He knew she was shy and would force her into interacting with others. She reviewed her list in her head before speaking. "I would like three reams of Cartesian white, as well as one ream of calculating paper, one-quarter inch squares. And do you carry Astronomy pads that include longitudinal rules?"

The shopkeeper had been nodding along as she ordered. "Absolutely, young lady. We just brought in a stock of them last week, anticipating the demand. I assume you're a Penwick student, then?"

"Yes, I am," replied Eleanor.

"Well, then I wish you the best on your studies. While I get together the paper, would you like to browse through the pencils? I'll point out that we've got a new box of Silverwood reds. The real things, mind you, not the counterfeit ones you'll find in other shops." This last part was said with the air of someone with firm ideas about pencils.

As he rumbled about the store, slipping boxes of paper out of piles that by some miracle stayed upright, Eleanor and her uncle bent over the counter looking over the various boxes of pencils on display. The Silverwood reds were quite attractive, and taking one in her hand Eleanor felt the weight was just right. Jacob Weatherby, a boy in her class, had a Silverwood red. He claimed that he had never had to sharpen it the entire year even though he used for all his classwork. He said that sprites in Silverwood had enchanted great redwood trees to grow the pencils like little branches. When they had gotten to the right length the sprites snipped them off, polished them, and sold them on to merchants. Eleanor didn't believe it was true, but they were very nice pencils. Last year she had gone through an entire box of twenty Fingerling Number Fives and by June she was working with tiny nubs of lead.

"You look smitten, Eleanor," said her uncle.

She looked at him, hopeful. He'd appreciate a solid argument, preferably one that showed she had thought it through like a Numerist. Thinking a second she thought she had it. "Well, they are very nice. But also much more expensive than standard models. However, rather than having to buy a box of twenty, I would only need one, and maybe a second just in case. In addition, these last so long that we wouldn't have to buy new pencils next year, either. It seems like they might be a wise investment."

Her uncle regarded her for a second, and then seemed gave the slightest nod of his head. "You're on to me, Eleanor. But that makes good sense. Let's get you two this year. But," he said, pointing his slim finger down at the case of Silverwoods, "I expect that you will treat these accordingly - as investments. They are not to be left jostling around loose in the bottom of some rucksack."

She flashed a smile at him. "Thank you."

The shopkeeper trundled up behind the counter, the five reams of paper Eleanor had ordered bound up with twine. "Now," he said, "what can I offer you to write on this fine paper with?"

"I'd like two of the Silverwood reds, sir," Eleanor said.

"Ah, excellent," said the shopkeeper as he extracted two of them from the little display rack. "If you don't mind, I over-heard your conversation, and they should be treated with care. These are quite valuable. I have, somewhere...." he said as his head disappeared behind the counter and they could hear him rummaging around in some boxes. "Aha! I have a perfect box for you. Holds two pencils, and will keep yours nice and safe as you move about school. That's on the house, for you." He handed over a sturdy if somewhat nicked up black box. It had two little brass clasps on one side. The shopkeeper popped them open and nestled two of the Silverwoods into the case, closed it up, and handed it over to Eleanor.

"You keep them in good condition and they can keep you safe," said the shopkeeper. Seeing the confused look on Eleanor's face, he continued. "The lore is that Silverwood can absorb magic. Just a story, of course, but just in case you run into any wizards from the Warren you can fight them off with these," he said, chuckling.

"Thank you, sir, very much," she said.

"Think nothing of it, young lady," he replied. When her uncle had paid, and taken hold of the reams of paper, the shopkeeper disappeared again into the back of the shop.

"Well then," said her uncle, "we've got a few more shops to visit, don't we? Best be on our way."

They made their way back out into the hubbub of activity on Norfolk Road. They stopped by a cobbler to pick up new shoes for Eleanor, as a growth spurt this summer had left her existing pair snug around her toes. They also procured a small mirror for the wall of her new dormitory room, as well as a supply of candles that could be used at her desk. Having wandered up and down Norfolk Road the entire morning they sat down at a small cafe set off on a quiet side street and enjoyed lunch while their feet were able to rest. Once the final plates were cleared away Uncle William gathered up several bundles and Eleanor loaded her arms up with the rest.

"Now," said her uncle, "all we need to do is get you to school." Eleanor felt a leap in her stomach at that. It was again a combination of anxiety and excitement. She would no longer be one of the first-year students paraded in front of everyone at the opening convocation and stumbling about the grounds in search of classrooms. She would be allowed into the library without an escort, and could choose to study in her room at night rather than in the first-year common area. She would be treated, she thought, more like an adult.

"Then we should get going," said Eleanor and they weaved their way as best they could, loaded down with packages, through the crowd on Norfolk Road. With a little effort they mad their way back to the alley where Mr. Adler lived.

Arriving at the front door a quick tug of the bell-rope brought Mrs. Hill, who insisted they pile their goods inside the entry-way and sent them scurrying upstairs to retrieve their remaining things while she rushed off to the rear of the house. Eleanor could hear Mrs. Hill yelling for Reuben to bring the horse-cab around as she packed her clothes into her small bag and headed downstairs.

"Mr. Adler apologizes that he can't be here to see you off, but he had to be out for a meeting," said Mrs. Hill as Eleanor and her uncle stood with their bags in the entryway. "You," she said, looking right at Eleanor, "take care of yourself. Be careful to eat enough, it will keep your energy up. And vegetables, make sure you eat plenty of them as well."

"I will," said Eleanor and, surprising even herself a little, gave Mrs. Hill a hug.

"You know," said Mrs. Hill, "that you are always welcome here, and if you ever need something do not hesitate to send a note."

"You're too kind, Mrs. Hill," said Uncle William, "I appreciate it."

"Don't be silly, Mr. Wigton," she replied, straightening her apron. "You may need all the help you can get, but your niece seems like a wonderfully capable young lady."

Eleanor gave her uncle a quick look, but he was taking the ribbing in stride. "I will miss you too, Mrs. Hill," he said, and led Eleanor out the front door to find the horse cab tied to a small post at the foot of the stairs. He heaved the bags into the rear area where Reuben had already stowed their packages from the morning.

"Thank you, Mrs. Hill," said Eleanor, waving, and they trotted off down the alley towards Norfolk Road. At the corner Eleanor was surprised to see the thoroughfare calm, perhaps as people were still indoors for lunch. Regardless, with the good fortune of light traffic they were quickly down the road and found themselves at the foot of what was formally known as the Ravenna Greyjoy Lovelock Heartwick Bridge, but which all the locals called the Heartspan. It was wide enough for three wagons to drive abreast across the tightly fitted cobblestones. The bridge reached a height of twenty feet above the waters of the Heartwick, which was at least two hundred yards across at this point. They could not see them as they trotted over, but the bridge was supported by ten massive columns of stone that the dwarves had sunk into the riverbed wide enough apart to allow small barges and boats to pass through.

As they crested the bridge and began to descend they had a full view of the Stewards' Castle occupying the point of land that sat where the Silver River joined the Heartwick to head down to the sea. The castle had seven slender towers in its perimeter wall, and from within that wall rose the great Stewards Tower, a massive four-sided block topped out with an Observatory that spilled across the top of the tower and was open to the sky to allow a full view of the heavens. Despite this Eleanor could see that almost all of the telescopes were pointed downriver towards the sea. The Steward cared less these days about charting stars

24

than about identifying ships coming up the Heartwick towards the wharves that spread out down the banks to the south of the city proper. People said that from the height of the Tower on a clear day the Steward could identify ships that were as many as five days out.

Coming down the bridge they entered the area people called the Point, just to the north of the Steward's castle. The road remained wide and paved with the same brown cobbles that were used on the bridge. To their right lay the homes of some of the wealthiest residents of Flosston Moor. They were cramped together, similar to those across the rest of the city. Their wealth was represented not so much by the decadence of the architecture but by proximity to the castle. To their left the castle proper lay about three blocks away but the intervening area was populated by a nest of various offices and departments that supported the Steward in his governing of the sprawl of Flosston Moor. Moving about were numerous Wardens in the red and black livery of the Steward. Outnumbering them by a factor of ten to one were citizens and functionaries, the former hoping to convince the latter to fund some local project or another. In and amongst the general throng were knots of sailors being led to or from hearings regarding some dispute about gambling or ships pay.

Eleanor stared and took in the scene as they picked their way across the Point. The amount of activity centered on the Steward's castle was at once both exhilarating and disturbing. A Norfolk had served as Steward for one hundred years even though the office was not traditionally hereditary. However, when Samuel Norfolk had arrived back from the Cinnamon Islands with his holds full of not only the namesake spice but several other varieties that no one had ever even heard of before, he had risen to become not only the wealthiest but the most powerful man in Flosston Moor. Within several years the King had approved his appointment as Steward and since then the Norfolks had held onto the office with a tight fist. Few would argue with the arrangement, it was true, as Flosston Moor had gone from a sleepy port town to the largest trading city along the entire Mandlebar coast. The Norfolks dredged the river and built the wharves. They contracted with the dwarves to install the sewer systems and replaced the old ferries with massive bridges. In the end, to get anything done one had to work through the Stewards office and the Norfolk family. But looking around, Eleanor thought, you couldn't deny that things did get done.

They passed by the last of the outbuildings of the castle and came upon the second bridge, the Silverspan, which had not even been given a full name after everyone realized it would never be called anything else. The Silver River was not as wide as the Heartwick and the bridge was not as impressive. The horse clopped over it and they found themselves on the west bank of the river. Once across the change in the tenor of the city was palpable. The traffic was slower, the crowds smaller, and the buildings were older. Down the riverside to their left ran some small wharves and Eleanor could see the outskirts of the Warren, whose ancient stone buildings climbed across each other like plants searching for the sun.

Turning instead to the right as they came off the bridge, they followed a street full of smaller shops, each set into buildings that were constructed of great irregular stones rather than the uniform bricks that made up most of the rest of the city. There were patches of moss on many of the storefronts, and great vines snaked their way up the front of most, hiding the upper floors behind plumes of green. The avenue they were traveling down now had once been the commercial center of the city before Samuel Norfolk changed everything. Here the shops tended to be family businesses from five or six generations back, and there were particular residents of this section of town that took great pride in not having crossed the Silverspan in years.

As the rows of shops petered out the most ancient resident of this part of the city loomed in front of them: Penwick Academy. The stones of the school were black from centuries of weathering. A low wall just barely taller than Eleanor's uncle ran around the grounds of the school, which sat wedged between the riverbank and a small hill. As they approached up the road Eleanor could make out Morgan Hall set behind the main gate.

Off to the left of Morgan Hall were several smaller class buildings including one with a thin spire emerging out of its center, the Astronomy Tower. Behind them all, built up against the hill itself was the Library. However, it was far more than just a collection of books. It consisted of a whole series of separate buildings that clustered together against the hillside like mushrooms. Each individual one had the style and architecture of the year in which is was built, and as they spanned centuries it created a riot of conflicting colors and textures.

At the front of the Library stood the Entry Hall, constructed only one hundred and fifty years ago. It was a formal looking white marble building with two stately columns guarding the heavy wooden doors set behind them. It represented the only way into the mass of interlocking libraries, which poked up above the Entry Hall as if they were trying to spy over its shoulder. The first of those nosy constructions was the New South Library, a plain looking brick building with tiny windows set at uneven intervals running up its facade. The New South Library was itself three hundred years old, and the Old South Library that was just visible next to it was another three hundred years older, its gray stones showing every year. No one enjoyed going into the Old South Library as the drafts were awful in the winter, and it was always damp and dark.

Also visible right behind the Entry Hall was the Solarium, built of large white-colored stones but looking much more spry than the Old South Library. The top floor was encased in a greenhouse where Apothecary students learned to raise the plants that they then ground, mushed, ripped, and burned up in order to create various ointments and medicines. Below that, the floors of the Solarium held not books but racks and racks of dried plants and a collection of preserved insects, birds, and small animals.

The other library visible to Eleanor and her uncle as they rolled through the gates of Penwick was the Navigation Tower, a slim building trimmed out with lustrous dark wood brought back from the Cinnamon Islands and topped with a series of flagpoles at which students would practice signaling. Below were floors full of shallow but wide drawers holdings maps of anywhere one could think of in the world. There was also a floor devoted to nautical instruments such as telescopes and sextants. Included there were samples of clocks used to keep accurate time on board ships, useful in calculating their longitude. You had to be careful to not be there on the hour, as the entire floor erupted into a cacophony of bells and whistles to mark the time.

Hidden behind those buildings were at least twenty more libraries, housing other specialty collections. The exact count wasn't known. The builders of the libraries had not only chosen to use different styles, but had shown an almost pathological dislike of the other buildings, trying to muscle them out of view. The result of this was that some of the earliest libraries were completely surrounded and cut off. It was said that they had completely forgotten to cut doors and passageways into one of the oldest, and it stood like a tomb of unknown books in the middle of the overall structure. As it was, reaching any of the collections could be a bit of an adventure as the buildings ran up against the hillside and often the floors of one did not match its neighbor. There were short cuts in and around the maze of buildings that students had manufactured or found over the years, and much of the education at Penwick consisted of learning how to find your way from one collection to the next.

There was a bit of a crowd just beyond the main gate. 6th year Proctors were ticking off names as students passed through, and Eleanor and her uncle were sent on to Prescott Hall, the dormitory in the very back corner of the grounds, a common home for second years. As her uncle brought the horse cab to a halt in front of the mossy two-storied building her class advisor, Mr. Hanford, came out of the door.

"Ah, Eleanor, how nice to see you again," he said, giving her a pat on the shoulder.

Mr. Hanford had been their class advisor last year as well, and would be until they joined specific Halls at the end of this year. He was responsible for seeing that they were able to succeed academically, but also was the one who resolved squabbles involving roommates, ensured that students did not miss meals, and handled all of the myriad problems that fifteen twelve-year olds could generate.

"Thank you, Mr. Hanford," Eleanor replied. "You remember my uncle."

"Of course, Mr. Wigton," Mr. Hanford said, extending his hand. "I'm sure you don't need to be told, but Eleanor has been an excellent student, and we're looking forward to great things from her. I understand that you have some interest in the Hall selection process coming this fall."

"I try to stay out of it," her uncle said, in a bald-faced lie. "But I will admit I'd be happy to see another Numerist in the family."

"Well, sir, it's an excellent Hall," said Mr. Hanford. "But Eleanor here will have her options open to her, if she continues to perform as well as last year." He smiled back at her as he said this.

Eleanor tried to not blush but she couldn't help it. She had to admit she did enjoy being noticed for having done well. She had studied hard, she figured, and had earned some praise. Although she didn't want to tell anyone else this she hadn't found the first year all that hard. Her uncle had prepared her well for Penwick, and most of the material had come quite easily. Her roommate, Miriam, had worked much harder than Eleanor and not done quite as well. There's nothing wrong with being smart, Eleanor told herself. She could put in the hard work; it just hadn't been necessary yet.

"You'll be wanting to know your room, then," said Mr. Hanford. "You and Miriam are in number five. She's up there already, so if you hope to have any say in decorating you'd best get moving. Some of the porters will bring up you trunk in a bit." He shook her uncle's hand again, and then moved on to a wagon that had pulled up behind them. Taking several of today's new packages with them Eleanor and her uncle made their way through the door and into the foyer of Prescott Hall.

To the right through double doors lay a common area. Several tables with four chairs a piece were set about the room, and a few bookshelves manned the spaces alongside the fireplace. The room was lined with dark wood, and it seemed a little drab given the bright summer weather. Come winter, however, it would be a much happier place. To their left was a single door, ajar at the moment, and inside they could see the apartment of the housekeeper. She was likely out and about helping students

31

find their way and unpack their trunks. There was a wide staircase in front of them leading to the second floor and next to that a door that must have led to the first-floor rooms. If she was on the second floor with the girls then that meant the boys in her class would have rooms downstairs.

The made their way up the stairs, and onto the second floor landing. There were a few doors to the right and Eleanor saw Violet Higgins and Willa Beaumont outside of one of those rooms. They gave her a quick wave. Eleanor went to the left and moved past two doors before finding room 5 at the end of the hallway.

The door was open and Eleanor edged her way into the room. Miriam, her dark curly hair pulled back with a green ribbon, was balancing with one foot on her bed, tottering a little as she attempted to hang the end of a lacy blue curtain over the window. Startled by the sound of Eleanor dumping several packages onto the other bed, Miriam wobbled even more and landed with a thud on her rear end.

"Eleanor," said Miriam, "you scared me!" But if falling had made her angry that would make it the first time in her life. She was unfailingly chipper, at times to the point of annoyance to the other girls. Two enormous green eyes dominated her round face, and she always seemed about to giggle. She came at Eleanor with a rush, "How are you?"

Eleanor caught her and gave her a hug, "I'm good, how was your summer?"

"Oh, fantastic. Lots of riding, of course." She straightened her dress out a little, which seemed to break her train of thought.

32

"Hi, Mr. Wigton," she said, pumping his hand even while he was trying to hang onto the stock of parcels he had in his arms.

"Hello, Miriam," he said, letting the packages tumble onto Eleanor's bed. "I'm sorry to have missed your parents."

"Not a problem, sir. You didn't miss much. My grandparents brought me this year, they wanted to see the school. My grandmother made the curtain, do you like it Eleanor?"

Miriam grabbed it off the bed and held it up in front of her face. It was light blue and was a torrent of loops and teardrop shapes with little tassels dangling down every few inches. It was uneven and one end appeared to be coming apart.

"It's lovely, Miriam. Why don't you give me a moment and we can hang it up together?" Eleanor said, smiling. It was impossible to say no to Miriam.

"Well, you're not doing anything before I say goodbye," said her uncle. Hugging him close she looked up and gave him a quick kiss on the cheek. It struck her at that moment that a year ago she wouldn't have been able to do that. She'd grown perhaps three inches over the last year and was now almost as tall as her mother. It was an odd feeling, she thought. To her, people like Uncle William and her father had always been gigantic, and now they seemed to be on the same scale as her. Knowing that she'd have more freedom at school made her feel more adult, but it hadn't settled in until that moment when she realized she was of a height with her uncle. The feeling was more terrifying than exciting.

"I love you, Uncle William," she said.

33

"I love you, too, sweetheart. Study hard, write home to your mother when you can," he replied. "Take care of her, Miriam," he shouted over her head.

"I will, Mr. Wigton!" said Miriam.

As her uncle let her go and turned to leave a large bell began to peal across the schoolyard. The bell was rung on the first day and on the last day of the school year. Today, it meant that the Convocation would begin soon and they would officially begin their second year. Eleanor's uncle had disappeared into the hallway while she had glanced out the window towards the main hall's bell tower.

She felt relieved that her uncle was gone, and then felt awful for feeling relieved. She was impatient to begin the year, more independent than the last, when as first years they were herded by Mr. Hanford the entire time. They would be on their own for more of their time now and would be expected to perform well without constant oversight. Eleanor had spent much of her first year chafing at the close monitoring and looking forward to this moment when she would be left to fend for herself.

A voice broke her chain of thoughts. "Come on, Eleanor, we've got to get going!" said Miriam as she rummaged through her trunk for a moment before producing a thin blue scarf that she slung around her neck. She then pulled a tiny mirror out of her pocket and carefully checked that her hair was curled in exactly the right way. Miriam had a habit of doing that, pulling out the mirror what seemed like one hundred times a day.

"Are you going to wear anything, Eleanor?" Miriam asked.

34

Eleanor had almost forgotten. One of the small but very meaningful benefits for second years was the permission to wear modest personal touches in addition to their plain black dresses. She turned to find the package from one of the shops they had visited this morning, and pulled out a faint pink scarf of her own.

Wrapping it around her neck Eleanor grabbed Miriam by the hand and they raced down to the entry hall. There they saw several of the other girls from their class already assembled: charming Darcy Ellington, talking with the inseparable Violet Higgins and Willa Beaumont at the bottom of the stairs. Near the door were Cassidy Smithwick and Amelia Norfolk, giggling about something. Most of the eight boys in their second year class were leaning up against the wall, somehow looking as if they had just come in from wrestling in the dirt outside.

As Eleanor and Miriam came down the stairs they exchanged some quick hellos with the other girls before Mr. Hanford came in and told them it was time to go. He had managed to find time to change into a long, dark green robe.

"Students," he said with a big grin, "welcome to your second year. If you'll follow me to the Entry Hall, we'll make that official." He spun on his heel, the robe whipping around behind him, and led the students out onto the grounds.

They joined several other groups of students pouring out of the dormitories and large houses along this side of the campus. The older students were arranged by Hall, with the Numerists all wearing dark blue robes and the Navigators the same dark green of Mr. Hanford. The Historians stood out in their deep red even though there were only four in the entire school. The flood of Barristers streamed out of the largest dormitory dressed in brown, while behind them the Apothecaries clustered together in their simple grey robes.

As second years Eleanor and her classmates remained in the standard black but she did not mind not having earned any robes at the moment, given that the sun was pounding down on the school this afternoon.

The doors of the Entry Hall were wide open as they approached, the massive wooden doors propped open by thick steel pins set into holes in the ground. As they approached there was a distinct smell of parchment and leather. It was intoxicating, a more tangible signal of entering the Library than passing through the doors itself.

Their class began to crowd together with the older Halls in the small antechamber. There was little here except for a few ancient tapestries hung on the sleek marble walls looking down on them. With some hassling and bumping, the teachers coaxed the students through the smaller set of doors leading farther into the building. The light dimmed as they went farther in, the daylight finding it hard to maneuver around the doors and into the depths of the Entry Hall.

Eleanor and her classmates waited while the Halls were called forward through the long hallway they were waiting in. Finally a voice from down the hall called for second years and Mr. Hanford led the way forward. The hallway was lined with smaller blocks of marble that gave off a cool sensation despite there being a

36

host of milling young students bumping up against each other and generating heat. At the end they emerged into a grand room that reached two stories high, a balcony running around the perimeter. Massive staircases led up to the balconies in the back corners of the room. There were also three archways spaced along the opposite wall from where they entered. These were the entrances into the maze of collections and libraries beyond. As if to remind everyone of the fact that they were distinct buildings the light from the Entry Hall appeared to stop right at the archways, and the openings were pitch black.

Miriam tugged her hand and Eleanor realized they were being shuffled towards a set of benches set up across the center of the hall. As second years they sat towards the front, on the left. Across from them was an empty bench where the first-years would be put as soon as they were brought in. Behind them the Barristers were settling into several rows and on the other side the remaining Halls were arranging themselves. After having settled his charges Mr. Hanford went to stand up in front of the assembled students along with the other assorted teachers.

There were a few remaining mumbles as the students arranged themselves, and then a striking woman with light brown hair, but with grey streaks showing, stepped forward from the set of teachers. The Headmistress wore the deep red robes of a Historian but around her neck hung the heavy gold chain of the Headmaster of Penwick. While of a slight build she appeared to loom over her surroundings, her dark eyes scanning her students until there was complete silence.

"Welcome back to Penwick," she said, her voice echoing about the gigantic room so that she had to pause before speaking again. "We look forward to another excellent year with you, and to joining with you in new discoveries."

The Headmistress turned slightly and one of the teachers handed forward an envelope. While opening it, she spoke again, "Our new first-year students are eager to join us, so it would be best to begin, I think. Please remember that you all were once in this position, and that first-year students have quite enough to do without serving as either porters or waiters for upperclassmen." With that she gave a long look at Eleanor's second year class, which, if hundreds of years of tradition were to be preserved, would soon be the ones ordering the new students about campus on various errands.

"Arnold Bagely," the Headmistress announced loudly, and out of the rear hallway came a lanky boy who walked as if he was slightly unsure as to how his legs worked. Eleanor and the rest of the students clapped politely while he found his way to the end of the bench at the front. "Maxine Fiddlescoop," was the next name and the process continued through the rest of the thirteen new students until they filled up most of the bench opposite Eleanor and her classmates.

The Headmistress handed the roll sheet back to one of the teachers and returned to speaking to the assembled student body. "This is the seven hundred and sixty eighth group of students to have passed through Penwick Academy in its illustrious history. I am hopeful that you will take this privilege as

38

seriously as your predecessors" she said, the comment echoing about the chamber.

There followed a series of short announcements regarding new hours for the kitchens, areas of the city like the Warren that were off-limits to students, and curfews for being in their dormitories. The Master Keeper, a man looking just as old as the libraries he tended to, then wobbled forward to give them a standard recitation of the rules regarding food, drinks, and fires in the library. Eleanor nodded along with everyone else at these pronouncements. Just as she felt her attention starting to drift, the Master Keeper came to a conclusion and the Headmistress stepped forward again.

"Well then," said the Headmistress, allowing herself a quick smile, "we begin yet another year at Penwick. Let's get to work."

CHAPTER 3

_____

THE DELIVERY

SHEETS of yellowing paper danced in the air as Eleanor flailed with her free arm, trying to keep her balance as her foot slipped on an old stone step. Sliding down one step before she righted herself, she muttered a string of curses at her own clumsiness. She picked her way down the remaining stairs, plucking up the Silverwood pencil case, and snatching sheets of paper out of the air before shoving everything into her rucksack.

It was going to take an hour just to sort out the Physiology notes, Eleanor figured. And with part of her evening already scheduled in the Observatory it was going to be a late night. Reaching the bottom of the great stone staircase, she paused and adjusted the black ribbon holding her hair in place. She was finally feeling a little more composed when a high-pitched screeching voice almost made her drop her bag again.

"Ms. Wigton," said Mrs. Arbuckle, who taught Botany. Her long black robe and sleek ink-black hair made it seem as if her disembodied head were emerging from the shadows of the hallway that led off towards the dining hall. "I presume that you have a reason for rattling about during class hours?"

"Yes, Mrs. Arbuckle," said Eleanor, taking a deep breath to try and get her heart to slow down. "The Headmistress sent for me, and asked me to come right away."

41

"In trouble, are you?" asked Mrs. Arbuckle, looking surprised.

"No. Not that I am aware of, ma'am," replied Eleanor, which was the truth. Valerie Spalth, a fifth-year, had arrived in the Geometry room with a note for her teacher, Mr. Gatwick, asking him to send Eleanor to the Headmistresses office. In her whole first year, and now almost two months into her second, Eleanor had never even been put on dish duty in the kitchens. So Eleanor had no clue as to why the Headmistress had asked for her today.

"Well, then," said Arbuckle, dismissing her with a wave, as if Eleanor had been the one who had stopped *her* in the hallway, "off you go." She appeared to float up the stairs without effort, which only served to remind Eleanor how clumsy she had been.

Turning, Eleanor hurried off again down the main corridor of Morgan Hall. She came to a halt in front of a set of ancient wooden doors. They were carved to look like two facing pages of a gigantic book. The text etched into the wood was from Fredrickson's *History of the Mandelbar Coast*, which Eleanor had to read last year. Next to the right-hand door was a great fabric rope that hung down from a hole in the ceiling above her. It had a massive knot tied in the end that sat just above the ground. Eleanor felt her mouth go a little dry. She had never before been into the Headmistresses office, and she still did not know why she had been summoned. Repeating to herself that it would be fine she reached out and gave the fabric rope a long pull. From behind the doors she thought she heard the faint echo of a bell but she couldn't be sure.

Nothing happened immediately but just as Eleanor was wondering whether she should pull again the left-hand door gave a shudder and then swung open towards her. Light from the room inside spilled out into the shadowy hallway.

"Oh, excellent, Eleanor, the headmistress will be glad to see you're here," said a plump little woman wearing a long dark purple shawl over her plain dress. It was Mrs. Puddlemump, who, as always, had a cheery smile on her face. Eleanor smiled back as she followed the older woman inside the door. The presence of Mrs. Puddlemump made her feel much more at ease. It was she who served as a bit of a surrogate mother for the children here at Penwick, dropping by with snacks when students were studying late for tests, or finding time to sit with them and cheer them up when those tests had not gone so well.

"Have a seat, dear. I'll go let her know you're here," said Mrs. Puddlemump as she pushed her way through a much smaller wooden door on the wall opposite where they had entered.

Eleanor sat in one of the series of straight-back chairs lining one wall of the room. Across from her was a small wooden desk, it's surface hidden beneath organized stacks of paper, one of which held up the eyeglasses that normally hung around Mrs. Puddlemump's neck. The room was much cozier than one would have guessed from the outside, with great velvety green curtains hanging down around the one window that rose above the desk.

A moment later Mrs. Puddlemump came back and with a wave of her hand indicated that Eleanor should go on in. Eleanor thanked her and walked through the open door into the office beyond.

The first thing that struck her was the high ceiling. It was dark, dark blue and had stars painted upon it. She didn't recognize any patterns or constellations.

"Southern hemisphere, I'm afraid. You'll only get to them if you decide to pursue Navigation," said the Headmistress, sitting behind a great claw-footed wooden desk that held a brass globe in one corner, a pile of pencils and papers in the middle, and a small brown package perched on the opposite corner. The walls to either side were covered in bookcases, small books up top, and great ironbound tomes as high as Eleanor's waist resting along the bottom shelf. In and amongst the books were various brass instruments, only a few of which Eleanor could name. A fireplace tucked into the back corner gave the room pleasant warmth.

The Headmistress herself sat tall in her high-backed chair. She did not look, up close, as imposing as she always seemed to Eleanor during assemblies or in the dining hall. While she may have seemed slight in person, the impression of terrible intelligence was even more pronounced. Her hair was pulled back into a simple bun, although several stray locks had refused to cooperate and had been tucked back behind her ears. She wore a set of gold-rimmed spectacles, resting towards the end of her nose. She looked over those at Eleanor now.

"Eleanor, how is your uncle?" she asked. The question threw Eleanor for a moment.

"He's fine," Eleanor replied. How could I forget that? Her uncle had told her before last year that the Headmistress had been his History instructor here at Penwick when he was a student. "I'm looking forward to seeing him next summer."

"Excellent. Please tell him that I said hello," said the Headmistress as she dropped her eyes to the papers on her desk and started shuffling through them. Was that it? This was all so that the Headmistress could extend some pleasantries?

Eleanor was just about to turn around and walk out, thinking the meeting was over when the Headmistress raised her head and spoke again. "Mr. Farragut tells me that you took the top grade on the History midterm. Well done."

Top grade? Eleanor knew she had done well, but didn't realize she had beaten everyone. That was a nice surprise, she thought. She said a quick "Thank you," to the Headmistress.

"Overall, you've been doing very well, dear," the Headmistress continued, "Even better, I dare say, than your uncle," and with that she gave Eleanor what could only be described as a mischievous grin. It was a word that she would never have thought of using to describe the Headmistress. For Eleanor and the other students the Headmistress had never seemed very human. She had always appeared to be some kind of scholarly force of nature.

"I have a little task for you, Eleanor. Something to break up the drudgery of another school day," she said as she rose up out of her chair and smoothed down the front of the dark red dress she wore. "Both of my Proctors are furiously attempting to study for a advanced Cartography test this evening, so I would rather not bother them. You've got a free afternoon today, which means you won't miss out on much. And," she said as she came around to the front of the desk, "I know I can trust you."

"Of course, ma'am," said Eleanor.

"Good. I need you to deliver this," said the Headmistress, picking up the small brown package from the top of her desk, "to the Steward's Tower. You are to drop it with a clerk named Wellsby. He'll be expecting someone to bring it along, so just mention at the main gate that you are delivering it on my behalf."

"Steward's Tower. Wellsby. Got it," Eleanor repeated, adding "ma'am," at the last second.

The Headmistress nodded. "Good, go grab a shawl and run along. Don't forget that the doors close at eight o'clock, so no dawdling along the way," she said with a stern look on her face.

"Of course not, ma'am. Thank you," said Eleanor as she took the package from the Headmistress and headed out of the room.

In the anteroom Mrs. Puddlemump helped her push open the massive outer door, and wished her luck as she ran off down the hall. Once out of Morgan Hall she ran to her dormitory and took the steps two at a time to reach the second floor. She pushed open her door and stepped over the pile of notes Miriam had left on the floor. She grabbed a deep blue scarf and a black shawl, as the weather had turned cooler in the last few weeks. It would be getting even colder once the sun had set. Wrapping up, she hustled back out the door, almost forgetting to take the package with her.

She raced back down the dormitory steps and cut across the grounds, which were empty at the moment with everyone else in classes, and approached the main gate. Her footsteps echoing on the smooth stones, she trotted through the gates of Penwick, not even pausing as she passed the pair of retired Wardens that served as the official Penwick security force.

It was already getting cold, she noticed, and she wrapped part of the scarf up around her head to keep her ears warm. Heading down the walkway towards the city she wished she had slipped on some sturdier shoes. Hers were light ones useful for moving about the school but already her toes were feeling cold.

It's not far, she thought, and it'll just waste time going back inside. So she continued down the walkway and passed into the row of shops running along the riverside. It was quiet at this end and she saw no one on the streets. A block or two farther, though, she could see and hear the bumble and noise of people moving about

She attracted a few glances from townspeople out doing their business. Penwick students didn't often come into town alone and usually not on a Tuesday. Her plain black shawl and dress marked her out from most of the people moving in much more vibrant attire. She passed Dixon's, the bakery, slowing down to peer more closely at several enticing desserts in the window. Then she reminded herself that there was plenty of time to obsess over these next Sunday afternoon. She hustled on down the road.

After another block she had passed beyond the typical range

47

of Penwick students on an outing. She looked up and to her left, and could see the Steward's Tower poking above the rooftops. With the tower in sight, she'd figured she would get there quickly enough. It looked like it would only be a few more blocks to get to the Silverspan Bridge.

Craning her neck up at the tower had kept her from looking at the street in front of her, and so only at the last second did she hear the clop of hooves and the rattle of a harness as a delivery wagon bore down towards her.

She yelped and jumped backwards towards the buildings lining the street. The front wagon wheel clipped her shoulder and she spun as she fell backwards, losing her balance and falling to the ground.

"Aye! Watch where you're walking, missy!" shouted the driver as he clopped down the street. Several people across the way stopped long enough to stare but none offered to help. She picked herself up and wiped some mud off her shoulders, cheeks burning with embarrassment. Just keep walking, she said to herself, but that thought was interrupted by a voice.

"Hello, there. Looks like you dropped this," said a tall brown-haired boy wearing an incredibly messy leather apron. He was also rather handsome looking, with tiny dimples next to each of his blue eyes. This did nothing but make Eleanor feel even more embarrassed.

"Yours?" he tried again, holding out the brown package towards her. It was dripping in mud and had gotten soaked in the puddle Eleanor now found herself standing in. This was

48

turning into a complete disaster.

"Oh no!" she cried, and grabbed the package, scooping chunks of sticky mud off of the wrapping and watching little rivulets of water run down out of the corner. "Oh, this is awful. The Headmistress trusted me with this!" she said to no one in particular.

"Eh now. Can't be all bad," said the boy. "Let's get that all cleaned up for you. We've got some towels in the shop," and pushed open a small white door behind him, beckoning for her to follow.

Numb with worry she stepped inside. Inside there was a single counter and on top of it lay a massive slab of what she guessed were the remains of a pig. A round man stood behind the counter holding a long knife in one hand, and a gigantic pork chop in another.

"Right. What's all this then?" he said to the boy. He was clearly the father. If you took the boy and sort of mushed him down into a ball, the man behind the counter is what you'd get.

"She had a bit of a scare, that's all. Just going to wipe down her package here and send her along," said the boy and he reached behind the counter top and flipped through a pile of rags, looking for the least dirty one.

Eleanor was too nervous to say much of anything. She let the boy wipe the mud off of the package and tried to avoid the father's eye, which wasn't hard as he had gone back to butchering up the pig laying right there in front of her.

After a moment the boy said, "This wrapping is soaked

49

through, do you mind if I take it off? It's just going to get whatever's inside all wet as well."

Eleanor wasn't sure what to do. The Headmistress hadn't said anything about the package. She didn't even know what it was, to tell the truth. Was she allowed to open it? It was for the Steward, and even if it was innocent it wasn't her business to know what was inside there. Then again it also wasn't her business to ruin whatever it was by dumping it in a mud puddle.

"Fine. Go ahead," she said faintly. Then, recovering a little, added, "thank you."

"No problem, miss. I'm Jack, by the way," he said, and gave her a quick smile. He had ripped the paper off the package and had swallowed up the contents inside of a thick grey towel.

"Eleanor," she replied.

"Well, nice to meet you then, Eleanor. So, you're a Penwick student, then?"

"Yes," she said, "second year."

"So, all dusty old books up there, isn't it?" Jack asked, his voice displaying a bit of skepticism as to the usefulness of such things.

"Well, I guess so," Eleanor replied, "but there is a lot more too it than just reading old books. It's rather hard to explain, actually."

"To a butcher?" asked Jack.

"No, no, that's not what I meant," Eleanor said, flustered. This was a disaster. It was like her mouth was acting as clumsy as her feet today. She hadn't meant to imply anything about

50

Jack. He was being nice. "It's just very satisfying to be able to find answers."

"Depends on the question, I guess," Jack said, apparently less than convinced. He unfolded the towel in his hands and pulled out the contents of the package, a leather-bound book with some obvious water stains on the cover.

"Oh my," said Eleanor upon seeing the damage. She grabbed the book out of his hands. She flipped open the cover to see how the pages had fared. A folded sheet of paper that had been tucked just inside slid out and fell on the floor.

Reflexively, Eleanor reached down to grab it and before she could remind herself that this was private correspondence, read:

> To the Lord Steward,
>
> I hope that you find this volume to your satisfaction. I apologize for the delay in locating it, but you understand some of the conditions in the Library. Please do let me know if we here at Penwick can be of any further service.
>
> Sincerely,
> Olivia Wheedle, Headmistress
> Penwick Academy

She folded up the letter quickly as if that would somehow erase her memory of what she had read. The book was still in her left hand, open to the title page.

"*Botanical Field Notes of the Cinnamon Islands, Simon Tratford*," read Jack over her shoulder. He straightened up. "That, without a doubt, sounds like the most boring book ever written."

51

"Perhaps the Steward would like to educate himself on the source of so much of his wealth," said Eleanor, feeling a bit defensive.

"That so?" replied Jack. "Never really took the Steward for the scholarly type, eh Dad?" His father grunted something that might have meant agreement.

"There's nothing wrong with trying to inform yourself," said Eleanor.

"No, I guess not," replied Jack. "Good thing, though, that you've managed to get it wet already. It'll hide the drool marks when he falls asleep trying to read it," and gave her a wink.

Eleanor was now hopelessly unsure as to whether she was supposed to be a partner in, or target of, his joking. She felt flustered at feeling a bit picked upon, nervous at having marred the book, and had a fluttering in her stomach with no apparent explanation. It seemed best to escape before something else happened that made her feel foolish.

"I really need to be going," she said. "Thank you for your help."

"Any time," said Jack. He waved goodbye as she backed out the door and into the street, being careful this time to keep her eyes up for any approaching wagons.

Hustling now, she found the bridge quickly and was able to make it to the gate of the Steward's Tower without any further incidents, her small size allowing her to weave through the crowded streets outside the Tower. Two bored-looking Wardens in silver helmets stood at the main gate of the Steward's Castle.

The heavy iron gates were open. She explained that she was delivering a book from Penwick for a Mr. Wellsby, and the guard waved her on without much thought.

Passing into the courtyard she realized she had no idea where in the castle she was supposed to find Mr. Wellsby. Turning about for a moment, everything looked identical. There were twelve doors set into alcoves along the sides of the courtyard and in front of her was a massive iron portcullis blocking a stone archway leading further into the castle. I hope, she thought, that Mr. Wellsby isn't through there.

"Could I help you, young lady?" said a voice from behind her. Eleanor spun around to find a short man, just taller than she was, standing before her. He had on dark blue robes, but there was a noticeable brown stain down the lapel. He was a round man, with a round nose on a round face. Even his hands looked round.

"You look like you're unsure of where to go," he said, gesturing around the courtyard with one of his rotund hands.

"Yes," said Eleanor, feeling a bit embarrassed. She must have looked like a little child. "I need to find a Mr. Wellsby."

"Ah, Wellsby! Easily done, young lady. I can take you right up to his offices. I'm headed up to the Harbormaster's myself," he said, gesturing towards the last door on the right side. Eleanor got the impression from his tone of voice that going to the Harbormaster's office was supposed to be rather prestigious. She didn't have the heart to tell him that she had no idea who the Harbormaster was.

53

"Thank you, sir," said Eleanor as he opened the door for her and pointed her up the stairs that lay beyond.

"A Penwick lady, I'm guessing?" he said. Without waiting for her to answer he rambled on, "I could tell by the black dress. I was at Penwick, myself, you know? Barrister Hall, of course. Can't get very far around here with much else. Any thoughts on which Hall you'll be joining?"

"Not entirely, sir," she replied. They had come to a landing with three different hallways leading off of it. She hesitated, waiting for the round man to point the way.

"Ah, yes. Straight ahead, then, miss." She headed down into the dark hallway. There were several doors along the way, but the round man didn't indicate she should stop so she kept walking.

The man was puffing along loudly now and Eleanor was beginning to wonder if he was doing all right when he spoke up.

"Here we go, then. The last door, yes," and he stepped past her to push open a low wooden door at the end of the hall.

"Thank you, sir," Eleanor said, and passed inside to a small office with a weak fire going in the fireplace. There was a skinny old man sitting at a writing desk, and with what appeared to be an immense amount of effort he stood up to greet them.

"Mr. Tubman," said the old man in a surprisingly strong voice. "You appear to have brought me a rather unusual delivery."

"Yes, Mr. Wellsby, I guess so. It was rather funny, actually, I - "

"That will be all, Mr. Tubman," said Wellsby, turning away from the fat man.

"Of course, Mr. Wellsby," said Tubman, bowing slightly as he backed out of the room.

Eleanor felt a little uncertain with Mr. Tubman no longer there. This Wellsby man looked frail, but she had an uneasy feeling being alone with him. He stood there assessing her with a look that reminded her of her father eyeballing a horse. She realized that he was staring at the book in her hands, which she had almost forgotten about.

"Mr. Wellsby, sir. The Headmistress from Penwick asked me to deliver this to you," she said, holding out the book towards him. She was hoping he would just take it and she could go. There was something about the old man that made her feel unsure of herself.

"Yes, the book, of course," he said coolly. But his wrinkled claw snatched it from her with obvious desire. He spent a moment flipping through it, his eyes flicking over the pages like a hawk, searching out something specific. He swept pages back and forth for a few tense moments.

"Page one-hundred eighty three is missing," he said harshly.

Eleanor felt a pit in her stomach. Had she lost it when she dropped the book? She didn't remember anything coming out of the book other than the letter. It had to have been missing before she delivered it.

"I'm sorry sir," she said. "I don't know where it is."

Wellsby peered at her with his tiny, black eyes. It was com-

55

pletely disconcerting, and Eleanor wished she could melt into the floor. To her surprise he put the book down suddenly. "And who exactly are you, young lady?"

"My name is Eleanor Wigton, sir," she said, hoping that was sufficient.

"Wigton, yes," he replied. Eleanor wasn't sure, but it seemed from his response as if Mr. Wellsby had somehow expected this. Did he know who the Headmistress would send? How? There's no way he could have asked for her, the Headmistress had only chosen her because the Proctors were all busy. She was just imagining things.

"Well, Ms. Wigton," he said as he moved to his desk and began writing out a note. "I presume that if I send you back with a note for your Headmistress it will arrive there without being opened?"

Eleanor felt her self go flush. Of course he knew. He would have expected the book to be wrapped and it was not. He could see the stain on the cover from the mud. She had made a complete mess of this, and he was writing the Headmistress a note to tell explain what Eleanor had done. She'd be punished, most likely with kitchen work for at least a week. How could she have been so clumsy?

"Of course, sir," she said, almost in a whisper.

"Good, then. You'd best be going. I'll assume you can find your way out," he said, and sank back into his chair, which had the effect of making him seem aged and decrepit again.

"Yes, sir. Thank you, sir," she said, bowing and running out of the door and down the hall. Her legs kept pumping as she raced down the stairs and out of the courtyard. She realized that people were staring at her as she ran through town to the bridge but she didn't care. By the time she reached the gates of Penwick she was bright red and out of breath.

CHAPTER 4

AN UNUSUAL MEETING

ELEANOR spent the next few days in a state of almost constant agitation. Having delivered Mr. Wellsby's note to the Headmistresses office, she had been waiting for her punishment to be handed down at any moment. Miriam asserted that it would be entirely unfair to wait more than three days to decide the matter, and declared it closed. Eleanor appreciated the sentiment but remained skeptical that the Headmistress was terribly concerned about Miriam's sense of fair play. Finally, after several more days with no news, and an increasing amount of class work taking up her time, Eleanor began to believe that Mr. Wellsby had not asked for her to be punished.

The weather, which for the last month had flirted with the idea of snow, had now made up its mind. The peaked roofs of the school were pure white as if they had been frosted like a cake. In contrast, the open square around which the school buildings huddled was no longer so pristine, with the remaining snow smeared brown from the continual trudging of boots. Getting through the drifts between the library and the dormitory was a frigid expedition requiring a fur-lined cloak, extra socks, and a good sense of direction. For all that, Eleanor found something about the sight of Penwick buried underneath the snow very comforting. The atmosphere around the school was quieter at this time of year, as the cold drove most students into the common rooms where there was little to do other than continue to work on the increasing piles of class work.

An additional effect of the snow and cold was that students tried to move between buildings as little as possible. Eleanor, who in better conditions would have spent her free time between morning classes swinging by the kitchens for a snack and reading in the courtyard, had now taken to huddling in a front-row desk near the fire in Mr. Farragut's classroom while waiting for History to begin.

One very cold day, Eleanor shuffled herself into Mr. Farragut's room and took up her normal spot. She was near enough to the fire to warrant taking off her bulky outer cloak, and draped it over a chair near the fireplace to dry out. After letting her fingers warm for a moment she sat down and pulled out some Geometry homework. Once she had settled in and was scribbling away she realized that there were voices coming from the open door of Mr. Farragut's office. While they were muffled she could make out most of the conversation.

"I've enough to do already without all this," said a voice that Eleanor was quite sure belonged to Mr. Farragut.

"Ernest," replied a woman, almost certainly the Headmistress, "I understand. However, I would like you to take this on as a personal favor. None of the Numerists would bother with it. Most of the work will be done by the students we select, regardless, so you should only be required to help keep them on task and point them in the right direction."

There was no audible reply, and Eleanor could only assume that Mr. Farragut had agreed to whatever it was the Headmistress was proposing to him. After the pause, though, a third voice came floating out of the room, a man's voice that sounded old but very clear.

"As to those students, Olivia, I have taken the liberty of making up a list." The muffled sound of paper shuffling came through the open doorway.

"A list?" said the Headmistress, "Really, Lewis, did you think we were incapable of identifying our own top students?"

"Not at all," said the man, "you are the highest authority, of course. I do, though, think that these students would be particularly useful for the purposes of this project."

"Let me see that," said Farragut, and there was another shuffling sound as the paper changed hands. "Millsap, fine. Newberry, fine. Both top marks for several years and have shown some interest in this kind of thing. Wallace? Do you mean Sean or James?"

"James," was the answer from the unidentified man.

"Right. He was a decent student, nothing special," said Farragut.

"He's one of Gerhard's aces in Navigation," said the Headmistress, "despite your opinion of him."

"Hmph," was Farragut's reply to that. There was a pause and he continued, "Now what about this? This girl's too young, and even though her marks were good last year that's just in the introductory classes. What good is she going to be on this?

61

There are a handful of top students that would be more useful."

"Nevertheless," said the other man, with a firmness that implied he was not planning to argue, "she is someone that I would like on the project."

"She's gotten excellent marks through all her classes, Ernest," said the Headmistress.

"That may be, Olivia, but she just won't have had the practice to be a useful contributor," said Farragut. There was no immediate reply and Eleanor guessed his objection had fallen on deaf ears.

"Now," said the man, "I was hoping to introduce myself and the project to them all this evening."

"Tonight?" said the Headmistress, "You can't mean them to begin work now, Lewis. They've exams to study for. This seems like something that can wait a few weeks."

"Olivia," said the man with a tone of familiarity. He sounded to Eleanor like someone who had known the Headmistress for a long time. "While I don't expect these students to fail out of Penwick on my account, if I could have my way I'd have gotten this information months ago. Time is of the essence. I was hoping to encourage them to get started."

"I suppose that is fine," said the Headmistress with reluctance. "Ernest, why don't you meet tonight in a reading room after dinner. I'll have Mrs. Puddlemump send notes around to the students involved."

"Hmph," was again Farragut's only reply.

"Well, then, we shall be going, Ernest, and let you prepare

62

for class," said the Headmistress. There was a screech of chairs on stone floors and the shuffling of cloaks. Eleanor saw Mr. Farragut hold his door open wide and two shapes emerge.

The first was the Headmistress, buttoning a thick blue cloak about her, a fur hat on her head. She saw Eleanor and gave a quick start, perhaps surprised to see someone in the room. The other man was behind her, older as Eleanor had thought, but not frail-looking. This man had flecks of gray about his temples and in his close-cropped beard, and while he was wrapped up in a long gray cloak he looked lanky and thin. His face was rough and his eyes were piercing.

The Headmistress looked back and forth between Eleanor and the man for a moment, a quizzical look on her face. The man either did not notice or did not care. He walked right over towards the fire and stopped in front of Eleanor's desk. Eleanor was put off for a moment as she realized that she might be in trouble for having eavesdropped on their conversation. Had she heard something she wasn't supposed to?

"Ms. Wigton," he said, which shocked her even more, as she had never seen this man before. Then his weathered face relaxed into a smile, "It's very good to meet you."

She failed to answer, thrown by his recognition of her. The man waited, his face remaining in a tight smile. "Uh, and you too, sir," she said. Then feeling as if she must explain herself in some way, "I usually work in here between classes. To stay out of the cold."

"An eminently sensible thing to do, young lady," said the

63

man. "But I am being incredibly rude as I know your name, but you obviously do not know mine. I am Lewis Madigan." He held out his hand. Eleanor took it and gave it a quick shake. She had the impression that he expected her to recognize him, but she was certain she had never heard the name before.

He continued, "We should of course be getting out of your and Mr. Farraguts way, Eleanor." He walked back towards the Headmistress, "Olivia, perhaps you will let me plow a trail for you back to your office. There are a few last items I'd like to discuss with you." Pulling on a woolen hat he led the Headmistress out of the classroom door and Eleanor was left staring.

"Throw another log on the fire, Ms. Wigton, if you don't mind," said Farragut, startling her back to the moment as he stuck his head out of his office door. "Class is going to start soon, best have it warmed up for the students."

While Eleanor stoked up the fire more students started to filter in, shaking snow off their boots and hanging damp cloaks up on hooks across the back wall. Cassidy Smithwick and Amelia Morgan came and sat down next to Eleanor.

"What was the Headmistress doing in here?" Cassidy asked.

"I'm guessing we aren't so lucky that she sacked Farragut," said Amelia. "But she should, after making Darcy cry last week over that stupid research assignment."

"No, sorry," said Eleanor. She wasn't sure how much she should tell the other girls. It had clearly been intended to be a private conversation, and the Headmistress, Mr. Farragut, and the perplexing Mr. Madigan probably would not appreciate her blabbing about it all over school. Cassidy and Amelia, though, worked friendships like conspiracies. Telling them something exclusive would put her in a special relationship with them. Being drawn into their knot of whispering was not important to Eleanor and she decided to stay mum.

"I didn't hear anything, really," she said. "I think it was just some administrative stuff."

"Then who was the tall man with the beard?" asked Cassidy. "I've never seen him before. He isn't a new teacher, is he?" She looked at Eleanor with her gigantic eyes wide open like an owl's. She seemed so desperate to get some gossip.

"Sorry. I really didn't hear anything," said Eleanor, feeling some pride about keeping it secret.

"Well, Eleanor," said Amelia, "if you're going to lurk around in classrooms, you could at least pay attention." The other girls both giggled at that, and huddled together to chew over some other rumor they had picked up earlier that day.

The class had filled up, and there was a final rush of shuffling chairs and papers as Mr. Farragut swept out of his office and took up position at a small wooden lectern. He rather enjoyed his encyclopedic knowledge of history, and took great pride in never using any notes. This caused problems, as he would forget that not all of his students shared such a passion for, or ability in, historical details. Darcy had been an unfortunate victim of that attitude last week when she had failed to include some meaningless battle that he found crucial in her summary of the First Ardic War.

"Good afternoon, everyone," began Mr. Farragut, "Today we'll be continuing on with our discussion of the origins of the Second Ardic War, focusing on the diaries of Cletus Borgia that were found several years ago." With that Eleanor began to take notes, trying to keep up with Mr. Farragut's lecture. History classes were so dense with information that they left her right hand stiff and aching afterwards. Still, it was generally enjoyable, and while he could be somewhat arrogant about it, Mr. Farragut's ability to speak coherently on the material for an hour and a half without notes was rather impressive.

After he had finished, Mr. Farragut dismissed them. This was not as relieving as it should be, seeing as how they all had to make it across the snowbound courtyard to the dining hall for lunch. After stuffing themselves back into cloaks, gloves, and hats, the students milled about in the outer hallway hoping that someone else would take the lead in plowing through the drifts. Jacob Weatherby finally exclaimed that he was more hungry than cold and opened the door. Eleanor and the rest of her class filed out behind him, heads bent against the wind, shuffling as fast as possible in the snow towards the relative warmth of the dining hall.

Eleanor made it to the second-year table, and settled in with the rest of the girls in her class. All the girls collected at the end of the table closest to the fireplace while the boys occupied the other end. By unspoken agreement there was a buffer zone between the two sides of the table, with enough room to make sure that no girl spoke to a boy by accident.

As they sat down servers from the kitchens appeared, including several students who were working as punishments for various infractions around campus. Plates of warm bread and bowls of hot soup appeared. Eleanor and the rest of her table went for the soup, giving it a chance to banish the cold in their bodies from the inside out. It was mainly vegetables but bits of chicken from yesterdays dinner appeared now and then in the bowl as Eleanor pushed her spoon around. The smell of cardamom filled the room, one of the many flavors that had become common around Penwick, and all of Flosston Moor, ever since the discovery of the Cinnamon Islands. Her grandmother would faint, Eleanor thought, if she knew how much of the rare spice the school used for a regular lunch on a Tuesday. When her grandmother had been growing up, enough cardamom for just one bowl of soup would have cost as much as a new team of horses.

Eleanor was enjoying the smell and the warmth in her stomach when someone calling her name made her start.

"Wigton! Wigton! Where are you," shouted Belinda Cromwell across the dining hall. She was near the door, waving something in her hands. "I've got a message from the Headmistress for you!"

There was no need for shouting, as Belinda had to have known full well that Eleanor would be sitting with the second years. But Belinda very much enjoyed being a Proctor, and always made sure that everyone was aware that she worked in the Headmistresses office. As Belinda threaded her way in between the various tables of students, though, Eleanor had more important concerns. Was this the order for detention? Had the Headmistress finally decided on a punishment for dropping the book in the mud? I was just starting to think I was going to be alright, thought Eleanor, so delaying like this seemed cruel.

"Wigton, right, here you go. From the Headmistress," said Belinda again as she stopped at the table and dropped an envelope in front of her. "It's sealed," she said, loudly enough to make sure everyone heard, and therefore everyone knew it was important. The Headmistress never bothered to seal short trivial messages. Did this mean that her punishment was particularly awful? Oh no, thought Eleanor for a moment, what if I've been expelled? The idea had flitted by her mind after the botched delivery, but it had been too terrible to even contemplate. The Headmistress wouldn't expel her for that, would she? And surely not with a note during lunch, not with Belinda Cromwell crowing it about so that everyone would know.

"Thank you, Belinda," said Eleanor quietly. She stared at the envelope in front of her, vaguely aware of Belinda behind her, now shouting for "James Wallace!".

"Well, Eleanor, open it," said Miriam. Cassidy and Amelia stared across the table at her, salivating at the prospect of inside information. The other girls had leaned in to look at her, and even the boys were all looking over. Eleanor felt herself go red. This was terrible, she thought. They're all going to see me cry when I get expelled.

"It's not going to bite you," said Violet from the end of the

68

table. "Just get it over with."

Eleanor still hesitated for a moment, taking a deep breath. It's nothing, she told herself. It's probably nothing. Once she got hold of the note she almost tore it to pieces getting it open, her heart pounding.

> Ms. Wigton,
>
> You have been selected to participate in a special research project under Mr. Farragut's supervision. Please report to reading room number 17 in the Library after dinner this evening.
>
> O.W., Headmistress

It took her a moment to realize what the letter meant. The whole episode from this morning, they were talking about her? But didn't Mr. Farragut think she was too young? More puzzling was that she was certain Mr. Madigan had insisted on specific people. And now she was one of those people. She had done well at Penwick so far, but why would Mr. Madigan know about it, and what did he want her for? Well, it's better than getting expelled, she decided despite the confusion.

"So," said Miriam, "what does it say?" Which was a bit of silly question as Miriam had practically climbed up her left arm, and was clearly reading the note over her shoulder. "You've got a special project to work on? With Farragut? What did you do to deserve that?"

"Not surprising, I guess," offered Darcy. "You're clearly his favorite in class." She seemed relieved, as the fact that is was just a boring research project with her least favorite teacher meant that it wasn't something to be envious of.

"Kind of an odd group, don't you think?" said Violet. She had craned around, as had many of the other students to see who else was getting the notes. "James Wallace from Navigation. And that's Millicent Millsap from Numerancy. Aren't they both 4th years? Who's that other boy at the Numerancy table?" She almost stood up on the table to see over the Barrister's in the way. "Adam Newberry, a 6th year."

Eleanor shrugged. She had no idea what to think about the project. She was the only one who wasn't already in a Hall, and had not done any focused training. 1st and 2nd years took a range of classes in all areas. The older students would have very specific skills and be aces in the Library. What did Mr. Madigan want with her? Was it some kind of mistake?

There wasn't a lot of time to worry over the situation as the bell rang then to signal that lunch was ending. Students stuffed spare bread in their pockets and drained soup bowls. Filing out, Eleanor and Miriam dropped their dishes at the kitchen and wrapped back up to make their way across campus to Geometry. They made it just as the warmth of lunch was escaping their bodies, and they took a minute to dry out in front of Mr. Gatwick's fireplace before sitting down to class.

Eleanor didn't take very good notes in Geometry or in the Astronomy class that followed. She was preoccupied with speculation about the project and why she had been included. She racked her brain trying to think of any connection with the other students, but the best that she could come up with was that Millicent Millsap had been one of the Numerancy assistants in the Library last year and had helped Eleanor find a book on algebra.

She fidgeted through dinner, not eating much, wondering how soon she could head over to the Library. The others appeared to be having similar nerves, which made Eleanor feel somewhat better. Millicent and Adam were among the first people to get up and clear their dishes, each looking around to try and see if the others were coming. They all found themselves huddled in the entryway, tucking into gloves and hats.

"A bit mysterious, eh?" said the boy from Navigation as he loped in behind the rest of them. "I'm James, by the way, I don't think we've met." He held his hand out to Eleanor. His hair was dark, almost black, and he looked athletic. He had an easy way about him and was the only one who didn't appear to be outwardly nervous.

"Eleanor," she said, taking his hand and giving it a small shake.

"How's tricks, Millie?" said James to the other girl.

"Fine, Jimmy," she said, exaggerating the name, which Eleanor figured meant that she hadn't been happy to be called 'Millie'. She pulled at her hair absently with one hand, her face pinched and sour looking.

"I'm Adam," said the older boy, looking over the rest of them. "I'll lead the way," he said and pushed open the exterior door. If anyone had a different plan he seemed unconcerned, and anyway there was nothing wrong with letting someone else take the brunt of the wind across the open courtyard.

Her feet felt like bricks by the time they had made it to the Entry Hall and they stopped to drop wet cloaks and boots in some alcoves in the main chamber. Tracking water into the Library would get you expelled, and the various collections stayed a pleasant temperature year-round. Some students said the dwarves had installed a heating system when the Entry Hall was built.

In the grand hall the benches had been replaced by several long wooden tables on which were stacked various books that were to be shelved by the Keepers who oversaw the various collections. They skirted around these and passed by the archways, instead taking one of the staircases up to the balcony level and then around to reading room 17.

Someone was there. Eleanor wondered if it was Mr. Madigan. He seemed very keen on the project, but the note had only said it involved Mr. Farragut. As they all emerged into the room Eleanor saw that both men stood at the opposite side of a long table, talking too quiet to be heard. They noticed the students and walked forward to meet them.

"Good evening," said Mr. Farragut. He face suggested that he was still unhappy about this particular assignment. Mr. Madigan gave no indication of even noticing Mr. Farragut's displeasure as he smiled at the students.

"Yes, good evening. I believe you all know Mr. Farragut, but most of you do not know me," said Mr. Madigan. Eleanor felt self-conscious as the other three looked at each other and her, trying to figure out who already knew the strange man. It's not like she really knew Mr. Madigan, as all they had done was introduce themselves in the classroom. She did her best to act like she didn't know what he was talking about.

"My name is Lewis Madigan. I have requested your assistance for an unusual research project. Your Headmistress and Mr. Farragut have been very kind to allow you to participate alongside your usual studies."

Millicent raised her hand, but did not wait for Mr. Madigan to acknowledge her before speaking. "Is this part of our required classes? Will there be marks given?"

If the interruption bothered Mr. Madigan, his face did not register it, "Ms. Millsap, the answer to both questions is no. This is something in addition to your regular work. It is not compulsory, however, and you are free to turn down this opportunity. I'd only ask that you at least let me explain the project before making a decision." Millicent seemed ready to interject again but a stern look from Mr. Farragut made her swallow the question.

"Why don't we all have a seat, and I can explain this all in a little more detail." He motioned towards the table and they all shuffled about the massive chairs, sitting in a cluster at one end of the table with Mr. Madigan at the head. He sat silently while they settled themselves, his fingers held together and his chin resting on their points.

Once he had their attention again Mr. Madigan pulled a paper from inside his cloak. He laid it out in front of him, smoothing it with his weathered hands.

"I have a bit of a mystery," he said, tapping the paper with his index finger, "and I need several smart people such as you to help me figure it out."

Eleanor looked around at the other students. Adam and Millicent looked confused. James looked curious. She just felt more than ever like she shouldn't be here. Mr. Madigan passed the paper to Mr. Farragut, and indicated he should pass it around. When it came to Eleanor she saw that it was two lines of numbers:

$$8\ 26\ 4\ 12\ 14\ 19\ 2\ 6\ 25\ 7\ 11\ 12\ 12\ 3\ 16\ 17$$
$$12\ 41\ 22\ 21\ 15\ 33\ 15\ 7\ 43\ 22\ 26\ 26\ 39\ 35\ 44\ 34$$

"So what's the mystery?" asked James as Eleanor set the page back in front of Madigan. "Is there something special about these numbers?"

"I don't know about the numbers themselves," said Madigan, "That is what I am hoping you will be able to find out for me. But the origin of these numbers is what tells me they are important."

James looked intrigued and even Adam and Millicent's interest had picked up. This was not going to be like her regular assignments, thought Eleanor.

Madigan continued, "The two lists of numbers were found on separate sheets of paper. They were obtained from a man whose past would suggest they have a dark purpose. He is one of the Forgotten, as many people call them. They are a set of -"

Mr. Farragut interrupted Madigan with a pronounced cough. Madigan did not acknowledge it, but to Eleanor it seemed that he did rethink what he was saying.

"- criminals, let's say," Madigan finished. "These criminals have been searching for something, and I am determined that they not find it."

There was silence, but only for a moment.

"Searching for what?" asked James.

"And who are the Forgotten?" added Millicent.

Madigan was about to answer when Mr. Farragut cleared his throat. Madigan gave the teacher a piercing look, but answered, "To be honest, Mr. Wallace, I have no idea what it is that they are after. I'm not even sure it's relevant at this point."

To Eleanor it seemed as if it might be a crucial piece of information, but Madigan did not seem inclined to elaborate.

"And Miss Millsap, the Forgotten are a collection of danger-ous - criminals, as I said," continued Madigan, giving a sideways look at Mr. Farragut. "They are known as the Forgotten be-cause they hide their true names and appearances from every-one, including each other. They use - ", Mr. Farragut cleared his throat all too loudly, and Madigan gave him another glare but kept talking, " - peculiar arts of deception. This allows them to move freely throughout the city, perpetrating their crimes."

"So, logically, anyone and everyone could be a member of this Forgotten group, right?" asked James. "How could you possibly know who they are if they are hiding in plain sight?"

Mr. Farragut leaned forward, "James, watch you tone."

While James had sounded rude, Eleanor found she was just as skeptical about the idea of these Forgotten. What did Madigan mean they were hiding their true names? She found a host of questions forming in her head, but held her tongue in front of the other students. James looked as if he was about to toss a retort towards Mr. Farragut, but Adam interrupted with his own question.

"Whatever it is or they are, what do you expect we're going to find? " asked Adam, frowning at the code.

"If I knew that, Mr. Newberry, I would not be here tonight," said Madigan, which made James snort out loud. "What I know is that there was some reason for these codes. A purpose. I must know that purpose." His voice deepened as he said the last, and a determined look crossed his face. He stood and began pulling on a thick winter's cloak.

"This is a test without an answer key," Madigan said, staring out at each of them in turn, then shrugging his cloak over his shoulders. "It is unlike what you are used to working on in class. However, it would be a great service to me to take this project on. If you are willing, Mr. Farragut has reserved this room for you to work in. I hope you will take up the challenge."

No one said a word. Madigan gave them a slight nod, turned, and disappeared into the dark as he exited the room.

CHAPTER 5

MR. MADIGAN'S PROJECT

AFTER Madigan had left there was silence in the room. Eleanor found herself uncertain of what to do. There had been a hint of something in Mr. Madigan's voice, a note of anxiety, almost desperation. The codes had captured her curiosity, a puzzle begging to be solved. The dutiful part of her replied that she was at Penwick to do school work, not run off and waste time on a wild goose chase involving codes and these Forgotten people. Eleanor wavered and as she glanced around the table. She could see each of the other students was engaged in a similar internal debate.

They ended up all looking around at each other, hoping that someone else would offer up an argument one way or the other. Mr. Farragut said nothing to help them decide.

Adam broke the silence. "It all sounds very questionable, if you ask me," he said, sounding as if they had all been waiting for his opinion.

Eleanor was surprised when she felt the bottom had drop out of her stomach. Adam wasn't going to do it? Would the others follow suit? If they did there would be no reason for her to try it alone. She was shocked at her own sense of disappointment at that.

Her stomach took another lurch, up this time, when James

spoke.

"Where's the sense of adventure, Adam? Curiosity?" he said, leaning back in his chair. "I know it all sounds a bit off kilter, but that's what's intriguing about it. I'm game. I'll work on it, Mr. Farragut."

The teacher just nodded and looked back at Millicent and Eleanor. Millicent was working a loose strand of hair in between her fingers, eyes half closed. Eleanor stayed silent, wanting the other girl to answer first, hoping that she'd say yes.

After what seemed like an hour Millicent's eyes fluttered open the rest of the way. "I'll do it," she said. "I'm assuming that if I start to fall behind in classes, I can just quit." At this she looked at Mr. Farragut.

"I'll promise you that, all of you," he said. "Neither Mr. Madigan, nor I, can force you to work on this. Your time is a favor to him and the Headmistress."

"Then I'll give it a start," said Millicent, dropping the wisp of hair from her fingers now that a decision had been made.

This was enough for Eleanor. "I'll do it," she said, and if the others cared they didn't show it.

"Good, then. Millicent, James, and Eleanor, this room will be available to you from now on. If you have any questions, or need permission to access archives, let me know and I will sign for you. Now, I think that it is getting late enough, so why don't you all head back to your dormitories."

They started to push back their chairs, but Adam stopped them.

"Alright, I'll do it," he said, managing to sound as if he had just given in to their demands. Millicent rolled her eyes.

"Well, thank heavens for that," said James, pushing his chair back and walking out without waiting for a response.

The next afternoon after classes had left off for the day Eleanor and the three others made their way back to reading room 17. On the table was Mr. Madigan's code as well as several stacks of blank paper. A moment after they had sat down Adam grabbed the code and set it in front of him.

"Well then, here's the plan," he started. Millicent made an audible groan, and James stared at the older boy with his mouth wide open.

Adam plowed ahead. "It seems obvious that this has to be some kind of substitution code. We should start by finding all the books we can in the libraries related to cryptology."

"And who decided that would be the plan?" said Millicent.

"I was thinking things over last night," said Adam, in a parental tone.

Perhaps noticing the looks of contempt from James and Millicent, he took a deep breath and went on.

"Look, I'm a sixth year and I've been a Proctor for Mr. Williams in Numerancy before. Of all of us here," he said with a sideways glance at Eleanor, "I've got some experience with this kind of research."

"I don't remember Madigan or Farragut asking you to direct the project," said Millicent.

"Right," said James, "I don't work for you, Adam." He snatched the code from Adam and scanned it over. "This may not even be some kind of alphabet substitution at all. It could refer to coordinates on a map. Like you said, there are a too many numbers outside of the regular alphabet range. I'd start with some maps."

"I don't need you telling me what to do, either, James," said Millicent.

"People," Adam interjected. "We have to have some kind of plan. We aren't going to get anywhere just running off doing our own thing. Let's start with reading up on how codes are formed, it's what makes the most sense."

Millicent and James both grumbled back at Adam. Eleanor remained quiet. She was the junior member of the project and didn't have a clear idea of what they should be doing. Adam was acting overbearing, assuming that he was in charge because he was a sixth year, but he did have a point. They had to coordinate their work.

But the others would not come to an agreement. James wouldn't budge off his idea of looking over maps and Millicent refused to accept that either of the boys had a valid idea even though she wasn't offering any of her own. They argued back and forth for several minutes before James took a blank sheet from the pile in the middle of the table and started copying out the code.

"What are you doing now?" demanded Adam.

"It's called writing," snapped James.

"You're such a bonehead. What're you going to do, make your own copy?"

"Yes," said James, "and then you can all do whatever you'd like. But I'll be getting on with doing something useful." He bent back down over the code, his pencil scribbling.

Millicent looked over at James for a moment, and then grabbed some blank paper herself and set to work making a copy by peering over James' shoulder. Adam sighed, took a chair on the other side of James and began on his own version.

Eleanor didn't move for a moment. She felt paralyzed. Even if she had her own copy she didn't know where to begin. The others were older and had ideas about what to do. She didn't like Adam or anyone giving her orders, but at least she'd have had some clue as to what to do. The others, though, were intent on their copying and the last few minutes had made it clear that they were not going to come up with a common plan. So, once the others had finished Eleanor took the list and began copying it out onto a blank sheet.

Millicent stood and tucked her copy into her bag. "I'll see all of you around the school," she said and walked out.

Adam and James shuffled themselves off with some mumbled grunts towards Eleanor and cold stares for each other.

Eleanor was left alone in the reading room copying down the numbers. Now that the others were gone she felt her self-control slipping just a little. This wasn't what it was supposed to be, she thought, sniffling back a tear that had somehow crept into her eye. She had been excited at the prospect of working on this, and in her head she had seen them all sitting in the reading room collaborating. Now she had a very neat copy of this list of numbers, but no idea of what to do with it. She felt lost and very much out of her depth. Why had Mr. Madigan asked for her? He couldn't have expected her to know what to do by herself. The older students were there to provide some guidance and all they had done was argue. It was not turning out at all like she had pictured.

She'd have to talk to Mr. Farragut, which didn't excite her. Despite being unclear on what to do she still prided herself on being one of the top students. Top students wouldn't be sniffling, she told herself. Nor would they run to Mr. Farragut first thing. Maybe she should at least try to come up with something first. Show them all that she wasn't helpless without a teacher's guidance.

Resolving that she would try to work independently for a few days first, she gathered up her things and stored them in her rucksack. She tidied up the stack of blank paper on the table and left the reading room for the chilly walk back to her dormitory, where she still had a few hours of regular schoolwork to do. It was going to be a long night.

It was two days later before Eleanor had time to head back to the library and begin working. She hadn't seen or talked to the others since their first meeting with Mr. Madigan, and had no idea whether they had already made any progress.

She made her way through the main doors of the Entry

Hall, but rather than heading for one of the archways leading into the collections she took the stairs up to the second floor. She emerged onto the balcony and walked towards two wooden doors, one of which was slightly ajar. It was open enough to let her slide through without having to push it any further.

Inside was a windowless room that took up almost the entire second floor of the Entry Hall. Long wooden tables ran in regular rows across the middle of the room, and there were perhaps two dozen students and a similar number of visiting scholars huddled over books and notes at those tables. Around the perimeter of the room were wooden cabinets that ran floor to ceiling, each containing hundreds of small drawers. A catwalk ran around the room halfway up, with skinny ladders on rails mounted to it. There were a few students up on the catwalk trying to slide open a drawer while not falling the six feet to the floor.

Most people, including Eleanor herself when she had first arrived, thought that the vast expanse of bookshelves and specimen trays in the tangle of libraries was what gave Penwick its prestige as a school. But there were archives of comparable size in several other cities. What made Penwick unique was this room and its walls of drawers. It had no official name. The students simply called it the Index.

Inside the drawers were cards, row after row of them, each one a little bigger than Eleanor's hand. At the top of each was written something: a name, a place, an idea, anything. Below it successive generations of Penwick students and traveling scholars had noted down which books these items appeared in, often down to the exact page. As a Penwick student advanced through the school they'd be expected to litter their own notations across this collection of information, tying the books of the archive into an ever-tighter web of connections.

There was a section of drawers organized by subject, and another set for specific people. Last year Eleanor and her fellow first-year students had giggled their way through the Index in their first few days on campus, looking themselves up. The novelty of that had worn off quickly. For most their card consisted of a newly lettered entry referring the reader to the *Penwick Student Registry, Volume 97, Book 14, section 5*, housed in the 3rd floor annex of the Old South Library. Those from Flosston Moor had also shown birth records on their card. The only interesting entry had actually shown up on Eleanor's card. Aside from her Penwick registration there had been an earlier note that listed her in something called *King's Inquest, Berry 1712*. Eleanor didn't know why she was listed in that book, or what a King's Inquest was. Her grandfather, who had lived in a village named Berry, had died in 1712. But he had died in a sailing accident, caught in a freak storm at sea, so why was there an inquest? Eleanor was never able to find the book on the fourth floor of the Hollowbrick Archive, where the card said it was located. Most likely it had been shelved in the wrong space, and now only a stroke of unbelievable luck would ever bring it to light.

Eleanor wasn't too worried about a dead end with her current search. Despite Adam's pushy manner she had decided that learning something about how codes worked was crucial for her. Substituting letters in for the existing numbers resulted in something like

```
H Z D L N S B F Y G K L L C P G
L ? V U O ? O G ? V Z Z ? ?  ?   ?
```

and she had no idea what to do with the numbers greater than 26.

Along the north wall she found a subject drawer labelled "Cod - Coe" and slid it out. Rifling through with her fingers she came across a large yellow card that just said "Code" on it, and beneath that were listed several variants on the word including "Code breaking".

Behind that main subject card were a series of white cards. Some pointed towards books in which someone had mentioned a code, but she did not want those. Digging further she found four cards that listed books about codes and code breaking. She wrote down the locations of these, relieved to find that they all were located within the New South Library and only separated by two floors at most.

Making her way back downstairs she went out the right-most archway, over which a small sign hung that read Navigation Tower. Last year Mr. Hanford had showed them a short cut through a storage closet on the fourth floor of the Navigation Tower that led into a stairwell of the New South Library. The wooden floor of the closet had rotted away from some ancient leak, so you just had to be willing to walk over a thick plank some students had laid down over the gap. She made it to the closet in just a few minutes.

Reminding herself to not look down, Eleanor crossed the plank and came out near a door to the third floor of the New South Library. She was able to find the first two volumes on code breaking that she had looked up without too much trouble. She pulled them off the shelf and left two "In Use" tags in their places.

The other two books she wanted were on the fifth floor. After discovering that the first stairwell only went up to the fourth floor she doubled back and found a thin wrought iron spiral staircase in the center of the stacks that took her all the way up. One of the code-breaking books was missing and an "In Use" tag was in its place with the name "M. Millsap" printed on the bottom. Millicent. It was disappointing but not surprising. Even Millicent had to realize that Adam's idea about reading up on codes was a good one.

Stuffing the books she did have into her rucksack, she made her way back down the spiral staircase, over to the first stairwell, and across the plank to the Navigation Tower. As she emerged into the Tower, she almost stumbled backwards into the gap in the floor when two of the Keepers startled her. They were pale-skinned and dressed in brown robes, pushing a battered cart filled with musty books. Both of them looked at her blankly, but said nothing. The Keepers lived somewhere in the library complex itself, but none of the students knew where. They tended to the libraries as best they could, trying vainly to keep the vast collection of records organized.

Eleanor mumbled a quick "excuse me" as she slipped past the Keepers. They made her and many of the students feel uncomfortable, and she was glad to get out of their sight. They never said a word but peered after her until she disappeared around a corner. She made the quick trip to reading room 17 where she could see light coming out from the open doorway. She entered and saw James standing in front of a massive ocean chart that he had pinned to the wall.

"Oh, hello Eleanor," said James when the sound of her books hitting the table startled him.

"Hi," Eleanor replied quietly.

"Reading up a little on the mysterious world of cryptology, eh?" he asked. She nodded. "Hoping to find out if there is some meaning to the numbers 41, 33, 43, 39, 35, 44, and 34?"

Eleanor stopped cold. "How did you know that?"

"Millie was around yesterday, going through the same stuff as you. I'll save you tedium of looking all this up. Your standard code allows you to use numbers as well as letters. So 41 stands for the number 15, as in twenty-six plus 15 equals 41."

"That doesn't - ," said Eleanor.

"Help?" finished James. "No, Millie didn't think so either. You still end up with some garble like L 15 V U something or other. I'm telling you all, it's not supposed to translate into words."

Eleanor felt deflated. She was behind everyone else and engaged on a wild goose chase to break this code if James was right.

He must have noticed the defeat in her face because he lost the flippant tone. "Eleanor, don't take it personally. It was worth checking the easiest options first."

She wasn't sure if he was just being patronizing, but it sounded sincere. It made her realize how wound up her insides had been about this whole project from the moment she got the note in the dining hall until now. "I - just - I really don't know what I'm doing here. I feel like I'll rubbish the whole thing."

James sat down in the chair next to hers. "Look, Madigan picked you out for a reason. Maybe you don't see it yet, but there is a reason."

"How could you be sure of that?" Eleanor asked.

"One second with Madigan and you can tell he doesn't leave things to chance. It reminds me of playing cards with my dad."

Eleanor was a little lost and gave James a quizzical look. "My father has been playing cards forever," James explained, "and he knows the deck back and forth. He always knows what you're going to play even before you do. Madigan strikes me as the same kind of man."

"But what game is Mr. Madigan playing, do you think," asked Eleanor, to herself as much as to James.

"That I just do not know," said James.

Having been somewhat reassured Eleanor set to work with the codebooks she did have. Over the next two weeks she returned to room 17 at least once every day to read about various ways of constructing alphabet codes. She did not have any clear concept of what she was looking for, but was hoping that brute force was a worthy substitute for inspiration. She tried various schemes that presented themselves. Letting B equal 1, C equal 2, and so forth, with A equal to 26. Letting C equal 1 and D equal 2, and so on. She tried each remaining letter of the alphabet as the first letter. None of those worked. She tried other options. Going backwards through the alphabet with Z as 1 and A as 26. Letting the higher numbers wrap around so that 33 acted just like a 7. Skipping Q and Z so the alphabet only used 24 letters.

During this time she often saw James. His map was filling up with strange marks and pieces of twine stretched between various points. Some almost lined up on islands on the map, and others ran at odd angles out to the middle of nowhere. Millicent was around at times and had built a small fortress of books around one space at the corner of the table. James enjoyed asking her if she planned on digging a moat. Adam was spending his time elsewhere and Eleanor never saw him.

She didn't see many people at all, at least not outside of class. She spent time in the library working on the project in the afternoon, which meant that she only made it to the dining hall at the end of service. The second-year girls would be gone already, back in their dormitory doing classwork. Miriam tried for the first week or so to linger long enough to eat with Eleanor, but eventually she was absent as well. Dinner became a solitary event, sipping soup while she got started on her actual schoolwork. Eleanor tried to ignore it, but her singular existence at

Penwick was starting to wear on her.

Relief came from an unexpected source. It was a typical night in the dining hall, with only the sounds of the students serving out detentions in the scullery breaking the silence. Eleanor was working at some of her Geometry homework when someone jostled the table, breaking her concentration. It was Millicent, who set down a tray of food and several books across the table from Eleanor.

"Do you mind some company?" asked Millicent.

Startled at the intrusion, and shocked that Millicent had even spoken to her, it took Eleanor a moment to reply. "Oh. Sure. Yes, of course," she said and started to tidy up the books and papers she had strewn about the table.

"Thanks," said Millicent and somewhere behind her typical sour expression Eleanor thought she noticed what might qualify as a smile. The older girl set her own books out on the table, a weak defensive position compared to the fortress she had erected in the reading room. She set to work on something that looked like Astronomy homework and said nothing else, her fingers twirling at the loose brown hair that hung down over her papers.

Eleanor watched her for a moment, and decided it was best not to push her luck by speaking to Millicent any further. The presence of someone else made an incredible difference to her mood that evening. The hollow feeling that had settled into her stomach the last few weeks receded. They both studied for another hour before the head of the kitchens shooed them out for the night. Millicent gave Eleanor a nod as they separated outside.

Over the next few days their silent collaboration became routine. Eleanor, arriving first, would eat dinner and start studying. At some point Millicent would come along, sit down across from her, eat quickly, and then set to work. At most five or six words would pass between them, but for Eleanor it was enough to lighten her mood and give her a fresh energy in working on the code. She now had a significant stack of notes detailing all of the ways that Madigan's code did *not* translate into meaningful words.

The lack of progress had apparently hit Millicent as well, and about two weeks after she first sat down with Eleanor it elicited their first real conversation. They had both been studying as normal, and Millicent was perturbed about something. She kept muttering to herself. It was becoming a little distracting, and Eleanor was wondering if she should interrupt when Millicent said something that caught her attention.

"Why carry them separately?" muttered Millicent.

"What did you say?" asked Eleanor.

"What?" responded Millicent, her train of thought clearly broken.

"What was that you just said?" asked Eleanor.

"Why carry the codes separately?" said Millicent. "It's just odd that someone wouldn't write them down together on the same sheet."

That's right, thought Eleanor. She had been so focused on

91

the numbers themselves that she had forgotten Madigan said he found the two lists of numbers on separate pieces of paper. What would be the point of that? Did it mean something?

"Separate messages?" asked Eleanor.

"Maybe, but neither makes sense by itself," replied Millicent, still annoyed at the interruption.

"What if that is the point?" asked Eleanor, an idea creeping into her consciousness. "Neither code makes sense by itself but only when combined with the other."

Millicent's frustration appeared to fade as she sat thinking. "One is the key and the other is the message, perhaps?"

"Could be," said Eleanor. "If someone intercepted one of the codes it would be useless without the other. There would be no way for the person who delivered one of the messages to figure out what it meant. Only once both were delivered could the recipient figure it out."

Millicent didn't reply, but pulled a sheet of paper from her bag and started scribbling. She seemed so intent on her work that Eleanor bit her tongue and let her work. After a few moments Millicent looked up and a tiny smile escaped from her face.

"I think this might be it," Millicent said. "The first list is the key. It tells you where to start in the alphabet for each letter. The second list is the actual message. So the first letter is a 12, but the key tells you that A is equal to 8. If A is equal to 8, then 12 is equal to D."

Eleanor saw what she meant and it was quick work to match

Millicent's method. Subtracting the number on the first line from the second, she now had a single line of numbers reading

4 15 18 9 1 14 13 1 18 15 15 14 27 32 28 27.

After working with the codes so much these last two weeks she could translate these to letters in her head,

D O R I A N M A R O O N 1 6 2 1.

She looked up at Millicent. "Dorian Maroon? 1621?" Millicent nodded furiously.

"I think we've got it, Eleanor," said Millicent. "Now we just need to figure out who Dorian Maroon is. It's a weird name, but 1621 is almost exactly one hundred years ago. I wonder if that is supposed to be the year he was born."

"I've never heard a name like that before," said Eleanor. "Are you sure it's a person?"

"I'd guess so," said Millicent. She glanced up at the great clock hanging over the fireplace. "It's already very late and I have to be up early for a History class. I'll see you around. Tomorrow it's worth looking in the Index for Mr. Maroon."

She packed up her books and left the dining hall, which was almost empty. Eleanor sat for a while longer, staring at their breakthrough on Mr. Madigan's project. She tried to study some more but couldn't keep herself from thinking about who or what Dorian Maroon was. It wasn't clear to her whether Millicent meant that they should look in the Index together, or if she was planning to do it herself. Unable to concentrate, she gave up, stuffed her books into her rucksack, and headed back to the dormitory.

Sleep didn't come. Her mind whirled around, planning out where she would look next for evidence of Dorian Maroon. There were birth records in the Library, as well as house deeds and records of wills and inheritances. That assumed that Dorian Maroon was actually a person, of course. But what else could it be?

Despite getting in so late she was up before Miriam the next morning, and raced back to the dining hall to wolf down some oatmeal before heading to the library. She didn't have class until afternoon so she had a few hours to work.

Returning to the Index she visited the wall holding cards organized by people's names. She located the skinny drawer labelled "Mar - Mas" and opened it up. Marblehead, Marek, and Marlebone all rolled by. Her heart caught when she spotted a card with the name Marook on it. Slowing down it took only five more cards to reach one labelled with the last name Maroon. But it was for someone named Stephen Maroon, not Dorian. The next card was for a Gretchen Maroon, followed by Donald Maroon, and after that came someone with the last name Maroot.

No one named Dorian Maroon at all. Fighting down her disappointment, she copied down the references she found for the three people sharing the Maroon last name. It might be that they were related to Dorian and perhaps would provide a clue to figuring out who he was. She used shorthand to take down the locations, a pattern every student learned early on in their time at Penwick. Stephen Maroon's birth record she wrote down as -2 V 14 3 B. The -2 V meant that the book containing it was in the second sub-basement of the Vellium, an ancient tower nestled in the middle of the collection of libraries. She'd have to traverse the maze of the Old South Library, and then climb up three stories in the Obelisk just to reach the right stairwell to descend to the sub-basement of the Vellium. Once there she'd have to find her way to aisle 14, the third bay of shelves, and look on shelf B to find the book with Stephen Maroon's birth record. She scribbled down similar codes for the other two people with records in the Index and hustled off to find them.

It took her twenty minutes, but she found herself in the dull light of a few lanterns lining the walls of the sub-basement in the Vellium. This library was deep in the heart of the complex. Even the upper levels received no light through their windows, as further additions had been snuggled right up against them. Being on the fourth floor wouldn't have been any different from being down here in the sub-basement.

The books were musty and Eleanor was careful in extracting the birth records lest the pages disintegrate in her hands. Finding Stephen Maroon took a while, as she had to flip slowly through the crumbling volume. In the end it did not seem worth the effort. He did not show a Dorian Maroon as a parent, and he had been born almost three hundred years ago. Gretchen Maroon's records were located just a few floors up in the Vellium, but she also offered no evidence regarding Dorian Maroon.

From the Vellium she worked her way through a maintenance tunnel that opened into a hallway in the lowest floor of the white-marbled King's Stacks. This was the most pleasant of the many different buildings making up the Library, the white stone of the walls reflecting enough lamplight to let Eleanor fool herself into thinking there were functioning windows. Something about the nicer surroundings had led generations of students and scholars to take better care of this library. The books stood as straight as the King's own soldiers, and there were far fewer stacks of overflow volumes piled in aisles.

It took her a few minutes to reach the sixth floor, where she was able to locate a book of aged Sherriff's records citing Donald Maroon with public drunkenness. Again, nothing there contained any hint about a Dorian Maroon.

While not surprising, the lack of information was still disappointing. The thrill of cracking the code had given her a rush of energy, but the hunt this morning had sapped all of it. Dorian Maroon could still be a person that existed somewhere in the stacks and stacks of books here in the library. However no one had ever found him - or her? - worthy of noting in the Index. Without that it was hopeless. There were just far too many books to look through.

She shuffled back down the stairs of the King's Stacks and then towards the Entry Hall. Along the way she passed through the Old South Library. A wrong turn somewhere ran her down an aisle of shelves that dead-ended against a brown stone wall. Hung on the wall was an ancient painting. Only up close could she see that it was a picture of a sailing ship. From the looks of it the ship was several centuries old and the captain was portrayed in a dramatic pose, standing on the forecastle looking through a golden telescope.

Her grandfather would have enjoyed a good laugh at this, she thought. He had spent the early part of his life as a sailor and then captained a ship himself before settling down to raise her father and uncles. The ship had been called something like the *Red Peacock*. Or was it the *Purple Raven*? She couldn't remember, except that it was an odd name with a color in it, and it had always made her laugh as a child.

Turning to find her way back out of the dead end it hit her, a color in the name. *Dorian Maroon*. What if it wasn't a person, but rather a ship? Thousands came and went from Flosston Moor, and perhaps Madigan's Fogotten were after some kind of illegal cargo? With nothing to show from the three people named Maroon, it was worth a try.

She found the wrong turn she had taken, and was soon back in the Entry Hall. She nearly ran up the stairs to the Index and got several annoyed looks as she dumped her bag on a table. Ignoring them, Eleanor hunted down a special section of drawers on the second level. Shipping was of such importance in Flosston Moor that long ago Penwick students had started keeping track of individual ships in the Index. They pointed towards entries in the Harbormaster logs kept in the Navigation Tower.

Her heart was pumping hard as she climbed one of the thin ladders and scooted her way down the catwalk to the set of drawers reserved for ships. The "Di - Do" drawer was located rather far up the wall, and she had to stand on tiptoes to slide it from the rack. Bringing it down gently she set it on the catwalk and started to pick through the cards. She tried to remind herself to stay calm, as this was likely to be a dead end as well, but she couldn't stop her pulse from racing.

She almost missed it in her haste. An old card, yellowing around the edges, and at the top in neat cursive was *Dorian Maroon*. There were seventeen entries listed on the card, each referring to a Harbormaster logbook. The last one was dated 1621.

"I've got it," she said out loud, and received a distinct "shh-hhhh" from several people working just below her.

The thrill made her hurry down the ladder, and her hands nearly slipped. Taking a deep breath she continued down and found her bag at the table. Pulling out a blank sheet of paper and a Silverwood pencil from her pocket she copied down all of the entries on the card for the *Dorian Maroon*, although she was sure it had to be the one from 1621, given the code.

Back into the bramble of books and shelves she went, but not for long, as the Navigation Tower was the first you reached after leaving the Entry Hall. From there she worked her way up a spiral staircase in a corner of the collection until she reached the sixth floor, where the logbook from 1621 should be contained.

She found the correct aisle and saw that it was nothing but old Harbormaster logbooks. Working her way along the aisle, she was able to find the books from 1621 about halfway down.

They were in decent shape for being almost one hundred years old. There were three volumes for that year, and her notes from the Index said the listing was in the third.

After pulling down the massive leather-bound volume she laid it on the floor and flipped it open. The Index hadn't mentioned a page number so she would have to go through the whole thing. She fanned through page after page as a whirl of ship names ran by, each listing a destination, the date of departure and return, and a list of crewmembers and cargo. It was monotonous but the excitement of finding out the meaning of Madigan's code kept her going.

The end of the volume seemed to be coming fast, and Eleanor was getting worried that the ship's entry was missing when it appeared before her. The *Dorian Maroon* had left Flosston Moor on November 15th, 1621 bound for "Pembleton Island and beyond". Pembleton was the way station where most of the spice ships coming into Flosston Moor would pick up cargo. Beyond it were the Cinnamon Islands themselves. Few ships sailed beyond Pembleton any more. The islanders were more than happy to deliver spices there and trade them for goods from Flosston Moor.

But this was one hundred years ago. Not only that, but it was barely two years after Samuel Norfolk had first discovered the Cinnamon Islands. The *Dorian Maroon* must have been one of the first ships to follow up on his famous voyage, hoping to explore the Cinnamon Islands further. What did Madigan's mysterious Forgotten want with an exploration ship almost one

99

hundred years old? Whatever spices they might have found were long gone.

She read down the page and saw the crew list. There were 37 men that left Flosston Moor on the *Dorian Maroon*. From the notations in the log it appeared that only 14 had returned. Sailing to unknown islands was always a dangerous affair, but this ship appeared to have suffered a severe loss of life. Figuring that Madigan would want everything, she sat down on the floor and started copying out exactly what she found on the page.

While noting down the crewmembers names she spotted a listing for Mortimer Hassleford, the ship's navigator, who had perished on the trip. Something about the name tugged at her consciousness but she couldn't put her finger on it. There was also a Simon Tratford, listed as an Apothecary. He may have gone along to find new plants and serve as the ship's doctor, a typical role for one with his training. The return cargo was packed with cinnamon, nutmeg, elder flowers, and mace. It was lucrative and would have made the remaining fourteen crewmembers wealthy, particularly one hundred years ago when those spices were much rarer in Flosston Moor.

Questions whirled in Eleanor's head as she wound her way back out of the Entry Hall. She hungered to keep digging now that she had found a connection, but the clock indicated that she had already worked through lunch and her afternoon History class was about to start. She sprinted across the grounds. Mr. Farragut gave her a disapproving glance as she snuck into the room just as he was about to close the door. She sat down tired but elated, impatient to tell Mr. Farragut and the others about what she had found.

CHAPTER 6

MISSING INFORMATION

EXCITEMENT at having found the *Dorian Maroon* soon gave way to disappointment and frustration. Eleanor had rushed after class to tell Mr. Farragut about what she had found. He had agreed to send notes around to the entire group requesting a meeting in reading room 17 after dinner. He also said he would try to contact Madigan, but that night the old man was nowhere to be seen.

It was perhaps for the best that Madigan wasn't here, Eleanor thought as she sat in the reading room with the others that evening. They were picking apart her idea.

"It's nice work figuring out that code," said Adam as soon as Eleanor had finished describing what she had found. "But what do we know now? It's a ship. Flosston Moor is thick with them. We still don't know the reason for the coded message."

"I hate to admit it," added James, "but I think I agree with Adam on this. Madigan wanted to know the purpose of the note, not just the translation." Both he and Adam were doing a poor job of hiding their annoyance with Eleanor and Millicent cracking the code first.

Eleanor had hoped that Millicent would at least mount some defense, as she was the one who figured out how to decode the message. Eleanor had been careful to mention that fact first

103

thing when the meeting began. However, the older girl sat in a determined silence, not making eye contact with Eleanor or the others, arms crossed over her chest.

"I know it's only a start," pleaded Eleanor, "but now we have something to go on. I was thinking that we could look for the crewmembers in the Index, maybe find out if they have anything suspicious in their past." She looked around at the rest of them.

"We?" said Adam, "None of the men on that ship will be in the Index, they're just sailors. I was looking through Sheriff records to find out if there were other occasions of criminals using similar code messages and - "

James cut him off, "you haven't found anything yet."

"No I haven't," Adam shot back, "But I'm not playing with yarn all day, making an art project." He waved his hand at James' map, which now had even more strands of colored twine pinned between different points in the ocean.

Mr. Farragut held up his hands to indicate to the boys that they should stop. "That's enough bickering. As Mr. Madigan left no explicit instructions on how to conduct this search, there is no right way forward."

He turned to talk to Eleanor. "I appreciate that you've got something tantalizing. However, it is not immediately clear that investigating the crewmembers is the right avenue. I wouldn't recommend that the others stop their own research to focus on this." Adam and James nodded in agreement. Millicent continued to stare off in another direction.

Eleanor felt deflated. Was she giving herself too much credit? Did she think this was important just because *she* found it? The others were all more experienced at research, and didn't seem to think that looking into the crew was going to be fruitful. Were they right? But in her gut she knew this ship had to hold the next clue.

"All that being said, Eleanor," said Mr. Farragut in his typical flat voice, "I also wouldn't tell you to stop what you're doing. As I said, Mr. Madigan gave us no real direction here. The only thing he told me was to let each of you follow your instincts. So feel free to research this all you like."

"Does that mean we can go?" asked Adam, standing up from the table, clearly annoyed with the whole meeting.

"Of course," said Mr. Farragut, who also began to rise. James swept up some papers in front of him, and began packing his rucksack as well. With some muttered goodbyes they all left, leaving only Eleanor and Millicent in the reading room. Eleanor began packing her own things when Millicent finally broke the silence.

"That's what you get for stealing someone else's idea," spat Millicent.

Eleanor was unprepared for the comment. "Stealing? I didn't steal anything. You noticed a connection; I did some work to see if it led anywhere. I was just trying to help."

"Help? Is that what you call it? More like trying to hog all the credit," said Millicent, now glaring at Eleanor.

"I told everyone that it was your idea, first thing!" snapped

105

Eleanor. "And in case you didn't notice, it's not like it was such a fantastic idea in the first place. No one thinks it amounts to much. So I'm the one who looks stupid. Not you."

That caused Millicent to stop glaring and instead stare down into her own bag as she stuffed in some paper. "Fine. It's your problem, then. Have fun finding nothing about those sailors." She buttoned up the bag and hoisted it over her shoulder before stalking out of the room.

Eleanor wanted to cry. This seemed unfair. Just last night she had finally felt like she belonged on Madigan's project, and now she was back to feeling out of her depth and useless. The boys and Mr. Farragut were skeptical of the whole idea and couldn't get out of here fast enough. Millicent thought she was a thief.

The smart thing to do would be to drop it. Madigan had said they could if the project interfered with their regular work, and that was starting to come true. Plus, all this project had done was make her even more of an outsider in her own year and convince several upper year students she wasn't any good at research. Why should she bother?

Even though part of her was screaming to just walk away, one corner of her mind kept insisting that she go the next step. Madigan's mystery was still unsolved, and not knowing was eating at her. What did the Forgotten want with the *Dorian Maroon*? Who were the Forgotten, for that matter? With no answers, her brain wouldn't let go of the mystery. But she promised herself that if she couldn't find anything after two weeks she would give up.

It was three days before Eleanor could get back to the search. Tests in two classes had taken up all her time, and although they were difficult the study groups that the second-year girls held before-hand had given her a chance to feel like a normal member of the school once again. She had enjoyed staying up late to study with the other girls, even though this just confirmed for them that she was a little weird.

Back in the Index, Eleanor pulled out the Harbormaster log sheet she had copied down. Despite the others dismissal of the idea, she had decided to start by looking for each of the listed crewmembers in the Index. She was copying down the names of the fourteen survivors to a new sheet of paper when there was a thunk on the wooden table she was sitting at. She looked up and was surprised to see Millicent standing across the table.

"Eleanor, I didn't scare you, did I?" Millicent asked.

"A little, I guess," Eleanor replied. She realized her heart was racing, wondering what Millicent wanted. She took a deep breath to try and calm herself down.

"I wanted to know," said the older girl with a painful look on her face, "if you needed any help with looking into the crew of the *Dorian Maroon*."

Eleanor was a little taken aback. Millicent had accused her of stealing this idea and stormed out when Eleanor tried to explain herself. Now she was offering to help? It didn't make sense.

The look on her face must have shown the confusion in her

mind. Millicent spoke again, "Yes, well. I probably overreacted, alright? Can we just get on with whatever it is you're doing?"

Eleanor figured that was the closest thing to an apology Millicent could muster. It would do. She showed Millicent the list of fourteen names, and they agreed to divide it in half and look for any entries in the Index.

A boy sitting a few seats down had had enough of their talking and gave them a very loud "shhhhhh".

Millicent looked over at him with a frown. "Stuff it, Alex," she said. Alex looked like he was about to respond but thought better of it when Millicent glared at him.

"Let's start hunting," Millicent said, and Eleanor followed her over to the far wall of the Index.

Eleanor had taken the top half of the names, and was starting with Bartleby Bumblerump, who was first alphabetically as well as being the captain of the *Dorian Maroon*. If anyone on the ship was going to have a card in the Index, it was him. However, after flicking through the cards in the "Bul - Bun" drawer several times she had nothing to show for it. He wasn't listed.

The same went for Richard Cooper, Samuel Donant, and the rest of her list of names. Adam and James had been right, regular sailors just didn't make it into the Index. She was taking one last look through a drawer she hoped would contain a listing for Edgar Noonan when Millicent came bustling up.

"I've got one," she said, and Eleanor thought she detected something resembling excitement in Millicent's eyes.

"You did?" said Eleanor. "I've got nothing. Who is it?"

"Simon Tratford," said Millicent. "The Apothecary. He's got one listing for field notes from the Cinnamon Islands. He was also a student here at Penwick."

"So maybe his field notes can tell us something," said Eleanor, anticipation coursing through her. "Let's go find out what Mr. Tratford had to say about the voyage."

The field notes were housed in a building that students called The Rack. The Rack was a building crowded up against the west side of the library complex and it had an odd structure. It was seven or eight stories tall inside, and the bookshelves themselves were the entire height of the building. Metal catwalks had been run between the shelves at various intervals supported only by fearfully thin steel rods. You could look down through the grillwork of the catwalks all the way to the floor of The Rack itself. One of the third-years had told Eleanor you had to be careful walking around on the ground floor, as sometimes students above would throw up from getting vertigo. It probably wasn't true, but Eleanor had an uneasy feeling in her stomach nonetheless as they trudged through a series of hallways towards The Rack.

Getting into The Rack was an adventure in itself. The regular entrance on the bottom floor had been blocked for decades when part of the wall of the New South Library had collapsed. Instead a doorway had been cut into the stone of the adjacent Old South Library, but whoever did the work hadn't checked the location of the catwalks and therefore nothing matched up. It meant that they either had to jump down about four feet onto a thin catwalk or clamber up the rope that a long-gone student had thought to tie to a higher catwalk. Eleanor and Millicent decided to jump. Neither was sure they could shinny up the rope carrying their bags on their backs.

With a deep breath Eleanor hopped first off the edge of the doorway and tried to imagine herself being very light. Her feet hit the catwalk with a clang that reverberated down the shelves around her and across the rest of The Rack. Someone down below shouted at her to keep it quiet, their voice echoing off the stone walls and against the metal bookshelves. She decided yelling an apology would only make the matter worse. Millicent landed behind her with another loud clang.

Reminding herself to not look down, Eleanor shuffled her way towards the nearest ladder. They had entered on what was the fourth level of catwalks, but needed to get up to the eighth near the top of the entire structure. The ladders were made of the same thin metal bars as the catwalk and rattled against their supports with an alarming amount of movement.

Reaching the top Eleanor had to pause for a moment to get her heart to stop beating so fast after from the climb and the fear. They made their way around the catwalks to find the field notes of Mr. Tratford. They were supposed to be on a low shelf halfway down one of the aisles. Eleanor couldn't help but look down through the grates of the catwalk as she bent over to retrieve the book. The sheer scale of the drop to the floor was dizzying and she had to put a hand on the shelf to steady herself. She felt nauseous, and started to believe what the older students had told her.

Focusing on the shelf, Eleanor could not find the book. She figured it was due to her disorientation. Shaking her head to clear it she looked back at the line of books standing at attention. It should have been there. A gap on the shelf suggested that it may have been housed there at some point, but there was no "In Use" tag to indicate someone had removed it. That wasn't surprising, as oftentimes students were lax about using these, figuring that others were unlikely to want some obscure volume.

"It's not here," said Eleanor as she stood up and gained her bearings again.

"What? *Field Notes of the Cinnamon Islands, Simon Tratford*, right? Are you looking in the right place?" snipped Millicent.

"Yes," said Eleanor, "I'm not incompetent, you know."

Whether Millicent agreed or not went unsaid. She bent down to examine the gap in the stack that Eleanor had been looking at. She traced her fingers up and down the row of volumes and then stood up. "It's not here," she said.

"I just told you that," said Eleanor, but Millicent ignored her.

"Check around. Someone may have mis-shelved it," said Millicent as she started working her way to the left of where the book should have been. Eleanor went to the right and examined shelf after shelf. They worked for close to an hour, but could not find Simon Tratford's notes anywhere. If it was still in the Library it was likely lost to them.

111

The light was fading from the murky windows on the outside of The Rack when they gave up. Eleanor felt disappointed at being stymied like this. Most likely the field notes were nothing important, but now that they couldn't locate it Eleanor's mind kept spinning out tales about what they might have found inside: a treasure map, another secret code, or something else? Without speaking much the two girls picked their way back to the fifth level of The Rack and slid down the rope to the opening in the wall. A few minutes later they were back in the Entry Hall.

It was dinner time already, and as it was cold out they decided to cut through Morgan Hall to get to the dining hall. Inside only a few lanterns were still flickering, but it was still warmer than it had been outside. They turned down the main hallway which took them past the Headmistresses office.

Walking past the etched words on the wooden doors leading to the Headmistresses office it struck her. *Field Notes of the Cinnamon Islands, Simon Tratford.* It was the book she had carried, dropped, cleaned up, and delivered to Mr. Wellsby in the Steward's Tower. That man had given her the chills. What did he want with a book written by the Apothecary from the *Dorian Maroon*?

It ate at Eleanor all the next day, distracting her in class and causing her to miss out on several pages of notes that she had to copy from Miriam during lunch. Was it just a coincidence that Wellsby wanted that book? But what could he be doing with the same book that Madigan's coded message had led them to?

Why was everyone so interested in whatever plants Mr. Tratford had found while traveling?

That afternoon they had History with Mr. Farragut, and Eleanor remained in her seat after class ended. Mr. Farragut could tell that she wanted to talk.

"Alright, Eleanor, is there something that you have on your mind?"

It was hard to figure out what to start with. "Millicent and I looked up all of the men from the *Dorian Maroon*," she started.

"And you found something?" he asked. Eleanor couldn't figure out the tone of his reaction. Surprise? Disappointment? Mr. Farragut had such a monotone voice that everything sounded the same.

"We did," she said. "It turns out that there is a set of field notes from the Apothecary that was aboard."

"Is that all?" Mr. Farragut asked, apparently not seeing anything interesting in what she said.

"Well, no, it isn't," she said. Swallowing hard, she continued. "The field notes are gone. The book isn't on the shelf."

"Many volumes get waylaid in that nest of a library, Eleanor. I doubt it means anything," Mr. Farragut grumbled.

"There's just something odd about the missing book, sir," she said, even though it was becoming apparent that Mr. Farragut would very much like to leave.

"This whole project is odd, Eleanor. Honestly, I'm shocked that all of you haven't given up on this silly game already," he said.

As it surprised her as well, Eleanor couldn't honestly argue with what Mr. Farragut had just said.

"I know it's a bit strange, Mr. Farragut. But the missing book was sent over to a Mr. Wellsby in the Steward's Tower by the Headmistress," she said.

"And how," Mr. Farragut said, "do you know that?"

"I delivered it for her," she replied.

At this Mr. Farragut paused, staring off into the corner of the room for a few moments. "Wellsby, you said?"

"Yes, sir."

His shoulders seemed to slump a little, and he let out a resigned sigh. "I'll send a note to Madigan and see what he says. Until then you'll have to just sit tight."

"I will, sir," Eleanor said, puzzled at the change in his demeanor at this news. "Is there something bad about Mr. Wellsby having the field notes?"

Mr. Farragut gave a shrug. "I don't know for sure, Eleanor. But Madigan asked me to keep my ear open for the name. So I'll send him an note, like I said. I don't know any more that that."

With that he picked up his lecture notes and ducked into his office. Eleanor was left in silence to gather up her own things. She was able to see Farragut at his desk through the opened door. He was writing, and when he finished he opened up the bottom drawer of his desk and pulled out a large clay cup dotted with pebbles. He set the cup on the desk and then did a most curious thing. Taking up a candle, he held it to the note he had just written and set it on fire before dropping it in the cup. It went up in a brief shoot of orange flame, and then there was nothing but a few wisps of black smoke. Satisfied that the fire was out, Farragut took the pebbled cup and put it back into his lower drawer. Eleanor just stared for a few moments, wondering what that could have been about. He said he was going to write Madigan, but then he burned up the note? Why bother writing it at all if he wasn't going to deliver it? And Farragut seemed to have a special cup available just for burning things. Somehow that didn't seem strange to her, but as she crept out of the room her mind was spinning with questions.

The next few days oozed by. Eleanor's mind kept trying to figure out what could be in the field notes that would interest Wellsby. She had picked her way back to The Rack one afternoon to scan through more shelves looking for a clue. The volumes around Tratford's empty spot were all field notes or journals by naturalists exploring new places. Some of them were old enough, though, that those new places consisted of towns along the Mandelbar coast that had been inhabited for over five hundred years. In general the notes were endless lists of plants, often with sketches, and speculation by the author as to the value of those plants to Apothecary work. Many of the drawings were exquisite - the authors were gifted artists.

Standing alone on the catwalk that day she heard a clang from the direction of the opening in the wall. The banging and clattering came nearer and nearer as she listened. Very soon

Eleanor was convinced that whoever had entered the Rack was heading right towards where she was. She felt nervous for some reason, afraid that someone would find her here.

Another clang, and a figure came around the corner of the shelf and entered her catwalk. The light caught the figure's face. It was Millicent.

"I guess I'm not the only crazy one," said the older girl, dropping her satchel to the catwalk with a bang.

"What are you doing here?" asked Eleanor.

"Probably the same thing you are," said Millicent. "I've been trying to find Simon Tratford's notes. And in the meantime reading through a number of others. It makes me wonder what Madigan's mystery man is after. An exotic plant?"

Eleanor was a bit shocked. She hadn't thought Millicent cared that much about the project, but it sounded as if they had both been thinking along the same lines. "But Tratford sailed one hundred years ago, what did he find that isn't available now?" she said.

"I had the same question. Either we're on the wrong track," said Millicent, her fingers working again at her brown hair, "or what he found must be something remarkable and unique. The fact that this man Wellsby was interested in the book makes me think it's the second option. Tratford found something special, and maybe he didn't even realize it. But now someone is trying to find it again."

They spent some time picking through other books, neither able to find anything other than more sketches and descriptions

116

of exotic plants. They looked at each other and made an un-spoken agreement to give up. Neither said anything as they swung down the rope out of The Rack and wound their way back towards the Entry Hall.

Just as they were leaving the Library, though, Millicent made a comment, "We could use a Occlodex."

Eleanor had never heard the word before. "What is that?"

"An *Occludated Codex*, to be correct," said Millicent. The blank look on Eleanor's face made it obvious she didn't know what those were either.

"They're liquid books," Millicent explained. "A long time ago wizards in the White Tower decided that reading was too slow. So they cooked up some hocus-pocus to brew the words in a book into a potion. They called them Occludated Codices, but that was too long to say so people just called them Occlodexes. You could take a drink of one and have the whole text of the book in your head. It's like you had read the book and memorized it."

Eleanor was incredulous, "You can't be serious."

Millicent shrugged, "That's the story. I don't know if it's true or not. But in Mr. Bertram's class we learned about how closely Penwick worked with the White Tower for a long time. I suppose it might have actually happened."

"Liquid books," Eleanor said, "That's amazing."

"I think that's why they call it magic," Millicent replied.

"But there aren't Occlodexes any more, are there?" Eleanor asked, ignoring the other girl's comment.

117

"How would I know? I was just joking," said Millicent, shrugging. "I meant that we need a different source for the missing records. Something about Simon Tratford is important, and until we see his field notes we won't know what it is."

Eleanor could just nod in agreement. An answer, some answer, was hiding inside that book. But any ideas about getting the book back from Mr. Wellsby were dashed when Miriam came running up to meet them as they came upon Morgan Hall.

"Eleanor, there you are," shouted Miriam. "Mr. Farragut asked me to give you this note." She handed over a folded up piece of parchment that looked like it had scorch marks along the side.

"Did you try to light it on fire?" asked Millicent.

"No," said Miriam, as if this was something she commonly did to notes.

Eleanor unrolled it. It was from Madigan.

> *Eleanor,*
>
> *Excellent work, I knew that I was right to trust you all. Under no circumstances try to recover the book from Mr. Wellsby. I will inquire into obtaining the missing information, so please focus on your regular studies for the time being.*
>
> *Do not mention this to anyone else, including the Headmistress. I don't wish you to be deceptive with your head of school, but it is for the best if your discovery remains secret for a while longer.*
>
> *Madigan*

118

So she was supposed to just forget about the project? Just like that? Madigan didn't understand how it had dug its way into her brain by now.

Miriam must have noticed some distress on her face. "Is everything okay, Eleanor?"

Startled back to the moment, Eleanor replied, "Oh, sure. Uh, it's just a little disappointing, that's all." Miriam didn't know about the details of the project, and Madigan had asked her not to talk about it.

"Alright," said Miriam, not catching on to Eleanor's hesitation. "There isn't anything I can give you two a hand with, is there?" The look on Miriam's face was eager and expectant.

It hadn't occurred to Eleanor before that Miriam would have cared to participate. She had drifted away with the other second-year girls when Eleanor started working late on the project, but while the others were probably jealous, Miriam felt left out of her friend's world. Eleanor had gotten so wrapped up in her own situation that she hadn't bothered to notice the effect it was having on her own roommate.

"Miriam, I'm sorry," said Eleanor. "I know I've basically gone missing these last two months, and it wasn't fair to leave you alone with Darcy, Cassidy, and Amelia that long." That got a mild smile from Miriam. "Honestly, the note says that I'm supposed to do nothing now. Full stop."

"She's not lying," said Millicent, who had maneuvered herself so that she could read the note over Eleanor's shoulder. "You aren't missing anything, trust me. Good to get back to

119

regular school work, I'm behind in my Astronomy charts." With that the older girl turned and strode off towards the Numerancy house.

Miriam turned her giant eyes on Eleanor. "It seemed rather exotic, you know? Having this secret project to work on, while everyone else was just toiling away at the same old numeracy charts."

"Exotic is hardly the word I would have used. A lot of slow picking through old books in The Rack. Boring, boring, boring," said Eleanor.

"I guess so," said Miriam, although it wasn't the most convincing response. "How about we go to dinner at a reasonable hour. The kitchen should just be opening up."

"That sounds like a great idea," replied Eleanor.

They ended up having a very good dinner, and though some of the other girls pestered her for details on the project, Eleanor was able to deflect them long enough for the topic to turn to other matters. Fanny Gergson's hair, for example, which had turned a brilliant blue color after her experiment in an Apothecary lab had gone horribly wrong. She had a scarf tied around it, but you could see the sky blue locks peeking out around the edges.

That night Eleanor and Miriam worked together on several assignments in their room, Eleanor often needing some coaching on difficult items that she had been too distracted to catch the first time through in class. It was a very normal kind of night at Penwick, and to Eleanor it felt good to be normal.

Several days passed with a similar routine, and the problem of the missing field notes retreated to a far corner of Eleanor's mind. However, it hadn't disappeared and a few days later in the Index the project crept back into her consciousness. She was supposed to be researching a short essay on the Occidental Confederacy. Flipping through the cards in the "Occ" drawer her eye caught the word *Occludated*. She hesitated, telling herself that the whole concept was ridiculous, but in the end curiosity won out. She looked closer and saw it was indeed a card for *Occludated Codex*. She plucked the card from the drawer, finding it dense with references.

Not sure what she was looking for, she scanned over the card. Most of the entries looked ancient, but the last one on the back was for a history book about the White Tower published only a few years ago. It was located right in the New South Library, the collection adjacent to the Entry Hall. It would be easy to check it out. The person who had made the notation on the card had even been so good as to leave the page number for her.

So without stopping to think about it Eleanor was down the stairs from the Index and off to the New South Library. Without too much trouble she found the history book. Flipping it open to the correct page she found several paragraphs about the Occlodexes.

One clear example of how the White Tower continued to exert an influence on the city long after it was abandoned is the situation involving the Occludated Codexes, or Occlodexes as they are referred to.

121

Developed around the year 1400 by the White Tower, these liquid versions of books proved to be such a boon to researchers that Penwick quickly agreed to let the Wizards enchant any book in the Library.

While capturing all of the millions of volumes contained at Penwick was impractical, the White Tower did set up a facility inside the campus to capture a copy of all new books entering the Library as Occlodexes. Such was the force of inertia that it was only in 1644 that these conversions were stopped by the then newly-appointed headmaster Arthur Cavendish. The storage area for the Occlodexes at 14 Whiteheart Lane was closed only a year later.

This shows .....

Eleanor stopped reading, her head spinning. The Occlodexes sounded like they were real. And it sounded as if the Simon Tratford's field notes, written in 1621, could have ended up being converted into one. Were the Occlodexes still there in the storage area? If they were perhaps that was a way to get access to the record without having to go through Mr. Wellsby.

It wasn't much to go on, but it could get her further towards an answer to Madigan's mystery. Finding the actual storage area wouldn't be that hard. Even though she didn't know Flosston Moor's streets well she had heard of Whiteheart Lane. There was only one problem. It ran right through the middle of the one place in the city she wasn't supposed to go, the Warren.

CHAPTER 7

THE WARREN

ELEANOR sat watching as a trickle of carts and people shuffled past her little perch on top of a mossy stone wall. Most of them were making their way across the Heartspan bridge, which sat directly across the road from where she sat. To her left ran the row of old shops leading up towards Penwick. To her right the road ran under a stone archway that looked as if it would collapse if a stiff breeze hit it. Only a few people came and went under the archway. It was the unofficial gateway to the Warren.

After figuring out that there might be an Occlodex containing Tratford's notes, Eleanor had gone to Mr. Farragut. He had sent another note to Madigan. She had lurked in the doorway of the teacher's office long enough to see him again light the note on fire before dropping it into the pebbled clay cup. She had gotten a reply from her earlier message, so it couldn't be that Mr. Farragut was destroying the notes. It had to be some way of communicating, but how was burning a note in that cup sending the message? Magic?

She had waited impatiently for a reply. She had tried to return to a normal routine of classes and studying with Miriam, but her mind had other ideas. Four days had passed, then five. After a sixth day of waiting Eleanor had gone on a long walk outside of Penwick trying to burn off her anxious energy. The walk had taken her to the intersection where the Heartspan leapt across the river to the center of the city, and the shaky archway to her right stood as a warning that the Warren lay beyond.

For the next three days she had found an excuse to take a walk, and always ended up back at the archway. Today was no different, and she had been camped out on the stone wall for about an hour now. From her vantage point she could see several blocks down the main street into the Warren. The buildings were a tangle of different materials and styles, crowding the street so that the few people moving about had to work to avoid hitting each other. Looming over the top of them all was the White Tower, whose only apparent occupants were a flock of starlings perched on the battlements that rimmed the top.

The storage area for the Occlodexes, if it still existed, was only one block from the White Tower. That meant it was about six blocks from where she sat right now. Some moments it seemed ridiculously close, and Eleanor had to stop herself from walking under the archway. Then a burly sailor or some mangled beggar would amble past her on their way into the Warren, and she reminded herself that a second-year Penwick student did not belong there.

If Madigan would just do something, she thought. Send a message. Tell her he had found another copy of Tratford's notes. Show his face at Penwick again. Anything. It was eating at her, and she was wasting time lurking here at the archway hoping that some magical way of transporting herself to the Occlodex would appear.

She was so caught up worrying over all this that it took her a moment to realize that a tall boy carrying a brown package had stopped in front of her.

"You auditioning to be a gargoyle?" he asked. It was Jack, the butcher's son who helped her that day she delivered the notes to Wellsby.

"Excuse me?" Eleanor replied, startled out of her brooding.

"You're sitting there, just staring off down the street. I've seen you the last few days, not moving, just watching. Like a gargoyle."

He had a great skill in making her feel flustered. A few days? She had felt anonymous in her perch. There were enough people moving about that it didn't occur to her anyone would have noticed.

"Well," she started, uncertain of what to tell him, "I like getting out of the school. It helps me think."

"Think about what?" he asked.

She very well couldn't tell him about the project. And she was unable to think of something else, so she resorted to a tactic that worked sometimes with her father.

"I don't see that it's any of your business," she said, trying to sound a little offended that he had even asked.

"Ah," said Jack, not appearing at all apologetic, "girls and their secrets." He shook his head.

Despite herself, Eleanor replied, "And what's that supposed to mean?"

"Don't get all huffy. I don't mind. But girls like to be

125

mysterious, sometimes for no reason."

"Well, I have a reason," said Eleanor, not sure of why she was so worried about justifying herself to Jack.

"I'm sure you do. I did say sometimes," he said.

"So boys don't ever keep secrets?" Eleanor asked.

"Not the ones I know," Jack said.

"I find that hard to believe," she said.

"Look," said Jack, "there isn't a lot of mystery involved in being a butcher. Cut up the animal, package it, deliver it." He pointed to the package held under his right arm. "It's not like being a mysterious gargoyle."

He was this close to being infuriating, but Eleanor bit her tongue to stop herself from saying something stupid or mean.

"Alright, I've got to get this delivered," he said. "You have fun lurking over everyone on the street." With that he gave her a little wave and walked under the archway, into the Warren.

Eleanor was stunned. He's going in there? His father let's him? He had strolled under the archway without thinking twice. What if something happened to him?

"Wait," said Eleanor, and she hopped down from the wall. Jack stopped and walked back towards her. They met right under the arch.

"Going to spill you're innermost secrets?" he asked.

She ignored the comment, "You do deliveries in the Warren? Isn't it unsafe?"

"I do," said Jack, "and in answer to your second question the answer is: maybe."

126

"Maybe?" asked Eleanor, "What's that supposed to mean?"

Jack gave her a close look. "The Warren is filled with people who want to disappear. Some of them because they're in trouble with the law, but who knows? The most dangerous thing to do in the Warren is call attention to someone. If you mind your own business you can deliver a ham, for example, without a problem."

Eleanor considered this. It made getting to the Occlodex seem possible, at least. She was good at keeping quiet and staying out of the way. Maybe she could do this herself?

"Do you know where 14 Whiteheart Lane is?" she asked.

"Sure. It would be five blocks away. Not far," answered Jack.

"Six," she said automatically, thinking back to the map she had checked that morning.

"I guess you'd know," said Jack with a smirk, "see you around, gargoyle." He turned and made his way down the street, dodging the others walking on the cramped street.

He really was infuriating. She resisted the idea of a mean reply, mainly because she couldn't think of one. Instead she turned and headed the opposite direction towards Penwick, her mind spinning with possibilities.

The next three days were a battle between impatience and anxiety. Madigan still had not replied, but Eleanor was afraid of taking action to find the Occlodexes by herself. She ended up frustrated, both at the lack of knowledge about Tratford's notes, and with herself for being too scared to approach the Warren.

It got to be more than she could take, and while she hadn't worked up the courage to try the Warren alone, she figured she could be bold enough to ask for help. Eleanor hated asking for assistance of any kind. She had mangled a dress just last year because she tried to fix it herself rather than asking her mother for help or even advice, even though her mother was an excellent seamstress. The person she was going to ask wasn't going to make the process any easier, either, she figured.

Slipping out the front gate of Penwick after her last afternoon class Eleanor made her way down the street to the butcher's shop. Through the small window she could see Jack standing behind the counter, a knife glinting in his hand as he worked on some massive hunk of meat. She took a deep breath and pushed the door open.

"If it isn't the gargoyle herself," said Jack, giving her the same infuriating smirk from a few days before, "come to do some shopping or did you drop another book in a puddle?"

She almost turned and left at that. He seemed to take great pleasure in needling her, and the reminder of that day made her feel foolish all over again. However, she was able to keep her calm, and let the remark slide by.

"I was wondering if I could ask for some help," she said.

"You can," said Jack.

"I can what?" Eleanor asked, feeling like she was always operating one step behind the older boy.

"Ask for help," he said, "you asked if you could ask for help.

You are free to ask for help. Can't promise I'll do it, though."

Eleanor rolled her eyes. "You can be impossible, you know."

"My mother says that just about every day."

"I don't envy her, dealing with you," said Eleanor.

"And yet here you are," he replied.

Right, she thought. Somehow he always managed to get a conversation driven off in some random direction. She ordered herself to remain focused.

"I want you to look in on 14 Whiteheart Lane for me."

"Is that so?" asked Jack, "What's got you so interested in some place in the Warren?"

Here Eleanor reminded herself to be careful. She didn't want to reveal to Jack the whole story behind her request. Madigan had seemed keen in his message on keeping things quiet. But she had to come up with some kind of explanation for Jack without lying. She figured she could run close to the truth.

"I'm looking for a book and I think that it might be at 14 Whiteheart Lane."

"You're telling me that the gigantic nest of mismatched buildings full of books at Penwick doesn't have the one you are looking for?" asked Jack.

She tried to shrug as if it seemed silly to her too, but wasn't sure if she had succeeded. Jack was eyeing her. Eleanor could tell his wheels were spinning.

"What kind of books would there be in the middle of the Warren, about two blocks from the White Tower, I wonder," he said, "You aren't doing a little research into the black arts of witchcraft, are you?"

Eleanor was taken aback, but Jack was laughing. The truth was much less scandalous, but he could think what he liked so long as he checked out the address for her.

"Don't worry, Eleanor," said Jack, "I don't much care if you're trying to grow warts on some other girl's face."

Infuriating, she thought again.

"You'll do it, then?" she asked.

"Sure, why not?" he said, "If you wait here a moment, I've got to package up this leg of lamb. Then you can walk with me to the delivery. I have to go right past Whiteheart Lane." He grabbed the leg he had been working on and walked into the back room.

Eleanor felt her stomach sink. Had he misheard her? He just said that she could walk with him on the delivery, into the Warren. She didn't want to go *herself*. She wasn't supposed to go in there, and it seemed frightening despite Jack's opinions. Did he expect her to go?

"Jack?" she called, "Jack, I think I wasn't clear. I'm sorry. I was hoping that you might just tell me what's there when you get back."

He reappeared with the leg wrapped up in brown paper. "Don't apologize, I heard you just fine," he said, "I'll walk you there and back. You'll be fine, it's the middle of the afternoon."

"But -, " she stammered before being cut of by Jack.

"You are afraid," he said, "I gathered that. If the book is there then you'll have to go into the Warren to get it yourself

130

anyway. I'm not a delivery boy."

She glanced down at the package in his arm and she couldn't help it, she laughed. For the first time she was a step ahead of Jack.

He followed her gaze. "Right," he said, a touch of embarrassment on his face, "Got me there, gargoyle. My point is that you are asking someone else to do something you are too afraid to try."

"You're older, and you've gone before," she said as her giggle died away.

"And a few years ago I was your age, and hadn't. If I can do it, so can you. If you want this book, this is how it works," he said as he threw on a short woolen jacket.

Eleanor had expected to be back at Penwick this afternoon doing some homework. She had already congratulated herself on having the courage to even come down and ask for help, but Jack was raising the stakes. Was she willing to take Madigan's search this seriously? She could just wait for his reply, safe and sound inside Penwick. But the answer might be a few blocks away, and she had someone willing to show her the way. There had been a rumor that several of the sixth-years had been going into the Warren this year and nothing had happened. Jack had to know it better than they did, so she would be safe, wouldn't she?

"Alright," she said, cinching her cloak around her. "I guess I'm coming."

Jack stepped past her and held the door open. They walked

down the main street, Eleanor hustling to keep up with Jack's long strides. He didn't slow down as they approached the decrepit archway. She took two quick steps to catch up with him and that was it, she was in the Warren. No one gave them a second glance as they made their way into the maze of buildings.

The crowd was light, but Eleanor had to walk behind Jack to avoid bumping into people on the narrow street. Within a few blocks of entering the street had already twisted to the right so far that she could no longer see the archway behind them. The buildings jostled together, and the clash of styles from one to the next was disorienting. About half of the buildings were built from stone blocks worn smooth on the outside, similar to the one Jack's father owned. Wedged here and there between them, though, were plaster-walled houses in bright colors. A cluster made from sand-colored blocks of clay had marvelous decorative paintings outlining the doorways and windows. The colors were vivid, and seemed to be from a part of the rainbow Eleanor had never seen before. Scattered down the street were three-story wooden houses leaning over the street as if they were trying to whisper to their brick-made neighbors. Almost every building seemed to house some kind of shop or craftsman. A number of them were taverns, and the sound of sailors boasting and complaining about the life at sea filled the street.

Taking in her surroundings, Eleanor was not paying close attention and plowed into the back of Jack when he stopped.

"This is Whiteheart Lane," he said, pointing off to their right up another narrow street that had a gentle incline. Towards the

132

top she could see the base of the White Tower.

"I need to drop off the lamb over there," he said, now point-ing left towards a small brick building nestled between two of the decorated clay ones. "After that we can look for your book."

Eleanor nodded and followed Jack across the street. The little brick building was a restaurant of sorts, with four little tables in a small front room. The bell that had rung when they opened the door brought a short, brown-skinned man wearing a white shirt and colored vest out of the back. The vest was covered in an interlocking pattern of lines and squares colored in various shades of green and blue.

"Jack, excellent!" said the man, "we have a very nice dish to make tonight - my brother returned from Nalaband yesterday."

Jack handed the man the package, "If it's as good as the stew I had last week, he's a lucky man."

"It's better," the man replied, and then seemed to notice Eleanor for the first time. "Who's this, then? Your sister, Jack?"

"No, no," said Jack with a laugh, "this is Eleanor, she's a Penwick student. She's got something to pick up on White-heart Lane and I'm showing her the way. Eleanor, this is Mr. Barouch."

"Very nice to meet you," she said. Mr. Barouch gave a quick bow of his head and then a wide smile. His face was round and friendly. The smells coming from the rear of the restaurant were intoxicating. From the look of Mr. Barouch Eleanor imagined that the party for his brother would be a loud affair packed with family and friends.

"It is my honor, Eleanor. If you ever find yourself in our neighborhood it would be our pleasure to share a meal with you," said Mr. Barouch.

The idea of wandering down to the Warren for dinner seemed impossible to Eleanor, but she reminded herself to be polite, "Thank you, Mr. Barouch, it would be my pleasure."

"I'm sorry, Mr. Barouch, but we have to get going so that I can get back to the shop," Jack said.

"Of course," answered the older man, "please tell your father I wish him well."

"I will, Mr. Barouch," said Jack, "have a good day."

Jack answered Mr. Barouch's slight bow with one of his own. Eleanor bowed as well, not sure what else to do. This appeared to please Mr. Barouch very much, and he smiled even wider and bid them farewell.

"What did I tell you," said Jack as they crossed the street towards Whiteheart Lane. "The Warren's not full of boogey-men."

As if in response to Jack's comment, a stumbling wreck of a man burst out of a tavern right in front of them. He looked as short as Eleanor, but that was because he was hunched over at the waist. He had a ragged cloak around him that seemed more hole than fabric. There was a distinct smell to him, something between rotting vegetables and the rye whiskey her grandfather used to drink. Another man who must have been the proprietor of the tavern was berating him from the doorway, and threw a battered old pewter cup after him into the street.

134

Eleanor pulled closer to Jack and grabbed his arm, "So what's he supposed to be?"

Jack shook his head, "Just a drunk, Eleanor. Not a problem for you or me, just the tavern-keeper who he probably tried to short-change."

They passed by the ragged man, who was now collapsed against the side of a building, either asleep or unconscious. Eleanor wasn't sure. Whiteheart Lane was right before them and they started trudging up the inclined road. Jack explained that the place they were looking for was most of the way up the hill.

Eleanor's legs were starting to burn as the climbed up the street, which was much steeper than it appeared. After a few minutes they had climbed high enough to just peek above the lower buildings of the Warren, and could see the Steward's Tower in the distance. In front of them the White Tower was now a massive presence. Eleanor could see the few remaining flakes of white stone underneath the grime and dirt, and got a true sense of just how large it was. A wall surrounded the lower reaches, covering an area the size of six or seven regular houses. From inside that wall the Tower rose up, tapering until it reached a wide platform one hundred feet in the air.

"Just about there," said Jack, pointing towards a low brick building labelled with a large number 18 on the door. Bringing her eyes back down to street level and scanning both sides of the street, Eleanor spotted number 14 first. It was on her right and was one of the older stone buildings. At some point the owners had knocked out some stones and installed a massive mullioned window. Painted in peeling letters across the window pains was one word: *Apothecary*.

"Doesn't look like much of a place to find books, does it?" said Jack as they drew up in front of the window.

"No," said Eleanor. An Apothecary was hardly what she needed. Perhaps expecting a big sign that said *Find Occlodexes Here!* was hoping for a bit much, but it was disappointing nonetheless.

"Are we going in?" asked Jack.

Eleanor considered this. Her immediate thought was no. If number 14 had ever been a library for the Occlodexes, there seemed to be little chance that an Apothecary had saved them. The building wasn't even that large, she thought. It was only two stories high, and seemed quite narrow. It did not look like it could have held thousands or millions of Occlodexes. On the other hand, she had already come this far, overcoming any number of existing fears, so what did she have to lose?

"We might as well ask," said Eleanor.

Jack went to the door and held it open for her. Eleanor wished he would go in first, but she swallowed hard and slipped inside. It took a moment for her eyes to adjust to the dark interior. She almost ran into a low wooden counter that closed off the corner of the store near the door. Behind the counter she could see several long sets of shelves on which sat a dizzying array of various bottles, pots, and vials. There was a glass jar that must have held gallons of purple liquid, and Eleanor was quite

136

sure she saw something swimming around inside of it. Rows and rows of vials in varying shades of green sat on one shelf, each fizzing with bubbles. From the ceiling hung what looked like the dried carcasses of different birds and few lizards.

As far as they could tell there was no one in the shop beside themselves. A little bell had rung when they entered, just like at Mr. Barouch's. Unlike the smiling restaurant owner, though, no one came to greet them. They stood waiting for a few moments before Jack called out.

"Hello - is anyone there?" His voice seemed to die among the disordered stacks of pots and bottles. There was no apparent response.

"Hello!" he shouted even louder.

There was a rustling sound. It came from the wooden counter, or rather beneath the wooden counter. There was some scuffling, and then a thump followed by a man's voice making a muffled "Ow!". Eventually a frightfully thin man unfolded himself from behind the counter and stood up to face them.

"Eh, whaddya want?" said the thin man. He seemed to find their intrusion on what was his nap a great affront.

Jack looked at Eleanor and extended his hand towards her to indicate it was her turn to talk. She hadn't thought about what to do. How did she ask about Occlodex? Would the skinny man know anything? She couldn't well lie about the kind of book she wanted here.

"Sir, I was wondering if you have any Occlodexes?" Eleanor asked. She figured that if he knew what they were, she was in

137

luck. If not, then that probably meant they were gone.

"Occlodexes?" said the skinny man, scratching himself on his rear end. "Right, not sure I know that one." He seemed to be waking up now, and he made his way back between two overloaded shelves. His arms and legs picked their way through the clutter, reminding Eleanor of a spider as he moved. As he went, he called out various items that he thought might be a substitute for Occlodexes for some reason.

"Groat Oil? .... Lemming paste? .... Violet extract? .... Ballaroot seeds?" he called out. Eleanor gave up on saying "No" after the first few, and let the skinny man continue to bleat out the inventory.

Eleanor was thinking that she and Jack should just slip out and head back when a clanging noise from the back indicated that someone else had come into the shop. A low woman's voice called out.

"Vernon? What are you doing climbing all over? What is it that you are looking for?"

"Oi, Agatha, good that you're here. Got this young lady asking for ....," Vernon turned back to shout at Eleanor, "what was it again? Ligonin sticks?"

"Occlodexes," she called.

There was clatter as the woman from the back made her way to the front counter. She was short and round in shape, with white hair pulled back in a small bun. She had on purple robes that were stained along the sleeves with splotches of various colors, presumably remnants of her various wares. The

138

most noticeable feature, though, were her dark green eyes. They were a color Eleanor had never seen before. While her outward appearance was pleasant but untidy, the eyes were alert and piercing and reminded Eleanor of the Headmistress.

For a few moments the dark green eyes took in Eleanor, and some sort of calculation seemed to be going on inside her head. Finally she spoke. "Occlodexes, is it?" Her tone of voice sounded curious.

"That's right, ma'am," Eleanor said, swallowing her nerves, "I was looking for a book that was missing from the Penwick Library. My name is Eleanor. I'm a student there. And this is Jack. He showed me the way here."

"I'm Agatha Dobbins," said the woman with a smile and a curious look on her face, "do you know what you're asking for?"

"I believe so," said Eleanor slowly, "an Occlodex. The Occlodex, actually for some field notes from almost one hundred years ago. It has to do with some research I'm doing."

Ms. Dobbins' green eyes narrowed, making Eleanor feel uncomfortable. "And do you understand what a Occlodex actually is?"

"A liquid book, if I'm correct," said Eleanor. She ignored Jack's raised eyebrows. "A reference I found suggested that the Occlodexes were once housed here."

"So it did, so it did," said Ms. Dobbins. It took a moment before she replied, "You realize, of course, that this is now my Apothecary shop."

"That's very obvious, Ms. Dobbins," said Eleanor as an

139

apology, "I didn't know, and came here on the hope that the Occlodexes still existed."

"It's an odd magic for a Penwick student to be asking about," said Ms. Dobbins, her eyes studying Eleanor. "Very old, very intriguing magic, for all that. Not the kind of thing I thought the teachers at Penwick would have spent their breath on."

Eleanor felt disconcerted. She didn't want to reveal Madigan's project, but Ms. Dobbins was right about magic being rarely discussed at Penwick. "It's for a personal research project," she said, hoping that Ms. Dobbins wouldn't ask any further.

"I see," said the white-haired woman, nodding.

"I'm sorry to have bothered you, Ms. Dobbins. We'll move on, and let you get back to ... " Eleanor trailed off, waving her hand towards the cluttered shop.

" .. draining ginger beetles," Ms. Dobbins finished, and pointed to a green spot on her sleeve. "But where are you running off to, now that you're here?"

"Well," said Eleanor, confused, "this is an apothecary shop now, so I'll have to find another way to get my hands on the book I need."

"Dearie," said Ms. Dobbins, "this may be my shop now, but the Occlodexes didn't disappear. I've got them all down in the basement. Let's go have a look."

140

CHAPTER 8

A BOOK TO DRINK

JACK put his hand on Eleanor's shoulder and whispered in her ear. "Are you sure we should go down there?"

They had followed Ms. Dobbins into the back of her apothecary shop, past the rickety shelves full of things like begonia root and Clawfoot tonic. The rear of the shop rambled on through several rooms, including one spattered with bits of ginger beetles and smelling like a bad cheese. They wound their way back so far that Eleanor was sure they would going to come out on the other side of the city. But they were still inside the shop when Ms. Dobbins stopped in the middle of a room strung with drying garlic, onions, and other vegetables Eleanor didn't recognize.

Ms. Dobbins had pulled a key ring from inside her robes, and shoving aside some onions, had unlocked a battered wooden door. A lantern had appeared from somewhere else inside her robe and she had stepped through the door and started down the staircase that it concealed. Now Eleanor and Jack could see her below them, the lantern bobbing up and down as she made her way to the bottom of the stairs.

Eleanor looked back and forth between Ms. Dobbins and Jack. She could not explain it, but she did not feel afraid of the older woman, or what might happen. Ms. Dobbins seemed eccentric, but that wasn't enough to qualify her as dangerous.

141

"Yes," she whispered back. "I want to see if she's got the book."

"I told you the Warren wasn't that dangerous. I won't vouch for the basement of some batty old apothecary," he said. "You never said you were after magical books."

"Understood," Eleanor answered, still whispering, "You're free to leave if you want." She turned back to the stairs and started down, hoping that he wouldn't go.

Jack followed after a moment, the stairs creaking in turn as they descended.

"Ah, there you are," said Ms. Dobbins.

They stood in a small room with three doors. There were patterns of tiles inlaid on each door that reminded her of the mosaics in the Entry Hall at Penwick. Ms. Dobbins flipped through her keys to a fat brass one, and then unlocked the door on the right. Holding the lantern up she entered the room.

Eleanor followed, and saw racks and racks of small vials, each not much bigger than her Silverwood pencil. Their contents tended to take on a greenish hue, but she could see isolated examples of red, orange, and yellow as well. The racks ran from floor to ceiling, and the vials lay flat, resting in notches cut into the wood. Below each vial a tiny slip of paper was fastened to the wood with a small pin. Eleanor could see an accumulation of dust across everything.

"Well, dearie," said Ms. Dobbins, "welcome to what's left. All the Occlodexes one could ask for."

Following Ms. Dobbins down an aisle between two of the

142

massive racks, Eleanor could tell the basement ran on farther than she could see. If her bearings weren't off, it must run underneath the whole building. There would be thousands upon thousands of Occlodexes. Tratford's notes have to be here, she thought.

After a few moments walking they found themselves in a little clearing amongst the racks. On a solid wooden table was a stack of giant books covered in cobwebs and dust.

Ms. Dobbins set the lantern down on the table. "Here we go, dear," she said, "I haven't been down here in a long time. But let's see if we can't find out where your Occlodex lives. What's the title of the book?"

"Field Notes of the Cinnamon Islands, by Simon Tratford," said Eleanor, feeling her heart speed up in anticipation.

With the help of Jack, Ms. Dobbins wrestled several of the gigantic books aside until she found one labelled with an 'F'. It sent up clouds of dust when they flipped it open on the table. Ms. Dobbins turned over about a third of the pages, landing them on a page of books starting with 'Fi'. Rifling through more pages exposed even more dust, but got them to the right section.

"Here we go," said Ms. Dobbins. "Shelf four hundred twelve, position eleven. I'll be right back. Can't promise anything, of course, but it still might be there." She walked off down one of the aisles, muttering the numbers to herself. After going about fifty feet down the aisle, she ducked to the right and disappeared from Eleanor's sight.

"So what's so important about these notes?" asked Jack.

"I'm not supposed to say," said Eleanor, giving him an apologetic look. "And I'm not sure I know, anyway."

"Girls and their mysteries," he said.

Eleanor rolled her eyes at him, and then heard a clatter as Ms. Dobbins started making her way back down the aisle towards them.

"I've got it," she announced as she approached the large table. "It looks to be in good shape, plenty of bubbles." She held it up in front of her so they could see. It was a skinny tube like the rest, filled with a murky green liquid, and they could indeed see a noticeable fizzing going on inside of it.

"What do the bubbles mean?" asked Eleanor, curious about the Occlodex itself as the realization dawned on her that she'd have to drink some of this mysterious liquid.

"It means the information hasn't dissipated. The stopper has maintained a perfect seal. If you look around, some of the Occlodexes are flat. No bubbles. That means the words in the book have leaked away over time. They're just flasks full of colored water now," Ms. Dobbins said.

That was a good sign, Eleanor guessed. The book was still there, and there was still hope of finding out what was in Tratford's notes. But that information was apparently stored inside this tube and to get it she was going to have to drink some.

As if anticipating her worries, Ms. Dobbins reassured her. "It's not bad at all, dearie. They are pretty tasteless and you only need to take one decent swig. You don't have to drink the whole thing. Nor would you want to, or the whole book would be gone and you'd be seeing it in your sleep."

"What will it be like after I drink it," asked Eleanor, hearing her own voice quiver with trepidation.

"It's been a long time since I've used one," said Ms. Dobbins, "but it will be like a familiar picture in your head. It will take you a few minutes to get control of the pages. Your brain will jump forward and back without much of a pattern. You'll need to concentrate to slow it down so that you can read it."

Eleanor nodded. Ms. Dobbins worked the stopper a little, and then it came out with a pop. She handed it over to Eleanor.

"Bottoms up," said Ms. Dobbins.

Jack gave her a little shrug as if to indicate that he had no opinion on the matter. Eleanor noticed her hand was shaking and the liquid in the vial sloshed around inside. Taking a deep breath she raised it to her lips and took a drink. Ms. Dobbins was right, there was little taste, only a metallic tinge. It was cool, and she could feel nothing peculiar inside of her.

Then it hit her. An image swirled into focus inside her head and she could see the distinct layout of a page of text. There were times when she took exams that she could see the page of a book with an answer on it, but the answer itself stayed blurred. It was like that, but the words here continued to resolve. As a few seconds passed the clarity was perfect and she could read it as if it were laid out in front of her. It looked just like the other field notes she had dug through in the library. The page in front of her had a sketch of a large fern and a series of printed notes underneath. She tried to move her focus to the right to read the next page but there was a garble of black and white. The pages seemed to spin by, making her dizzy enough that she had to grab the edge of the table.

"Focus, Eleanor," said Ms. Dobbins, her voice steady and calm compared to Eleanor's head. "Take a deep breath, and don't try to get ahead of yourself."

She took the breath and forced herself to focus on the center of the pages whirring back and forth. It helped, and they slowed down. She still could not read them but they were no longer moving so fast that she felt nauseous. She was also able to discern what her own eyes were seeing - the figure of Ms. Dobbins in front of her with a worried look on her face - from the image inside her head. That helped steady her as well. She let go of the table.

That's when several things happened all at once. There was a crash behind her, causing her to turn, and this threw the pages back into a wild spin. Jack, who had been next to her, jumped into Eleanor, causing her to lose her balance and fall to the floor next to the table. The vial with the Occlodex flew out of her hand and smashed across the stone floor. A torrent of bubbles popped across the surface of the spilled liquid and then it soaked into the cracks of the floor, leaving only a dark stain.

Jack had dropped down next to her on the floor and was pushing her under the table. The swirling pages in her head kept her from being able to make out what was ahead of her, and she banged her head into the table leg. Jack was now under the table with her and yanked her by the arm to draw her out the other side.

"Go! Run!" he shouted, and shoved her forward down an aisle of Occlodex shelves. She was able to get oriented enough to look back and saw two men wearing grey cloaks climbing over the table. One held a thin wooden rod with metal studs around each end, and she was sure she saw a knife in the hand of the other. The weapons they were carrying didn't catch her attention, though, nearly as much as their faces. The man closest to her had an angular one, with a long scar running down his left cheek. Both of them had a look of malice that Eleanor had never before seen in a person.

"Come on," Jack insisted and he pulled her along with him down the aisle. Ms. Dobbins was nowhere to be seen.

They heard a loud crackling sound and a flash of blue light like a lightning bolt struck behind them. Eleanor glanced back again, and could only see a cloud of smoke at the end of the aisle. But could also hear pained shouts from the two men.

The end of the aisle came and Jack led them to the right, past several more rows of Occlodexes tucked into their wooden cases. "We've got to find another way out of here," he said, looking down each aisle as they passed. Eleanor could do nothing but follow along, as her head was still swimming in unwelcome images that kept her from focusing.

Jack pulled her down another aisle to their left, and they raced past row after row of red-colored Occlodexes. A useless part of her brain wondered if they tasted different than the green

147

ones.

They were now at what must have been the back corner of the basement. There was a wooden door ahead of them and in the corner was an enormous drain grate. Jack silenced her with a finger to his mouth. They could hear the stomping sounds of footsteps somewhere back in the aisles, and an occasional shout between the two men. Jack looked back and forth from the door to the drain.

He moved to the drain and pulled. The cover came off without trouble, exposing a hole large enough for them to fit through. Jumping back in front of the door he tried the handle. It was locked but the hardware was rusty and the door shook on its hinges. He raised up his leg and gave the lock a powerful kick. The door held but several nails fell out of the hinges. Another kick and there was a satisfying crack as the lock gave way. Jack pushed the door open.

Eleanor tried to move forward to the doorway as best she could but Jack swung her around and led her to the hole in the floor. He lowered her down. The drop wasn't far, as the drainpipe underneath was only about a foot taller than she was. After her, Jack lowered himself down, and then he reached up and maneuvered the drain cover back into place.

Jack grabbed her hand and they moved down the drainpipe a few feet. The had to step with care to not make splashing sounds in the few inches of water that ran down the middle. To Eleanor's great relief, the drain seemed to carry rainwater runoff and nothing worse. However, her muddled vision could make out some dark rat shapes scurrying out of the way of the intruders to their world.

Above them they could hear footsteps. They paused and then a raspy voice called out, "Over here. Back door!" The footsteps started again and then got muffled as the first man went through the doorway. A few seconds later a second set of footsteps did not even stop, and then disappeared after a few seconds.

They stood in the drain, catching their breath. Then Jack grabbed her hand and led them further down the drainpipe, into deeper darkness. After a minute of sloshing up the pipe, he spoke.

"Are you alright?" he asked.

"Yes," she said, "I guess so. What was that? What just happened?" She could feel herself getting frantic. The spinning mess of pages in her head hadn't slowed down and was making it hard to keep her emotions under control.

"I don't know, but they did not have anything friendly in mind," Jack said.

"Thank you," she said. "I don't know what I would have done."

"You're still flustered by that thing you drank. Are you still dizzy?" he asked.

"Not really dizzy, no," she said. The book had settled down now that they weren't running. "It's like someone is flashing pages in my eyes all the time, so it's hard to concentrate on what's in front of me."

"Well," Jack said, panting, "I think they took the bait. But we should keep moving. There has to be another way out of this drain and then we can figure out where we are. I don't suppose you happen to be carrying a lantern?"

"Sorry," said Eleanor. "How are we supposed to find our way around?"

"I can see some light coming down from up ahead. It might be another drain. We'll take it slow." His hand found hers in the dark and they shuffled forward, their feet drenched in drain water.

The light was indeed another drain, but Jack could not move the cover. Another dim glow was apparent ahead, though, and they moved down the dank tunnel towards it. Another drain cover, and again Jack could not make it budge. They continued like this through ten or twelve drain covers, Eleanor lost track. The darkness helped Eleanor get some control of her head, and she was able to shunt the pages of the notes to one side of her awareness. In its place was a muddle of varying shades of gray and black inside the drainpipe. After the last of the immovable drain covers, she was able to see some distinct change in the pipe ahead of them.

"I think we're joining up to a larger drain," she said.

Jack looked down the pipe for a moment at the vague smudge of lighter gray ahead. "I think you're right."

They moved on, and by the change in the echoes of their voices they could tell they had entered a larger section of the underground drain system. Conferring for a moment, they decided that the water seemed to be flowing to their right and agreed to follow the water that direction in the hopes that it would lead them to the banks of the river.

After just a few minutes of slogging down the larger pipe, though, they saw something even more encouraging.

"Light!" said Eleanor, pointing off to her left before she realized that Jack probably couldn't make out her arm in the dark.

There was a small opening in the sidewall of the pipe, and a strong steady light was flowing out of it. They swarmed to it like moths, and saw that it came from a tunnel that ran up out of the sewer. The tunnel was narrow, but they could crawl up it without trouble.

Jack insisted on going first, and crept up the passageway with Eleanor close behind. They climbed for about thirty feet when the source of the light became clear. There was a lantern hung from a little alcove cut into the ceiling. The lantern was not powered by oil or any source that Eleanor could see. It was just a round white ball contained inside a brass frame.

"Where do you think that comes from?" she asked. Jack just shrugged as best he could in the cramped tunnel.

After the alcove the tunnel turned downwards. This didn't seem ideal to Eleanor, but at the bottom they could make out what seemed like another lamp. That was promising, at least.

Going down backwards, they reached the second lamp, which was just like the first. Here the tunnel leveled out, tall enough now for Eleanor to just stand up, while Jack had to hunch over.

151

Ahead of them there was another source of light. Not seeing any other option, they pressed on.

As they came upon the next lamp, sounds started to intrude. They could hear a scratching sound, as well as a rough hum that sounded to Eleanor like it might be voices.

"Do you hear that?" she asked.

"What, the scratching?" said Jack.

"No, lower. Is that voices?"

Jack strained to listen, but shook his head. The continued to pick their way forward. The scratching sound didn't subside but Eleanor thought that the hum had disappeared. She was starting to wonder if they were creeping up on some disgusting sewer creature.

There was an eruption of noise and light in front of them. Several of the round lamps had been un-shuttered and blinded them. They both shielded their eyes and could only make out some vague shapes moving about ahead of them. The rough hum was now a rabble of low voices, none of which she could understand.

The lights moved closer and Jack and Eleanor both moved backwards. A voice spoke to them now, but not in any language they could understand. It sounded something like "Nerf hobben espang!"

Eleanor shuffled backwards again, and the voice shouted even louder. "Nerf hobben espang!" She froze in place. Jack did as well. The lanterns were still shining full in their face, and all they could make out was three dark shapes moving in their direction.

"Urpa pang dobble!" said the voice now. Eleanor glanced at Jack, who looked as confused as she felt. He raised his hands up above his shoulders. Eleanor did the same.

This somehow satisfied the figures. One of them said "Bleth!" and the lanterns were partially shuttered and pointed towards the walls. Eleanor took a second to get her eyes back into focus, and then struggled to ignore the spinning pages in her head as she looked down the tunnel.

The three figures approached them slowly. They each held in front of them a heavy looking hammer that had a nasty spike coming off the back of the head. They were short, standing upright in the tunnel, but while one seemed heavy set the other two were thin. They each had a leather belt around their waist with several tools hanging from it, and dirty clothes on underneath. Their faces were wide and their hair was tangled and scruffy. One of the skinny ones had a distinct beard, but the other two looked like Eleanor's uncle after a few days without shaving. It took Eleanor a moment to process what she was seeing, and then she realized it.

They were dwarves.

The heavy-set one looked back at the one with the beard and said something unintelligible. The bearded one turned and jogged off down the tunnel in the direction from which they had come.

Jack caught Eleanor's eye, and glanced behind them. She guessed he was wondering if they should try to make it back out of the tunnel. Eleanor was skeptical they could move fast enough. Jack shifted in the tunnel, and was answered by the heavy-set dwarf moving with surprising speed to smack him in the stomach with the hammer. He doubled over and fell to his knees. The dwarf backed away and said "Nerf etting purda".

"Jack," Eleanor said, not moving, "are you okay?"

"Yes," he rasped, grabbing at his stomach. "That was a good shot, but I'm alright. I don't think he hit me as hard as he could have."

Their little standoff lasted for a few more minutes, during which Eleanor's mind flew through possibilities. The most serious was that she could well be killed in a sewer by dwarves. The least serious of which was that she had a History assignment due tomorrow and was not going to be able to finish it. For some reason her consciousness could not seem to prioritize them, and both seemed terrifying. She could not get herself to focus.

Finally another lantern was seen coming down the tunnel. It was the bearded dwarf from before, accompanied by an older-looking dwarf who was not wearing a work belt. His clothes were not quite as dirty, but he still looked as if he had been engaged in some manual activity. White hairs covered his chin and sideburns but his head was close to bald. He stood in front of Eleanor and Jack, the other dwarves standing behind him.

"You have violated our territory by coming here," said the dwarf slowly.

Jack still seemed to be recovering from the blow to the stomach, so Eleanor spoke up. "We didn't mean to. We were trying to find our way out."

The dwarf took a moment, and Eleanor got the impression he was translating this in his head. "Why were you in the pipes? That is not a place for humans. That is the agreement."

"I'm sorry, sir," she said. "We were being chased, and the sewer was our only escape. We just wanted to find a way out, and followed the lights."

He considered this for a while. Then he turned and muttered some unintelligible commands to the other dwarves. Hustling around them in the tunnel, the two skinny dwarves got behind Eleanor and Jack and started to prod them forward.

"You follow me," said the white-bearded dwarf. They didn't have a choice, and crouched along the tunnel behind him.

The tunnel opened up into a larger one, and Jack could stand up straight. There were more of the lantern balls mounted along the walls here and the dwarves clicked little brass switches on the tops of their hand-held ones to turn them off.

They made their way along the larger tunnel, and Eleanor felt as if they were descending. The floor of this tunnel was clean and dry, and not part of the sewer system itself. The walls were smooth and tidy.

Different passageways connected to the main tunnel they were in, but they walked past a handful of them before turning into one of their left. At this point Eleanor lost her sense of direction as the new tunnel continued to fork and intersect with others, the white-bearded dwarf picking and choosing from identical passages but never slowing down. Other dwarves would cut across their path, or run by in the opposite direction. Most stopped and stared for a moment at Eleanor and Jack. Some made quick comments to the white-bearded one.

They eventually halted in a small room that contained what looked like a small desk, behind which sat another dwarf with coarse gray hair. He looked official, in some sense, to Eleanor. His clothes were a little crisper and cleaner than the others, and he had a serious look on his face. There were four different wooden doors arrayed along the wall behind the desk. They each had a small opening in them covered in thin iron bars. To Eleanor's distress it looked like a jail.

The white-bearded dwarf exchanged some words with the official. Eleanor could tell they were talking about her and Jack, as one of them would often gesture towards them. Then the official dwarf gave a quick whistle, and two dwarves came jogging into the room from a side passage. They wore similar dark blue clothes, and carried skinny versions of the spiked hammers. At a word from the official, they unlocked one of the doors behind the desk and came over to Jack and Eleanor. Grabbing each by an arm, the two dwarves pushed them into the cell.

"But we were just trying to find a way out," said Eleanor. She looked to each dwarf but saw nothing resembling sympathy in either ones face. The white-haired dwarf and his workers had left the room. The official dwarf came and stood in the doorway of the cell when his two deputies had gotten Jack and Eleanor all the way in.

"You have arrived here innocently," he said. His speech was much clearer and smoother than the white-bearded one. "But we cannot have you roaming free around our realm. You'll be held here until we can get a message to out to your Wardens. At that point your fate will be up to your Lord Steward, for this is a breach of our agreement."

"How long will it take to get a message out?" asked Jack.

"It's evening already, and it is unlikely anything will happen before morning. You'll spend the night here," the dwarf replied.

Eleanor's heart sank. All night? Had they noticed her absence at Penwick yet? She hoped they had, and maybe the Headmistress had already notified the Wardens, and they were looking for them. On the other hand, it might be better if the Headmistress didn't know. Maybe they could get out tomorrow and she could be back without anyone besides Miriam knowing she hadn't been in her room last night. She had a pit in her stomach, though, and knew that no matter what happened she was going to be in serious trouble. How had she gotten into this mess? The stupid project. Thinking about it tickled her brain and the pages of the ship's manifest spun back into her mind. They weren't as wild as before, at least. Now they just made her angry. Angry at her own foolishness for thinking she should have pursued this so far on her own. Angry at herself for putting Jack in danger because she hadn't been brave enough to try the Warren alone. If she had just waited for Madigan's reply she'd be in her room right now studying with Miriam.

The two deputies left them in the cell and walked out. The one in charge remained in the doorway. His face did not change but his tone of voice became less authoritarian. "My name is

157

Eldad, I'll be here all evening. Some food will be sent, along with some blankets. If you need anything else, just say something." He looked at Jack. "Is your stomach alright? Were you injured by the hammer?"

"No. Just winded," said Jack. Eldad seemed to relax at this. Eleanor wondered if he wasn't as worried about this as they were. Whatever agreement they had with the Steward was probably murky about the dwarves rights to hold humans captive.

"Good," Eldad said. "I'll return in a little while with the food." With that he backed out of the doorway and shut the door with a loud bang. There was a distinct clicking sound as he tumbled the lock closed. Eleanor couldn't help herself from gasping at the sound.

In response a voice came out of the dark back corner of the cell. It made her jump in fright.

"Don't worry, dwarf food isn't that bad," the voice said. There was a shifting of dark colors against the wall of the cell as a man stood up. He stepped forward into the weak light streaming through the little window in the door. He had a dark grey blanket around his shoulders, and above it his face was long and narrow. His hair was a tangled mess, with bits of straw from the ground stuck in it. Eleanor got a whiff of something that smelled like the drunk they had seen in the street earlier that day. This man had a steadier look about his eyes though.

"Blankets are rather comfortable, too," he said, holding up his arm to show it to them. "You'll like it here."

"We're not moving in," said Jack.

158

"Of course not," said the man. "But for tonight I appear to be your host. Let me introduce myself. I'm Hal." He held out his hand, which quivered.

Both Eleanor and Jack hesitated. Hal was earnest, though, and didn't put down his hand. Jack gave it a quick shake, saying, "I'm Jack Harris."

"I'm Eleanor. Eleanor Wigton," said Eleanor. Right as she said it, she was sure that she saw some twitch in Hal's face. Perhaps a flicker of recognition or surprise. It disappeared, and Eleanor figured it had been a trick of the poor light.

Hal gave a dramatic bow, "My lady, I am at your service. Am I right that you're from Penwick?"

Eleanor didn't like the idea that Hal knew something about her, but it was hard to hide the black dress. "I am," she said.

"An excellent school," said Hal, wavering where he stood. "They have a lot of books there, don't they?"

"A few, yes," said Eleanor, hoping that he would just go back to his corner.

"I've always liked books myself," said Hal. "You know I was considered the brightest boy in my family? I like to think that I could have done quite well at Penwick. Maybe I'll give it a go. Do you know if they take on older students?"

Eleanor wasn't sure whether to humor him or just remain silent. "I don't believe they do, no," she muttered.

"A shame," said Hal, taking a big step to his left to catch himself from falling over. "I've always liked books myself. Wait, did I say that already?"

"You did," said Eleanor.

"That's enough, mate," said Jack. "Leave off with the interrogation."

"Right-o, sir," said Hal. "You look like a tough customer. Don't want to offend anyone. Just go on back now to my corner. Don't worry. You'll like the food. Wait, did I say that already too?"

"You did, and now pipe down," said Jack with some menace in his voice, and he pulled Eleanor back against the opposite wall. They sat down on some matted straw. Hal took the hint and retreated to his corner. He would occasionally fire off a silly question towards them, asking if they knew the Steward, or had ever sailed to the Cinnamon Islands, or if they knew any of the sprites from Silverwood. They ignored him and he fell silent.

Eldad returned soon with the promised food and blankets. It was a full meal, and Hal was not lying. It was actually very good, even if Eleanor could not identify the meat in the main dish. She and Jack gobbled it up and Eldad returned with extra water when they had disposed of theirs in several quick gulps.

After clearing away their bowls and cups, Eldad locked them in once more. The lantern in the outer room was dimmed and the cell was close to black. Jack sat down in the corner of the cell, and Eleanor sat next to him. The excitement and terror of the day were receding, and her body slumped next to Jack's, leaning against his shoulder. She could make out a slow rhythm of his breath, and he appeared to be asleep.

The dark room and quiet surroundings let other things move

160

into focus in Eleanor's mind. The pages of Tratford's notes floated in front of her, more slowly then ever before. She was able to focus on more of the words. Trying to move one page over, the pages fluttered, but not out of control. Relaxing further as her body tried to sleep, her mind was able to get a better handle on the book. The pages slid by slowly now, and she was able to read through a whole page.

Sleep was fighting hard to overtake her, but curiosity was able to keep her aware of what she was reading. The pages slipped by, sketches and notes of plants and seeds and some animals. They looked similar to what she had found in The Rack. Nothing caught her mind's eye, and sleep started to pull harder on her.

Then she turned to page 183, the one that Wellsby had insisted was missing from the real book. Here she saw a drawing of what looked like gigantic raisins, oval shapes with a series of ridges all about them. Tratford's notes said he found them in a cave on something he called the Black Island. According to him they were an ebony color and were seedpods for one of the black-barked trees that gave the island its name. Seedpods? she wondered. Was all this about being able to plant an exotic tree? It made no sense to her, and as she drifted off her mind was a jumble of confused thoughts.

CHAPTER 9

THE NETHERDOOR

ELEANOR woke up lying on the floor. Jack had put his blanket down over the straw, and some time in the night laid her down on top of it. He was standing by the door, staring out. The light coming in was back at full brightness. Hal was snoring in the corner.

She rubbed her eyes as all the facts of her situation came rushing back to her. Would they be able to leave today? Soon? She had found the missing page from Simon Tratford's notes in the Occlodex. When could she let Madigan know about the discovery?

Jack heard her rustling and turned around. "There's something going on out there. I think I hear human voices."

Eleanor gathered herself up and joined him near the door. Outside the window she could see the desk that Eldad had been sitting at last night. He was no longer there. The sounds of voices were coming from just out of sight in one of the passageways. Jack was right, one of the voices sounded human. There were two or three dwarves too, it sounded like, and they appeared to be arguing.

They waited for a few minutes, and then Eldad came back into the outer room. He did not look pleased at all. He was mumbling to himself, but pulled a large key ring from his belt.

He spun on his heel and approached their door. "Step back," he said.

They did as they were told, and Eldad unlocked the door. "Someone is here to see you," he said, and from his emphasis they could tell that whoever this someone was, he did not meet Eldad's standards.

The next second a tall figure crouched to enter the cell. The light from the outer room kept him in silhouette for moment before Eleanor could get her eyes to resolve on him.

It was Madigan.

"I appreciate your understanding, Constable," he said.

"Mr. Madigan," said Eleanor, "I'm so happy to see you." The relief of seeing an adult, even one embodying so many unknowns, lifted the pit from her stomach. She went to the gray-haired man and he put an arm about her shoulders. The grip was reassuring.

"It's alright, Eleanor, we're going to get you out of here. And then I have a lot to apologize for," he said. The look in his eyes was warm, but the many lines on his face gave Eleanor the impression that he had not slept in quite a long time.

"How about the rest of us?" said Jack.

"You must be Mr. Harris," said Madigan. The old man extended his free arm towards Jack. "I have much to thank you for, and from what I understand it was your quick thinking that allowed you both to escape from Ms. Dobbin's shop."

"What was that all about?" asked Jack.

"A story that will have to wait, I'm afraid, for the moment.

The dwarves are upset by the intrusions they've been subject to these last few days, and they are reluctant to let go of some of the intruders," said Madigan.

"But it was all an accident, sir," said Eleanor. "What do they want with us?"

"Not you," said Madigan, "You're both free to come with me. It's him that is the problem," Madigan pointed towards the corner where Eleanor noticed the snoring had stopped.

"And what does their Constable think he's going to charge me with? I'm not the one who put that damn hole in the cellar where someone could fall through," Hal said as he pulled himself up from the corner.

"Unfortunately, the dwarves find your excuses are running thin, Hal," said Madigan. "They believe you are up to something."

Hal snorted, and waved his arm dismissively towards the door.

"You know him?" Eleanor asked, surprised.

Madigan let out a bit of a sigh. "I do," he said, "and I often tend to be in the position of removing him from sticky situations."

"You make out just fine in the deal," said Hal.

"I was not complaining, Hal, just making an observation," Madigan replied. He gave a kind look towards Eleanor, and then spoke to them all. His voice took on a solid tone, and to Eleanor it was clear that his words were not to be questioned. "We are going to walk out of here. You will follow me. First

165

Eleanor, then Jack, then Hal. You will speak to no one. I have only just barely convinced the dwarves to release you all to me, rather than waiting for the Wardens. Any false move, though, and they will not hesitate to put you right back in this cell. Am I understood?"

Eleanor and Jack nodded, Hal made a sound that could have been a 'yes'.

"Excellent," said Madigan. "Here we go."

He turned and stepped out of the cell. Eleanor followed, her eyes taking a few seconds to adjust to the lantern light. She hugged close to Madigan's back, though, almost stepping on his dark cloak as it swung behind him. She could hear Jack right on her heels, and a shuffling gait that must have been Hal bringing up the rear.

There were a number of dwarves coming and going in the tunnel they passed down, and while several slowed down to look them over, none made any move to stop them. Madigan led them without pause through a series of turns that left Eleanor feeling they must be right back where they started. However, they had appeared to climb upwards, and soon were back in a larger drain tunnel.

Sloshing across the water running down the tunnel Madigan led them into a small alcove. Inside of it was a ladder and above them Eleanor could see sunlight pouring down. It felt warm and intoxicating after being enclosed in the tunnels and cell for much of the last day. Madigan went up first, displacing the drain cover, and then helped up Eleanor and Jack. Hal hauled himself

166

up over the edge, landing with an audible groan on the cobbled street.

Madigan gave him a dark stare. "Go." Hal looked at the older man, appeared ready to say something, thought better of it, and ambled off down the street.

They were at the end of a dead end street. The houses were made of large irregular stones but there were no people about. Eleanor could see that the street connected to a larger one, where Hal was turning down now and disappearing from sight. The look of the buildings made Eleanor believe they were still in the Warren.

When Hal had been gone for a good minute, Madigan turned to them. "It's now time to get you both back to where you belong. Your father and mother, Jack, are worried sick. Eleanor, Penwick is in a bit of an uproar this morning."

The mention of Jack's parents made Eleanor think of her own. What would they say when they found out? Would they pull her out of Penwick, if they thought they couldn't trust her? Would Madigan let her tell them about the project, so that maybe she could explain her actions? They had always thought Penwick was a waste of her time, and now they might have an excuse to pull her out.

Despite the emotions flailing around inside of her, Eleanor was ready to follow Madigan back to the familiar grounds of Penwick. Madigan did not, however, start walking up the street. Instead, he turned around and stepped over to one of the houses behind them. He stood in front of the doorway, which was out-

167

lined in small stones, and looked over it. After a moment he spotted something, and then signaled to them to come over.

"We're not going to risk walking through the Warren again, given that someone was watching you yesterday."

"Who were those men?" asked Jack.

"Most likely thugs in thrall to the Forgotten. Real unpleasant types as you saw," said Madigan. He had paused in his response, leaving something unsaid. "They were watching out for strange comings and goings around the Warren. A Penwick student counts as strange."

Eleanor thought of Mrs. Dobbins and felt horrible for not asking about her sooner. "What happened to Ms. Dobbins? Is she alright?"

"Fine, Eleanor," said Madigan with a brief smile. "A little battered, but nothing that she can't fix up by calling on some of her own inventory. She gave as good as she got, stunning them for a few moments while you ran."

"Is my family in danger?" asked Jack, his tension apparent to Eleanor standing next to him.

"A very thoughtful thing to ask, Mr. Harris. But no, I don't believe so. I would suggest staying clear of the Warren, though, for a week or so," said Madigan.

"Not a problem," Jack replied, but his nerves had not seemed to abate.

"Now then," said Madigan. "Let us get you both back to someplace safe." He reached up to the door frame and put his fingers on one of the small stones. Eleanor could just make out

168

a small character or rune cut into the stone itself. I looked like a backwards, capital letter E. Madigan mumbled something under his breath that Eleanor could not make out. Then he turned and gave them a smile, his eyes glinting.

"Here we go," he said, and pulled open the door. The view was disconcerting. Through the door was not the interior of a house, but what looked like another street. Looking *into* this door, Eleanor felt as if she was looking *out* of another one.

"What is going on?" she asked. "What is this?"

"A Netherdoor," said Madigan. "Magic from an older time, when wizards were prominent residents of these parts. If you know how to find it, it often still works."

"So where does it go?" she asked. Part of her was flummoxed by what she saw. Another part was curious about the Netherdoor and how it worked.

"Every Netherdoor has a partner. If you invoke the magic, then when you open the door you can step out of the partner door. They provide some very useful shortcuts across the city." Madigan extended his arm in an invitation for them to step through.

"Unbelievable," said Jack, who had an uneasy look on his face.

Eleanor was entranced. She stepped forward, and felt a vague tingle in her foot as it broke the plane of the door. The tingle wrapped over her whole body as she moved through. And like that, she was standing on an entirely different street. The buildings were wrapped in ivy and looked tidy. She guessed that

169

she was no longer in the Warren.

Jack and Madigan stepped through. Jack just stared around in bewilderment. Madigan turned and shut the door behind them.

"I know where we are," said Jack, astonished. "We're a block from my parents shop!"

"That was the goal, yes," said Madigan, smiling. "You can see the advantages of using the Netherdoor."

Jack headed down the street. Eleanor and Madigan followed, and Eleanor realized that they were on a side street from the main avenue that ran from the Silverspan bridge up towards Penwick. Once they reached the intersection, to her right she could see the school looming only a few blocks away, and the butcher shop to her left.

"Jack," said Madigan, and the boy stopped. "We're going to leave you here to make your reunion with your parents."

"They're going to kill me for going missing," he said.

"My guess is that they will just be relieved to see you," said Madigan. "I had a visit with them last night, and explained as much of what happened as I knew. They understand you were the victims of circumstances."

"How did you know what happened?" asked Jack.

"I have many sources of information," Madigan said, a vague smile flittering across his face. "Many of which are not worth talking about. Suffice it to say that I was able to assure your parents that you were not to blame for this ordeal."

"Thank you," said Jack. He turned to Eleanor, "Well, I

170

guess I wasn't completely right about the Warren being safe."

Eleanor didn't know what to say, and found her head spinning. She bounced back and forth between wanting to cry and wanting to shout. Without thinking, she wrapped her arms around Jack and gave him a hug.

He hugged her back. "If you ever want to go back to the Warren, please don't ask me," he said, but he was smiling.

"Thank you," she whispered. "I'm sorry."

"We're both alright," he said, "so there's nothing to be sorry for."

With that he stepped back out of the hug and turned towards the butcher shop. He walked for a few steps, but then burst into a run and swung himself through the shop door with a clatter.

Eleanor watched him disappear, and then she and Madigan headed towards Penwick. They walked in silence most of the way. She felt like it was the first day of school again, with the alternation of anxiety and excitement fluttering around inside of her. It would be such a joy to be in her own room, but the thought of having to face the Headmistress was terrifying.

As if reading her mind, Madigan spoke. "We will need to see the Headmistress straight away, Eleanor."

"I see", she said, her voice dull.

"She, like Jack's parents, has already heard much of the story. Like them, she is relieved that you are unhurt," Madigan said in measured tone.

"But I'm still going to be in a lot of trouble for going into the Warren," Eleanor replied.

"She is unhappy about that transgression, yes," said Madigan. "But I would ask again that you refrain from divulging details of the project to the Headmistress though."

Eleanor stopped in the street. She was supposed to cover for Madigan, and take this punishment so that the Headmistress wouldn't learn about a project undertaken by her own students in the school she headed? That seemed unfair.

"Why can't the Headmistress know about this? What are you worried about," Eleanor asked Madigan.

He looked like a much older man at that moment, Eleanor thought. He gave her a weary smile. "There is a lot at stake here, Eleanor, things beyond your knowledge. I cannot risk that the Forgotten find out that we know anything about the code or the *Dorian Maroon*. The only advantage I have right now is their ignorance."

The comment about things beyond her knowledge irked Eleanor. It was unfair after what she had been through. However, Madigan's stony look did not suggest that he was willing to talk yet about those things. "And you don't trust the Headmistress?" Eleanor asked instead.

"I do trust her. But there is no reason to risk the exposure of what we know. That is all," said Madigan. "Until we know more about the reason for the interest in that ship, I ask you to keep this quiet."

Eleanor considered the request, and despite herself nodded in agreement. It was then that she realized she had not mentioned anything about the Occlodex to Madigan yet.

"But sir, I do know more about it. I drank the Occlodex. I saw the page last night before I fell asleep. I can read Simon Tratford's field notes, and the missing page. It's in my head."

Madigan said nothing for a moment but his eyes flashed with a mixture of triumph and pride. "You really are an exceptional girl, Eleanor. Remarkable. We will need to sit down and go over this in more detail when we are through with the Headmistress."

While Eleanor appreciated the praise, there was something else that struck her at that moment. She trusted Madigan. Despite his mysterious project, and the questionable things it had led her to do, she felt sure in her heart that he was looking out for her. From the looks of him he had been out all night searching for them, and it was not the Wardens or anyone else who had rescued her from the dwarves. It was him.

They marched the rest of the way up the small incline to the school, and passed by the aged guards. Inside the gates they approached Morgan Hall, and Madigan held the door open for her. They went directly to the Headmistresses office.

Mrs. Puddlemump all but leapt over her desk and enclosed Eleanor in a gigantic hug. She insisted on checking her over from head to foot, and gave Madigan a withering glare when Eleanor revealed that she had not eaten anything that morning. She promised to send for something from the kitchens and told them that the Headmistress was in her office.

For the second time Eleanor found herself in the lush confines of the Headmistresses office. The graying woman was staring out the window when they entered, and exhaled loudly when she

173

saw Eleanor. A second examination occurred, despite Eleanor protesting that Mrs. Puddlemump had already confirmed she was all right.

After settling Eleanor in a chair, the Headmistress took her own seat behind the desk. Her face firmed up and she took on the stern look Eleanor was familiar with. "Now we have to discuss your blatant disregard for school policy, Eleanor."

As Eleanor was about to speak, Madigan interrupted. "Olivia, please don't think too harshly of Eleanor. It was not her idea to visit the Warren. I suggested it to her in a note, and all but dared her to go. If anyone is to blame, it would be me."

Eleanor looked at Madigan in disbelief. He was lying to the Headmistress. Right to her face! The Headmistress must have seen the look on her face, for she turned back to Eleanor and asked, "Is this true?"

"Ma'am," said Eleanor, unsure of what she was supposed to do. Take the chance to escape from her fate, or own up to the offense? Wavering, she realized that it would eat at her every day if she tried to duck her own responsibility. "It wasn't Mr. Madigan. I went because I wanted to look –," she paused. Did owning up mean revealing what Mr. Madigan was up to? Things were a complete mess in her head.

"Yes, Eleanor?" the Headmistress prompted.

"I – I wanted to see what it was like. I didn't know things would be so awful," she said. It wasn't a complete lie.

"That is precisely why we forbid you to enter the Warren, Eleanor," said the Headmistress.

174

"About that, Olivia," said Mr. Madigan. The Headmistress gave him a withering look, but he remaining unperturbed. "If I'm correct, there isn't a rule regarding entering the Warren, is there? You strongly recommend that the students do not go, but I believe that there is no written order to that effect?"

The Headmistress stared at Madigan with fire in her eyes. When she spoke it was clipped and quiet. "No, Lewis. There is not."

"So if I may ask, Olivia, which rule has Eleanor broken?" He asked this in the same way that someone might ask about the weather. He ignored the furious look on the Headmistress.

"She missed Mr. Hanford's bed check last night," said the Headmistress.

"Ah, yes. That is a snag, isn't it?" said Madigan. "I am told that the typical punishment for such behavior is a few days in the kitchens, is that right?"

The Headmistress took several deep breaths. "My concern is not only with Miss Wigton, Lewis, but with the message that I send to the other students. I cannot tolerate such behavior, and if it is not punished other students will get ideas."

"And we can't have students with ideas, now can we Olivia?" said Madigan.

"You are aware of what I mean, Lewis," she replied.

"Do you not think that the story of Miss Wigton's terrifying escape from some street thugs, and subsequent jailing by dwarves a sufficient deterrent to your students?" he asked as he stared out the window of the office.

"It depends on the student, Lewis, as you are aware," the Headmistress replied. The way she said it made Eleanor feel as if this conversation was about more than her own situation, and echoed some long-standing disagreement.

"Yet Eleanor has shown herself to be quite a model student, apart from this episode. It hardly seems fair to start inventing rules just to punish her, doesn't it?" Madigan said, turning back to face the Headmistress.

The Headmistress looked back and forth between Eleanor and Madigan. The slightest slump in her shoulders was the only indication that she had conceded a point. "Miss Wigton, you will serve three nights of kitchen duty for missing your bed check last night. Your parents will be informed of this infraction, as is written school policy," she emphasized those words. "Before you even say anything, Lewis, no I will not be informing them of anything else. As you so gallantly swept in before the Wardens arrived, there is no evidence of anything to tell them about."

"Excellent. I think you've made a very wise decision, Olivia," said Madigan, a smile on his face.

"I'm sure you do, Lewis," she replied, frowning. "Now if you don't mind, both of you, I have many things to attend to."

"Of course, Olivia. We shall be off," said Madigan with the same even tone he'd been using the entire time.

"Thank you, ma'am," said Eleanor as she stood up. She felt like she should apologize more, but Madigan gave her a slight tug on the arm and urged her towards the door.

"You might consider your choice of colleagues, Miss Wigton.

They are not always what they seem," said the Headmistress as they exited through the door. Eleanor did not know how to reply to that, and pulled the door shut behind her.

"I thought that went rather well," said Madigan. Eleanor's stomach was only just now untying the many knots that had formed in it. If that was a good meeting, she was unsure she ever wanted to see a bad one. "I do apologize for the nights in the kitchen, I didn't feel that pushing your Headmistress on that front was wise."

"That's not a problem, sir," said Eleanor, just thankful have made it out of Headmistresses office still a Penwick student.

In the outer office, Mrs. Puddlemump bustled about Eleanor again, ensuring she was still all right. A tray of food sat steaming on the low table in the corner, and the smell drove any other thoughts from Eleanor's mind. With a muttered thank you to Mrs. Puddlemump she grabbed the bread from the tray and stuffed a large wad of it in her mouth. Mrs. Puddlemump talked to Madigan while she ate.

Once Eleanor had managed to consume all the bread, most of an apple, and some chicken, Madigan turned back to her.

"May I continue to use up some of your day, Eleanor? I have a few things I'd still like to talk about with you," he said, his voice even but a look of intense curiosity on his face.

"Of course," she said through a last mouthful of food.

Madigan led them out of the office, and across the hall to a lounge. It was decorated in a lavender color, with several small couches against the back wall, and a slim wooden table running down the middle. Several gigantic oil paintings of what Eleanor presumed were old Headmasters loomed over the fireplace.

Madigan indicated Eleanor should take a seat on one side of the table, and he pulled out a chair for himself on the opposite side. He gave a smile, but his face was serious. "I need to hear about what you've seen in that book, Eleanor," he said, "and then I've believe you've earned the right to know more about why I wrapped you up in this all in the first place."

CHAPTER 10

WHAT MR. TRATFORD FOUND

"CAN you see the book in your head?", said Madigan.

Eleanor nodded. The food had helped Eleanor settle the last of the nerves from the visit to the Headmistress.

"Very well, then. Slowly, Eleanor. Please tell me what you can see in the Occlodex," said Madigan.

She swallowed hard, and closed her eyes to help her concentrate. After the night in the dwarven cell she had not tried to look at the Occlodex in her head again, and was not sure how easily she could control it. But after a few stumbles she was able to fix page 183 in her head, and began to read what she saw.

While exploring the Black Island I came across a natural cave set into the side of the central mountain. The opening faced east, away from the prevailing winds. Inside the cave I found three black pods, which I surmise are the seeds from some of the black-barked trees we have found throughout the island.

The pods are wrinkled on their exterior, but the material itself forming the exterior of the pods is almost perfectly smooth, glass-like. The black color is deep and reflective. Each pod is approximately 12 inches long and about 8 inches high at the middle.

They are all ovoid in shape. They look like over-grown raisins.

The most notable aspect of each pod is that they all are quite warm to the touch despite being found in the cave, which is roughly twenty degrees cooler than the outside air temperature. They quickly absorb heat when put in the sun, becoming painful to touch.

The pods were also found beneath a pile of dried bones, almost as if they had been hidden away. We have not met any natives of the Black Island, and there are no other signs of human habitation here. Perhaps a large mammal had stored them for future use, although there seems no reason for animals here to hibernate as we see in our colder climates.

Eleanor looked up at Madigan when she finished. "Below that there is a sketch Tratford made of the seeds. It looks exactly like a giant raisin, as he said." He sat still in his chair but his eyes were focused on a distant point across the room, and she was afraid to break his concentration.

"Sir?" she said. "Mr. Madigan?"

His head snapped down. He sat forward on his chair and the intensity in his eyes ebbed. "I'm sorry Eleanor, I got lost a bit in thinking about what you just read. Are you sure there is nothing else written on that page?"

She closed her eyes and let the Occlodex resolve back into view. She looked over the page, sure she hadn't missed anything. But there was some scribbling in the bottom corner, she saw.

"There's a few extra marks that look as if they were made at a different time, perhaps," she said, feeling her eyes squint uselessly as she tried to focus in further on the page. "It's some letters and numbers."

"Read them," said Madigan.

"2 S 84 26 E," she replied. "What do you think those mean? They don't make any sense."

"Perhaps," replied Madigan, his fingers now tented in front of his chin, tapping against his beard. "They sound like nautical coordinates. 2 degrees south, and 84 degrees 26 minutes east. A location?"

Eleanor realized Madigan might be right. In their Astronomy classes they had worked on coordinates. Two degrees south meant 2 degrees south of the equator. The ship was from Flosston Moor, and those ships all used the Steward's Tower to mark zero degrees, so that meant Tratford's notes pointed to a spot 86 degrees away, or almost one quarter of the way around the world from where they sat now. She didn't know the maps as well as a regular Navigation student, but she was quite sure that it indicated someplace near -

"The Cinnamon Islands?" she blurted out.

"Quite possibly, Eleanor," replied Madigan. "I will have to consult with some more experienced cartographers, but that is likely to be the case. Mr. Tratford may have marked out the location of this Black Island for himself."

"So he could find it again?" asked Eleanor, and then something dawned on her. "Is that what the Forgotten are after, Mr.

Madigan? Do they want to find this island?"

Madigan's eyes flashed. "Very little gets past you, Eleanor. And yes it seems that they want this location. I fear the consequences if they should discover it," and his eyes unfocused again as he fell back into thought.

Eleanor waited again, her impatience growing. She had chased down the Occlodex and found this message, but Madigan still hadn't even told her about who the Forgotten were, and who sent the codes in the first place. He had stifled himself when he told them about the project. But now she felt entitled to some clearer answers.

The old man's face flickered back to life and he leaned back in his chair. Eleanor's frustration gave her enough courage to put her questions to him.

"Who are these Forgotten we're after?" she asked with what she hoped was a firm, forceful voice.

"We, Eleanor?" said Madigan, but a hint of a smile played across his face. For a moment she thought he would hesitate as he had before, but he scratched at his grey beard and went on, "The Forgotten are a collection of individuals with a wretched vision for the future of this city, and perhaps the kingdom. They are criminals, as I first mentioned at the meeting where Mr. Farragut had his ill-timed coughing fit. But they are more than thieves or smugglers. They are without conscience and will trample any who attempt to stand in their path to power." The look on Madigan's face was frightening as he spoke.

"Power over what?" she asked, almost in a whisper.

182

"Everything. Anything. It matters not to them, so long as others recognize their mastery," said Madigan, his eyes still doing a cold burn.

Madigan's voice gave no doubt that he took this possibility seriously, but what could give anyone that kind of power? Surely the Steward wouldn't turn over the city to the Forgotten.

"Why are they so dangerous?" Eleanor asked.

There was a pause, and then Madigan let out a deep breath. "They're wizards, Eleanor. True wizards, not some street artist or witch doctor."

"How can that be? You mean they're from the White Tower? They were all driven out long ago, after the Burning. There are no wizards left," she said, but her protests sounded hollow even to herself at that moment, only phrases from a history book.

"The wizards did disappear from view after the Burning, Eleanor, but they never left. They've always remained here in Flosston Moor," said Madigan. "The Burning was the result of a fierce battle within the White Tower, between wizards that were bent on exerting their own rule over the city, and those that felt our place was to exist alongside it."

It almost slipped past her. "Our place?" she asked, her eyes opening wide.

Madigan gave her a wry look. "You never do miss anything, Eleanor. Yes, our place. Perhaps this will not be very surprising any more, but I too am a wizard. The argument within the White Tower that caused the Burning never ended. I and several others struggle to keep the wizards who let loose the Burning -

183

the Forgotten - from doing it again."

A few weeks ago she would have dismissed his story, but having seen so many lingering scraps of magic about the city it did not surprise her to hear that Madigan was a wizard himself. But the idea that the Burning might happen again was shocking. The entire city had smoldered for over a year, the books said. Thousands died, but only because a few thousand lived in the city. If it happened now it would be devastating.

"But what do they want with this island?" she asked. It seemed to bear no connection at all to the wizards of the White Tower.

Here Madigan took a deep breath, and Eleanor was afraid some memory of Mr. Farragut had intruded on him and hectored him into silence. His face looked grim and sad, and Eleanor started to wonder if she wanted to hear his answer.

"It's not the island, Eleanor," Madigan said. "It's what Mr. Tratford found there that they covet."

"Seeds?" she asked. "To what end? Are they magical?"

"They are not seeds," said Madigan, staring down at his hands. "They are something far more valuable, far more rare, and far more dangerous. They are eggs."

Eleanor found her hands gripping the edge of her chair so hard she could feel the wood biting into her palm. Eggs? Eggs from what kind of animal? What made them so valuable? She said nothing.

"They are dragon eggs," said Madigan, as if reading her mind. "The bones Mr. Tratford saw were remnants of the

184

dragon's hunt. He was very lucky not to have found the cave while the dragon was still on the island."

The idea was shocking. It was one thing to see doors leading across the city or vials containing entire books. It was another to believe that gigantic creatures like dragons were real. "Dragons? The Forgotten want a dragon?"

"It would appear so, Eleanor. Dragons are one of the few things capable of reproducing the fierce fires that caused the Burning. The Forgotten would be able to threaten Flosston Moor, and the entire kingdom for that matter, with devastation. It would be a terrible weapon. They cannot be allowed to find these eggs," said Madigan.

Did the Forgotten already know how to find the eggs? The copy of Tratford's notes she had delivered to Wellsby had been missing the page describing them. Maybe they had taken it. But if they had, why were they sending someone codes leading him towards Tratford? So the Forgotten probably didn't know where to find the eggs. If they didn't know, then perhaps the city might remain safe. The coordinates were inside her head, and she certainly wasn't about to shout them out across the rooftops. The Occlodex had spilled when she and Jack escaped from Ms. Dobbin's basement, so that source was no longer available. Then again, all this talk about dragon eggs and wizards could be pure fiction - did she really believe such things?

"This is all rather astonishing," she said as these thoughts continued to twirl about in her head. "To find out that the fairy tales we were told about magic and dragons and wizards are true."

Madigan gave her a wry smile. "Well, not all those fairy tales are entirely true, Eleanor. However, they are all real in some sense. They have some truth hidden within them."

As he was talking Eleanor had been toying with the pencil case in her pocket. She pulled it out now. "Even my Silverwood pencils?" she asked. "People say they can protect you from magic."

"That is true," said Madigan. "Silverwood is quite useful to repel spells or cancel the effects of certain magic. Your pencils are small, but would be able to dispel magic that was not too strong."

She found the idea comforting now that she realized how much magic lived around her. In fact, having seen how useful magic could be it surprised her that it remained hidden beneath the surface.

"Why don't you come back out in the open? Return to the White Tower? People would see how useful your magic could be. It could give you allies against the Forgotten." she said.

"The Burning left a very deep mark on this city, Eleanor. The few who even entertain the idea that wizards continue to roam freely are almost always convinced they have dark purposes. And the Forgotten have infiltrated many places throughout Flosston Moor, hiding behind illusions to mask their true identities. It is difficult to move against them. They are everywhere. We operate best beneath the surface," he said.

"I can't believe that. I think the teachers at Penwick, for

186

instance, would fall all over themselves to have access to the Occlodexes," said Eleanor.

Madigan laughed. Eleanor wasn't sure what she said was that funny.

"They are welcome to go any time they want to use them. No one ever does," said Madigan. "For a long time, Eleanor, Penwick and the White Tower worked together. The teachers here helped determine the most important books to preserve as Occlodexes. It was also standard that a wizard of the White Tower could serve as a faculty member at Penwick."

"What?" said Eleanor, "So you could be a teacher at Penwick?" she asked.

"If I wished," said Madigan. "But there is no Magistry Hall anymore, is there? I don't think any students would be interested."

The idea of being able to learn about magic in a classroom sounded a lot more exciting than learning star charts or classifying plants. I couldn't be the only one who felt that way, thought Eleanor.

"Speaking of school," Madigan continued. "I believe it is time we returned you to your regular life as a student here."

The way he said it sounded rather final. Was this the end of the project for her? That didn't seem fair. She felt like she had a right to look further. "I don't like the sound of that, Mr. Madigan," she said.

He gave her a gentle smile. "Eleanor, you are a remarkable young lady. You have helped me a great deal. However, at this

187

point the hunt will become even more dangerous than you've experienced. I will not risk you any further."

Eleanor opened her mouth to reply, but the granite look on Madigan's face made her realize that there was going to be no arguing with him on this point. She was done with investigating. She was surprised at how empty that made her feel, given the recent events. There had been something thrilling about hunting down Simon Tratford's field notes. She had done things she never would have imagined a few months ago. Entering the Warren, drinking a magic book, meeting dwarves face to face. It seemed like the actions of a different person, a brave person. Eleanor liked the idea that she was brave. It was unlike when Madigan had first approached them about the project, when she had been so certain that she was in over her head. It reminded her of a question that had been bothering her for quite a long time.

"Mr. Madigan," she said. "Why did you pick me for this?"

Madigan raised his eyebrows, perhaps surprised that she had asked. "You are the top student in the second year, Eleanor. Your teachers all said you were bright and curious, two qualities I value," he said. "Given the events of the last few months, I'd say I made the right choice."

That was all very flattering to Eleanor, but there was still something gnawing on her brain. The day she had first met Madigan, in Mr. Farragut's room, he had acted like he knew her already. And she heard Mr. Farragut object to her inclusion, but Madigan insist on her presence. There was something more.

"You already knew who I was before you came to Penwick," she said, making it a statement rather than a question.

If he was startled by Eleanor's assertion, he didn't show it. He stared at her for a long time, though, appearing to weigh his reply.

"You are correct," he said. "I did know who you were. We met when you were a very little girl."

That explains how he knew her, but not why he bothered to pick her for this project. "That can't be why I was chosen, though," she said.

"No," Madigan replied. "I had a reason to include you. An instinct, really, more than anything."

"An instinct?" she asked.

"That you would be as persistent as a man I once knew. Your grandfather, Charles," said Madigan.

"My grandpa Charles? You knew him?" Eleanor asked, shocked by the idea. Just mentioning him brought up a well of memories and emotions about losing him when she was a child.

"I did," said Madigan, a clear expression of grief falling across his face. "He was a very close friend. We often worked together and he had the sharpest mind I've ever met. I took a gamble that yours was just as keen. I believe I won that gamble."

Eleanor sat without saying a word for a few moments. "I barely got to know him. I was five when he died."

"It was a terrible loss. I spent a lot of time with Charles. I'll tell you this, Eleanor. Going to find the Occlodex in the Warren was what your grandfather would have done. I think you're a lot like him."

Pride seeped into the emotions skittering around in Eleanor's head. Her grandfather was a legendary figure in her family: smart, strong, and respected. Being compared to him was an incredible compliment. But if Madigan knew him - .

"Wait, was he a *wizard* too?" she asked, not sure whether to hope the answer was yes or no.

Madigan laughed at that. "No, no. But he also was not afraid to recognize the presence of magic around him. He was one of the first catch on to the danger of the Forgotten. He put together a number of unconnected threads and found that they all led to the same place. He realized the danger the Forgotten posed, and spent much of his life trying to uncover the network of their membership. The hunt for the Forgotten is what occupied us for many years."

"Was that - ", started Eleanor, but she started to choke up.

"Was that what killed him?" said Madigan as the grief returned to his face. "I don't think so. Charles was a competent sailor, but there was a storm that day. I think he was simply lost at sea."

Eleanor was just able to keep herself from crying as she thought of her grandfather.

"I think that's quite enough for today, Eleanor," said Madigan. "Let's get you back to your dormitory so that you can get a bath and some sleep."

Eleanor nodded her agreement. She stood up and headed for the door.

"If you need anything, Eleanor, see Mr. Farragut to send me a note," he said, a smile on his face.

"I will," said Eleanor. His comment tugged at one other thing that had been bothering her. "What is the pebbled cup he keeps burning my messages in?"

Madigan laughed, the sadness at the talk of her grandfather disappearing from his face as he let her go. "It's a Smokespeaker. I have one as well. When Mr. Farragut burns a note in his cup with my name on it, it appears in mine."

"That explains the scorch marks on your return message," she said.

"A common side effect of the transmission, unfortunately," he said. "But still a rather convenient means to get a hold of one another."

"I'd like to have one of those," she said absently, not sure whom she would send messages too, as her family would never believe such a thing existed.

"I'll see what I can do," he said. "But I promise I'll keep you informed on what I find. I know you won't sleep if I don't. Worse, you might end up back in a jail cell."

"Thank you," she said, "and good luck."

She slipped out of the door and made her way outside to the dormitory. Almost everyone was in class, and she did not have to stop to talk to anyone. She was a tangle of emotions at the moment, and exhaustion was starting to settle over her. With just a few odd glances from some upper year students she made it into the dormitory, where she stripped out of the filthy

191

clothes she had been wearing for the last two days. Slipping on her robe, she made her way down to the baths, which for the first time in her life she had to herself. Filling the bathtub with the hottest water she could stand, she settled in and scrubbed herself clean.

She sat for a long time, turning over everything she had learned from Madigan. The connection with her grandfather gave her a jolt of confidence, and pushed down the doubts that crept through her head about everything she had done. The idea that wizards were still roaming about Flosston Moor gave her a thrill of possibility.

For now though she had to return to her life as a Penwick student. She could handle the nights in the kitchen she owed the Headmistress, and get back to her regular school work. If she was going to remain a top student she would have to work hard, but that didn't bother her. Part of her was looking forward to melting back into her regular school routine.

The bath was luxurious, but she started feeling so sleepy that she had to get out before she drown herself. Drying off, she headed back to her room and promptly fell asleep in her robe, lying on top of her blankets.

CHAPTER 11

EXAMINERS

RETURNING to a regular routine turned out to be impossible, Eleanor discovered. The next morning at breakfast it was clear that she had become something of a celebrity among the students at Penwick. The typical babble of voices in the dining hall first died down and then roared like a wave crashing on a beach after she entered. Several students turned around in their seats to look at her as she headed towards the service line to pick up her breakfast. They stared like she had green hair and an extra head.

She didn't have a chance to even pick up her spoon before the other second-year girls were battering her with questions about the Warren and the dwarves. What were you doing there? How did you get caught by the dwarves? Is the Warren really that scary? Did you go inside the White Tower? How much trouble are you in with the Headmistress? Are you going to be expelled?

The lure of hearing more was enough to break the invisible barrier in the middle of the table that separated the boys. They crept down the benches towards the girl's end of the table, until they were all but sitting on top of the table to hear what she had to say. The boys found the parts about staggering around in the sewers mesmerizing.

Luckily for Eleanor, the questions were so frantic and un-

193

ordered that she never had to explain *why* she had gone into the Warren in the first place. She figured that everyone assumed it had to do with the special project. That was enough for them. It saved her from having to come up with a crude lie on the spot.

One thing that she kept to herself was the Occlodexes. She felt possessive of them in an odd way. It felt like it would make them less special, less magical, if everyone knew about them. She very much wanted to go back to see Ms. Dobbins and try more of them. The looming question was whether she could do it without ending up staggering around in that sewer all over again.

She could see as she talked that some of the girls were reacting to the upending of the normal social structure at their table. Eleanor had always been quiet, talking mainly to Miriam if to anyone. Now she was the center of attention and this meant that Darcy Ellington and Amelia Norfolk were not. They could both be nice, but saw themselves as the queens of their little world. There were times when they battled each other verbally to be the sole monarch, but today they had joined together to keep things from getting out of their hands.

There was nothing cutting about what they said, but any expressions of doubt or disbelief came from those two. "Well, it's not like you're the only one who has ever been to the Warren, Eleanor. Seth Grafton in the sixth year has been many times," from Amelia. "Are you sure it was a cell? It sounds like it could just be a regular dwarf bedroom," from Darcy. They littered comments like that in between her answers to the other student's questions.

Eleanor had not ever been concerned with being the most popular girl, so their discomfort at the situation didn't worry her that much. In a few days, she was sure, things would go back to normal, and Darcy and Amelia could go back to being the self-appointed leaders of the second year girls.

The only rough part of the questioning was when she casually mentioned Jack helping her find Mrs. Dobbins shop. Darcy jumped in to ask her who Jack was.

"A boy I know from town," said Eleanor, not thinking much of it.

"You know him. Have you been seeing him?" asked Amelia.

"Seeing him how?" asked Eleanor, not getting at what Amelia was asking.

"You know, Eleanor," said Amelia, "is he handsome? Are you two a couple?"

Eleanor hadn't thought of Jack like that at all. He seemed much more like a very frustrating older brother. "No," she said.

"No what?" asked Darcy. "No he's not that handsome?"

"No," said Eleanor, feeling herself getting overwhelmed. "He's just fine looking."

"Oh, really," said Amelia, "and how do you know this Jack?"

"I met him when I was in town. He helped me when I almost got hit by a wagon," said Eleanor. That seemed like it had happened ages ago.

"A real hero, is he?" said Darcy. "Is that why you fell for him?"

"I did not fall for him," said Eleanor, "whatever that is supposed to mean."

"Oh, I think you know," said Amelia. Darcy nodded agreement, and they both got up from the table.

Know what? They walked off as if they had made some sort of point, but Eleanor didn't quite see what it was. She supposed that they just wanted to show everyone that they weren't enthralled by Eleanor's story. That was fine with her.

Unlike those two, Miriam had happily adapted to the new social order. She established herself as something like Eleanor's assistant, reminding people when a certain question had been answered already and calling on others who hadn't been heard yet. They had been going on so long that everyone was in danger of missing class, and Eleanor had barely had a chance to eat. Miriam shooed everyone away, insisting that Eleanor needed some quiet. She even pocketed some scones in case Eleanor needed something else to eat as they hurried to their first class of the day.

Geometry was a relief. No one could bother her, but she could hear Jacob Weatherby and Ronald Burns arguing under their breaths about how many dwarves she had seen in the tunnel. She tried to ignore them and work on the proof that Mrs. Arbuckle had tasked the class with.

After class, though, Mrs. Arbuckle stopped her to talk about the events of the last few days. The teacher expressed some concern for her ordeal, but seemed as interested as the students to hear more about the Warren. It was more pointed questioning

196

than she had gotten from the students, and Eleanor was only able to avoid talking about the Occlodexes by excusing herself to get to her next class.

This was history, and afterwards Mr. Farragut pulled her aside as well. Knowing more about the project, he didn't bother her for as many details. He seemed to be concerned that she was all right after the adventure, and offered to give her extra days to complete her latest assignment. Eleanor declined, as she didn't want to be seen as getting any special treatment.

Having assured himself that everything was fine he then proceeded to pepper her with questions about the dwarves, specific questions about food, clothing, and their style of speaking. She did her best to try and remember details, and on occasion Mr. Farragut would actually note something down that she said. Trying to recreate the dwarven words that were used was very difficult, as she had no idea of what they were supposed to sound like. It was a very tiring interview, and she was thankful when Miriam stuck her head back inside Mr. Farragut's room to remind them that they had to eat lunch.

The buzz at lunch was diminished but there were still plenty of random questions, including some from fourth years who were sitting at the table next to theirs. Amelia and Darcy had adopted a new strategy of indifference, and sat at the end of the table trying very hard to ignore everyone talking to Eleanor.

After lunch she and Miriam were walking to Astronomy when they came across James and Millicent.

"All hail the conquering hero!" said James, flashing a wicked

197

smile.

A few months ago the comment would have made her feel self-conscious, but given recent events she no longer felt like she had to defer to the older students on the project. "Very funny, James," she said.

"I'm guessing you're sick of talking about this, but how did you end up in the Warren?" asked Millicent.

"It was you," said Eleanor. "You seem to give me all kinds of crazy ideas." For a moment Eleanor was worried that she had hit a sore spot with Millicent, but it was hard to tell given that her normal look was one of annoyance. In the end, the older girl cracked a thin smile.

"You don't mean the Occlodexes, do you? Are they actually there?" said Millicent, her jaw almost falling to the ground.

"What's that?" asked Miriam, swiveling her head back and forth between Millicent and Eleanor.

"You've got to be joking," said James.

Eleanor considered what she should say. She didn't want the Occlodexes to be public information, but the main reason she could find for that was selfishness. Millicent had planted the seed. James was on the project. Miriam was her best friend at the school. She couldn't keep it secret from all of them.

"They're there. They're real," said Eleanor.

"I can't believe it," said Millicent. "That's incredible. Did you drink one?"

"Drink one what?" Miriam screamed. "What are you all talking about?"

"I'm sorry, Miriam," said Eleanor. "When I went to the Warren, I was looking for a library for books that have been turned into potions. They're called Occlodexes. You can drink them and see the book in your head."

"They're magic?" said Miriam, the astonishment clear on her face.

"They are," said Eleanor. "It's really incredible. One drink and the whole book is laid out in your mind for you."

"So you can see a book in your head?" asked James. "Right now?"

"If I concentrate, yes," said Eleanor. "It took me a while to get used to it, but now I can flip through it easily. The woman who owns the place has thousands in her basement, maybe more."

"This is all terribly confusing," said Miriam.

Eleanor gave her a smile. "I promise a full explanation tonight in our room, without everyone screaming questions." It wasn't clear from the look on Miriam's face whether this sounded like a good thing or a bad thing to her.

"We've got to get to class," said James. "Some time you'll have to tell me more about the Occlodexes. What a way to study."

Miriam and Eleanor said goodbye and then made their way to Astronomy class. After what seemed like hours of reading through star charts they were done for the day. With time before dinner they went back to Prescott Hall to try and study. When they got there a note was posted on the main door. Starting

199

the next evening there would be a series of talks given in their common room from the various Halls. It was getting close to the end of the year, and in a few weeks they would have to decide on what Hall to join. Eleanor hadn't thought about it at all, as she was so wrapped up in the project for Mr. Madigan. So while Miriam groaned at the demand on their limited time, Eleanor found herself looking forward to the meetings.

The next evening Eleanor and the rest of her second-year class crammed themselves into the common room, all focused on the three teachers and one sixth year student from the Apothecary Hall that sat at a small table. The teachers each took a moment to introduce themselves, even though they knew Mr. Bertram already from their anatomy class this year. The others were Mrs. Horace and Mr. Eglund. Each one talked about what kinds of classes they taught, and what kinds of things students could be expected to learn from them. Much of what they said sounded disturbing to Eleanor, involving things like extracting serums from rare insects and brewing tonics made from the leaves of various shrubs. She was reminded of Ms. Dobbins' ginger beetles, and the numerous stains all over her robes.

Eleanor was not sure that being an Apothecary sounded very fun. On the other hand, it did strike her that it might be the field that would know the most about Occlodexes. She wondered if the Apothecary teachers would let her pursue any research on the liquid books. None of the three teachers seemed like they were promising on that front. They all appeared to be precise and rigid, unlikely to let students stray too far off their standard course of study.

By the time Mr. Eglund has finished, Eleanor was quite sure she didn't want to be an Apothecary, as she couldn't see spending four years studying under any of the three. Students attached themselves to a specific teacher, and the Halls were just convenient groupings of teachers and students that shared some similar interests. So second years were trying to find the best match with a specific teacher, as that teacher would serve as their Examiner. The Examiner administered the oral exam each sixth-year had to pass in order to graduate from Penwick. A good relationship with your Examiner could be the difference from passing and having to remain at Penwick for an extra year or worse, expulsion.

Once the teachers had spoken, they asked if there were any questions. Violet and Willa asked a few, possibly trying to signal their interest in being Apothecaries to the teachers. The rest of the students sat mute. An awkward silence after Violet and Willa had used up their queries gave the teachers their excuse to leave. The sixth-year student then introduced himself as Thomas Healy. He gave his own brief comments on how much he liked being an Apothecary and then opened up for questions. With the teachers gone, Eleanor's classmates became much more inquisitive.

"Did Horace actually fail somebody last year?"

"I heard Eglund assigns twenty page essays every few weeks, is that true?"

"Are the rooms in the Apothecary Hall singles, or would I have to have a roommate?"

"How did Fanny turn her hair blue?"

"What's the story with Bertram? I heard he's a real prat."

Thomas did his best to answer without saying anything awful about the teachers. He assumed, and was probably right, that if he made any hateful remarks about the teachers in his Hall, it would get back to them and his Examination might not go well in a few weeks. Despite this handicap he seemed to get out enough information to satisfy them. By the end of the meeting Eleanor guessed that both Violet and Willa, as well as Derek Havermore, were thinking hard about becoming Apothecaries.

The next day was the delegation from Barrister Hall. There were five teachers and two upper level students from the Barrister Hall, and they generated far more questions and interest than any other. The Steward was always desperate for more hands to handle the flood of complaints, petitions, disputes, and contracts that followed all the ships coming and going from Flosston Moor. The students who didn't end up working for the Steward would probably work with one of the main merchant houses, spending their days creating the complaints, petitions, disputes, and contracts that their classmates had to work through. Miriam whispered to Eleanor that it all sounded horrifically boring, and Eleanor agreed.

As the Barrister teachers continued to talk, Eleanor's mind drifted off. She found herself sliding the Occlodex into focus, and paging through it looking at the descriptions of the fantastic plants that the *Dorian Maroon* had found in the Cinnamon Islands. Reading these was more engaging than whatever Mr. Howser from the Barrister Hall was droning on about.

Her mind kept drifting back to Simon Tratford. He had been a Penwick student and had sat through a series of presentations just as she was doing now. Perhaps he had been as bored as she was. He had ended up an Apothecary, and had probably been on the *Dorian Maroon* to catalog any new plants or spices they found, and identify the source of existing ones. It would have been an exciting journey, she supposed. She wondered if he came back to Penwick afterwards to do more studying in the Solarium, or if he had gone on more voyages? Did he use the coordinates he found to go back to the island?

Eleanor's consideration was cut short by the scuffling of chairs and feet as the meeting with the Barristers broke up. She had missed the teachers stepping out and the entire question and answer session with the upper level Barrister students. Miriam assured her that she had not missed anything important.

Over the next few days the meetings continued, and throughout them all Eleanor found herself drifting back to the questions surrounding Simon Tratford. Did he know that he had found dragon eggs? His notes seemed to indicate the answer was no, but had he figured it out later on? Perhaps he had let something slip long ago that had found its way to the ears of the Forgotten after all these years. These ideas popped about in her head, and no matter which Hall was talking, she found it hard to concentrate.

The Navigation Hall appeared to be the liveliest, which did break into her musings. The four teachers were all outgoing and seemed far less formal than the others. Several boys and girls in Eleanor's class were more taken with the Navigation Hall than with any other. It may have appealed to their sense of adventure. While many of them might end up cartographers like her uncle's friend Mr. Adler, a fair number would have the opportunity to work on ships. One of the teachers did try to keep expectations from getting too far out of hand. Navigators might spend fifteen years working on short-haul routes around the Mandlebar coast before they ever got to set foot on a trade ship going to the Cinnamon Islands. This did not seem to deter many of the aspiring Navigators in the room.

The contrast with the Numerancy Hall was marked. The three teachers were exactly what one expected Numerists to be: quiet, meek, and exacting. The students were, if possible, even more shy. It was not the most engaging presentation and Eleanor found herself feeling bad for the teachers as they seemed so uncomfortable trying to talk with the second year students. Eventually they were able to get across to the students that Numerancy was a nice quiet place to work without much disturbance, and that they tended to let the students dictate their own line of research. That part sounded appealing to Eleanor and she could see why her uncle fit in so well in the Numerancy Hall. However, the idea of managing accounts for a estate, which is what her uncle did, or working at one of the many new financial houses sprouting up around Flosston Moor did not strike her as the kind of thing she was interested in. Miriam, somewhat to Eleanor's surprise, was very intrigued by the Numerancy Hall. She bombarded Eleanor with questions after the presentation about what her uncle did every day.

The final night of the presentations was the History Hall. The Headmistress herself came, along with Mr. Farragut. All four of the students in the History Hall were there as well. The Headmistress explained that because of their small size they were a very close-knit group. The students affirmed later on that they were often helping each other with papers and research and that the Headmistress and Mr. Farragut spent a lot of time helping them with their studies. It sounded as if most of the students would end up either staying on at Penwick, or moving to other libraries along the coast after their studies were over. It did not seem very intriguing to Eleanor.

After the last meeting Eleanor felt as if she was no closer to choosing a Hall than before. None of them leapt out to her and grabbed her imagination. Over the next week she observed some of her classmates with jealousy, as they had such clear ideas about what they wanted to do. Violet and Willa talked nonstop about the Apothecary Hall, and how much they had enjoyed Mrs. Horace. Four of the boys in her class agreed to all go for the Navigation Hall, and she was sure they would fit in with the rowdy atmosphere.

Jacob Weatherby surprised everyone by letting it be known that he was going to try for the History Hall and wanted to study with the Headmistress. Two of the other boys tried to convince him that this was a terrible idea and that he should try the Barrister Hall with them. They both wanted to have Mr. Coverdale as an Examiner, as they had heard he was very good at placing students at merchant houses. Jacob stood firm and Eleanor envied his certainty.

It took several days for her to make up her mind, but Miriam told Eleanor that she was going to ask to be part of the Numerancy Hall. That didn't stop her from continuing to badger Eleanor for information about her uncle and what he did. It got frustrating enough that in the middle of some questions Eleanor told Miriam that her uncle often was called upon to wrestle live bears. Miriam's response was "Brown or black bears?", which had almost been enough to make Eleanor strangle her.

Between uncertainty about her choice of Hall and nagging questions about Simon Tratford, Eleanor was having a hard time keeping her head focused on schoolwork. A very welcome relief from the thoughts pinging around her brain came when she and Miriam returned to their room one night after studying late. A note had been tucked under the door, and it was from Mr. Adler. He had invited Eleanor and a guest - Miriam squealed her agreement when Eleanor asked - to dinner the next night at his house. It would be perfect to escape Penwick for an evening and clear her head. Eleanor's scrambled thoughts fell away as she drifted off thinking about Mrs. Hill's lemon tart.

CHAPTER 12

THE TALE OF THE *DORIAN MAROON*

THE next day Eleanor and Miriam spent some time after class preparing for dinner with Mr. Adler. Miriam insisted that they go through all of their scarves and hairpins before they could decide on what to wear. After assuring each other that their choices were perfect they hurried towards the main hall. They told Mrs. Puddlemump about the invitation and when they would return. Eleanor did not want to get in any more trouble with the Headmistress for leaving campus.

Having made their intentions known, they headed out of the gates of Penwick and into the city. The first few blocks were familiar to both and they chatted about nothing in particular as they moved down the street. Eleanor did peek through the window of the butcher shop to see if Jack was in, but all she could see was his father talking to a customer. Miriam spent most of the initial part of the walk pulling her tiny mirror from a pocket to check her hair, despite Eleanor insisting over and over again that it looked fine. Every time a breeze rustled them, though, Miriam pulled it back out.

Eleanor thought back to how frightened she had been just months earlier when delivering the book to Mr. Wellsby, and how the city had seemed daunting to her. It seemed less so now that she had been into the Warren. It also helped that the sun had decided to make an unexpected appearance, and it was pleasant to be outside without feeling as if one was going to freeze to death. Miriam was still nervous about the trip. She had never been beyond the few blocks next to Penwick without an adult. She stayed behind Eleanor as they wound their way across the Silverspan bridge dodging carts and foot traffic. Once they were on the Point the density of people picked up even further, and they held hands to keep from becoming separated in the bustle.

Over the Heartspan bridge they found themselves on Norfolk Road, where Eleanor recognized some of the shops that she and her uncle had visited at the beginning of the year, including Squint's Stationery. She pointed these and others out to Miriam, and they dawdled for a while in front of some of the dress shops, admiring and wishing. Eleanor dragged Miriam away so that they would not be indecently late for dinner.

The balance of patronage along Norfolk Road was shifting from the shops to the restaurants and pubs as they made their way towards Mr. Adler's alley. Eleanor barely recognized it in time, and they got an angry look from a cart driver when they darted in front of him to turn down the small street. As before, it was much quieter here than on Norfolk Road. Mr. Adler's house looked to be the only one with anyone present on this night. The rest were dark.

Eleanor pulled the thin rope hanging outside of Mr. Adler's door and heard the bell inside. A moment later came the creaking sound of an interior door and some muffled voices. Then the front door popped open and Mrs. Hill was there. She surprised Eleanor with a hug, and Eleanor felt herself relax in the embrace.

"My goodness, how good to see you, Eleanor. And who do we have here?" asked Mrs. Hill.

"Mrs. Hill, this is my roommate and friend Miriam," said Eleanor.

"Hello, ma'am," said Miriam.

"Well hello to you too, young lady," said Mrs. Hill. Having never met Miriam was not much of an issue for Mrs. Hill. She released Eleanor and threw an arm around Miriam's shoulder, guiding her into the front hall and eyeing her up and down.

"As I suspected," said Mrs. Hill, "You both appear to be studying too much and eating too little. Look at you both, all skin and bones." She plucked at the shoulder of Eleanor's dress, clucking a disapproving sound. "These Penwick dresses aren't doing you any favors either."

Neither of the girls had any reason to disagree with the last statement. Mrs. Hill scooted them back into the parlor where Eleanor and her uncle had waited several months ago. She was about to say something when there was a clatter from the front door and they all turned to see Mr. Adler come rushing in.

"Ah, excellent, excellent," he said, breathing a little heavily. "I got tied up with a captain and was afraid I'd kept you all waiting for hours."

"Not this time," said Mrs. Hill in a resigned tone that suggested she had long-since given up on expecting Mr. Adler to be punctual.

"Hello, Mr. Adler, thank you for having us," said Eleanor. "This is my friend Miriam."

"Thank you, sir, for inviting us both to come," said Miriam, adding a little giggle at the end. When she was nervous she giggled. For a Geometry exam last fall Miriam had laughed so hard she had been asked to leave the room until she could get herself under control.

"It's not me you need to thank, girls," said Mr. Adler. "Mrs. Hill is the one who all but beat me about the head with a broom until I wrote the note. I'd been meaning to ask for ages, but kept forgetting."

"You make me sound like a harpy, Mr. Adler," said Mrs. Hill. "You just needed some prodding, that's all." Eleanor felt quite sure that she meant prodding literally.

"Regardless," said Mr. Adler, "You're here now. Why don't you have a seat and I can catch up on all the excitement at Penwick."

"I'll bring in some tea," said Mrs. Hill. "Dinner will be ready soon." She disappeared into the dining room and through a door to the kitchen. Eleanor could hear her bellowing something to Reuben.

Mr. Adler sunk into one of the armchairs and motioned for the girls to do the same. He started to pepper them with questions about classes and their general life at Penwick. He was an easy man to talk with, never letting the conversation lag. Unlike most of the previous graduates of Penwick that Eleanor

210

knew, he was able to resist making unfavorable comparisons with his own time at the school. Her uncle had a tendency to do this, always insisting that the standards had slipped since his time, and implying that neither Eleanor nor her classmates were working that hard. Mr. Adler had the decency to keep those kinds of opinions to himself, instead inserting an "excellent" or "smashing" here and there when the girls told him about their classes.

Mrs. Hill delivered some tea, and then they strayed into uncomfortable territory for Eleanor as Mr. Adler asked about their choice for Halls. Miriam saved her by revealing that she was thinking of entering the Numerancy Hall.

"Well, that will make Eleanor's Uncle William rather happy," said Mr. Adler, giving Eleanor a wink. "What makes you think Numerancy?"

Miriam, to Eleanor's surprise and relief, launched into a detailed explanation of her thinking. It sounded like she had been rolling this over in her head for some time, and was now trying it out loud for the first time. She went through her enjoyment of her Numerancy classes, and how she enjoyed the precision of being able to find exact answers. It seemed incongruous to Eleanor, as Miriam was rather sloppy and clumsy. Perhaps the tidiness of Numerancy appealed to her by allowing her to instill order in one part of her life.

Miriam was still talking when Mrs. Hill returned to the room to announce that dinner was ready, giving Eleanor a chance to avoid talking about her own indecision. As they all stood up to go in to dining room Mr. Adler waved for Eleanor to walk ahead of him, and she had to maneuver around a low table set between the chairs. This forced her to skirt past a wall hung with some of Mr. Adler's map collection. Looking at the maps as she passed, she saw a name that startled her.

"Mortimer Hassleford," she said, almost in a whisper.

"What was that, Eleanor?" said Mr. Adler, behind her.

"Oh, nothing," she said. Hanging on the wall just several inches from her face were three different maps signed by Mortimer Hassleford, the navigator from the *Dorian Maroon*. She did not recognize the locations but they all seemed to be islands.

Her initial reaction was to keep the connection with the ship to herself. Eleanor did not want to violate Madigan's trust. As she made her way into the dining room she was wondering whether asking Mr. Adler about Hassleford would reveal anything. How did he get the maps? What were the locations on the maps? Were they from the *Dorian Maroon*'s voyage, or did they come from some earlier one that Mr. Hassleford undertook?

The arrival of the food kept Eleanor from having to decide exactly what to do, and kept Miriam and Mr. Adler occupied enough to not notice her distraction. Mrs. Hill's roast beef was excellent and there were heaps of vegetables on the table. Eleanor enjoyed the fresh bread right from the oven, which steamed as she cut it open. The food was a distinct improvement over Penwick's fare and both girls gobbled it up.

When all three were down to picking at what remained on their plates Eleanor decided that the chance of learning something about Hassleford outweighed any risk of exposing Madigan's hunt.

"Mr. Adler, I noticed several maps by Mortimer Hassleford hanging in your parlor. Where are they from?" she asked, trying to make it sound like an innocent question.

"Ah, taking some interest in Navigation, are you?" said Mr. Adler, who seemed ready to steer her towards a discussion of Halls.

"I'm not sure about that, Mr. Adler. But I came across Mr. Hassleford's name doing some research and just wanted to know some more about him," she answered, hoping that this would keep the conversation on track.

"Well, he was a very respected cartographer," said Mr. Adler. "The maps that I have are of some of the Angel Islands. They were extremely accurate for the time they were created, and were part of what made Hassleford's name. They've been surpassed since then but I always admired the art behind them. Nowadays the lines and notations on the maps we make are very mechanical. Hassleford's maps are more personal. You can see how the weight of the ink changed as he drew."

Eleanor listened but was not interested in the aesthetic value of Hassleford's maps. What she wanted to know was something about his trip to the Cinnamon Islands. She decided it was worth revealing more of what she knew to prompt Mr. Adler.

"He made a trip to the Cinnamon Islands, didn't he?" she asked.

"Yes, he did," answered Mr. Adler. "Not a very successful

trip for him, I'm afraid."

"How do you mean?" asked Eleanor.

"He died on the voyage," Mr. Adler said, his face looking dark. "He had gone along as a navigator on one of the ships that followed Samuel Norfolk's first visit to the Cinnamon Islands. The idea was to press past the barrier islands that Norfolk landed on, and explore more of the archipelago. Norfolk had traded with the Turgan - he's like the king of the islands - for his original haul of spices. Hassleford and others were trying to search out the actual source of the spices themselves. The Turgan was not pleased with their attempts."

"So was he killed by the Turgan?" asked Eleanor.

"Some were, but not Hassleford," said Mr. Adler. "At least as far as the stories go. It's not clear what occurred on Hassleford's voyage."

There was a mysterious tone to Mr. Adler's voice. If there was something special about that voyage it could be linked to the Forgotten's interest in the *Dorian Maroon*.

"It sounds like an interesting story," she said, trying to prod Mr. Adler on without sounding too eager. "What do you think happened?"

"Well, there are any number of legends that have grown since Hassleford's ship returned without him," said Mr. Adler.

"The *Dorian Maroon*," prompted Eleanor.

Mr. Adler gave her a surprised look. "You seem to know more than you let on, Eleanor," he said.

"I stumbled across the ship's name while I was doing some

214

other research, and that's where I saw Hassleford's name," Eleanor replied. It wasn't the truth, but there was no sense in revealing the original reason for her research.

It seemed enough to satisfy Mr. Adler. "As I'm an admirer of Hassleford's I've paid attention to the many rumors and stories that the sailors tell about the voyage. There are discrepancies among them, but let me give you the common elements. The *Dorian Maroon* sailed to explore and map more of the Cinnamon Islands, similar to several others launched after Norfolk's original route to the islands became widely known.

The *Dorian Maroon* hopped from small island to small island. One thing most people agree on is that they found the source island for nutmeg. However there were already several other ships from Flosston Moor lurking about, so the captain - Bumblerump or something if I recall - decided to press on further into the archipelago. They had heard of islands farther on that were supposed to be home to even more exotic spices. Hassleford would have been frantically trying to map out their route. Most likely he argued for slower progress so that he could create more accurate maps, while the captain wanted to push faster to stay ahead of other explorers."

Mr. Adler leaned forward, "Now, sailors that have been into the interior of the Cinnamon archipelago, and there are not many of them left these days, will tell you that there is something different about them as you go further and further. There are thousands of tiny islands teeming with plants and animals that no man has ever seen before. The islands themselves are hot and dark, canopied by gigantic, ancient trees. More than that, they'll tell you that these islands go beyond the normal dangers you'd expect from exploring unknown lands. One old mate explained to me that there was a palpable sense of evil, and that the islands seemed to conspire against the ships. Take this with a grain of salt, of course, but he insisted that deep inside the Cinnamon Islands there were shoals that appeared where none had been the day before, and islands that would disappear from sight overnight. They say many ships were wrecked on reefs that appeared out of thin air."

"And this is where Hassleford was going?" asked Eleanor.

"According to the stories, yes," said Mr. Adler. "The captain of the *Dorian Maroon* pressed the ship farther and farther, ignoring the pleas of much of his crew to turn back. Hassleford did his best to keep up, mapping out the islands they were passing and visiting for fresh water. There are people that would give an arm to see his notebook containing the charts from that voyage. No one knows where they ended up."

Eleanor felt her stomach do a little flip. If Hassleford's notes were lost, then perhaps Tratford was the only one who knew the destination of their voyage.

"What is so valuable about his notes?" she asked, hoping to confirm her theory.

"This is where the story gets even hazier, you understand," said Mr. Adler. "So you must take this as a fairy tale. There is nothing as prone to exaggeration as a sailor, and over one hundred years later the facts of the story have long since washed

216

away."

Eleanor nodded her understanding, but her heart was pounding with anticipation. She noticed that Miriam was leaning in towards Mr. Adler, anxious for the story to continue.

"They say the *Dorian Maroon* found a peculiar island that was unlike any other in the archipelago. Trees with bark as black as the darkest night. According to the legend - and mind you this is all just rumor - there was a spice that one could make from this black bark that was valuable beyond all measure." He said the last part with doubt dripping from his voice.

"More than saffron?" blurted Miriam.

"Yes," said Mr. Adler. "It was supposed to be wonderful to eat. One dash could transform a simple stew into the greatest food one had ever tasted. The stories say that it tasted different to each individual, giving them their favorite flavors," He shrugged his shoulders a bit to indicate he was not a believer. "Like I said, this is all a fairy tale made up by sailors."

To Eleanor, it sounded confusing. What about the dragon eggs? Perhaps what the Forgotten were after was nothing more than this spice. They wanted to be rich, not recreate the Burning. That sounded more plausible. Maybe, she thought, Madigan was wrong.

Mrs. Hill came bustling into the dining room, shocking Eleanor back to the moment and interrupting the conversation.

"What has you lot so serious looking?" she asked, grabbing plates and silverware and piling them onto a tray. "It seems like a good moment to bring out some desserts. Cheer you all up." She bustled back out, the dishes making a clatter in the kitchen as she deposited them on the counter. A moment later she backed her way into the dining room carrying a small lemon cake. Somehow she also managed to be holding a serving knife, three forks, three small plates, and a small pitcher of cream. It all ended up on the table without a spill.

"I knew you enjoyed this when you were here with your uncle, Eleanor," said Mrs. Hill as she cut slices of the cake for each of them.

Eleanor took a bite, and it was as wonderful as she remembered. Despite the incredible dessert she found herself wishing Mrs. Hill out of the room so that Mr. Adler would continue the story. She had numerous questions now about Mr. Hassleford, the other crew members, and if anyone had ever found the island again.

Mrs. Hill's entry seemed to pop the bubble around the story, and Eleanor was afraid that by reminding Mr. Adler of the outside world he would decline to continue. She decided to press him again to try and get the thread of the story back.

"What happened to Mr. Hassleford?" she asked.

Mr. Adler wrinkled his forehead for a moment, and Eleanor thought he was deciding on whether to continue or give her some kind of cursory completion to the story. For a moment she feared he had settled on the quick finish, but then he took a breath and went on. "That is an aspect of the story that generates the most disagreement. The ship loaded up on as much of the black spice as it could harvest in a short time. However, there were

218

problems. The stories are that the spice is cursed. When they went to sail for home, terrible things started happening to the ship, and many of the crew perished."

"That's awful," said Miriam.

"They limped into Pembleton Island," said Mr. Adler. "The story told by a few of the older sailors I've talked to is that the ship looked as if it had been burned, with black scorch marks up and down the hull and barely any rigging left intact. The remaining sailors told stories about flames erupting out of nowhere as they sailed."

"What about the spice?" Eleanor asked.

"That was enough for the captain, Bumblerump. He was convinced that the spice was cursed, and had it all thrown overboard. He was so concerned with the dangers of the spice that he decided on the way back to Flosston Moor to destroy the evidence of their journey there. He destroyed all of Hassleford's maps," Mr. Adler paused, "Hassleford himself had perished on the way back to Pembleton Island with the spice. So no one would ever be able to find the island again, except by dumb luck."

It took a moment for realization to set in. "So knowing where to find that island would be valuable to some people, wouldn't it? People who didn't believe in the curse?"

"I would think," said Mr. Adler. "There is always some captain convinced he can do what no one else has ever done, hoping to make himself rich in the process."

Neither Eleanor nor Miriam said anything for a moment. If

this were true, then the Forgotten were after the coordinates in her head so that they could find the island again. It could be that Madigan was completely turned around on what they were up to. It may not even be the Forgotten who were trying to find Simon Tratford's notes. It was only Madigan who had told her that they were behind the secret code.

The puzzled looks on the girl's faces must have indicated to Mr. Adler that he had gone far enough. "Ladies, I believe that is enough tall tales for one evening. If you are done with dessert, why don't I escort you back to Penwick. I have a captain to meet later this evening, and I'll be going out regardless."

They agreed, and thanked him for the meal. Mrs. Hill fluttered around them like a hen, fussing about their lack of warm cloaks for the walk back. She pressed a little package into each of their hands that included the rest of the fresh bread. Satisfied that they had eaten enough, and eliciting a promise from each girl to eat better at school, she released them out into the street with Mr. Adler.

The alley was already quite dark, but along Norfolk Road the lamplighter's were out and the street was awash in the red glow of the whale-oil street lamps. It was a pleasant walk as much of the day's traffic had died away. Mr. Adler pointed out several prominent homes to them once they crossed onto the Point, feeding them some tidbits of gossip about each to make them laugh.

Despite their protestations to Mrs. Hill, it had gotten cold out. By the time they had crossed the Silverspan bridge both

220

Miriam and Eleanor had their arms crossed and were shivering. At the gate to Penwick Mr. Adler bid them farewell, and the two retired Wardens gave the slightest nod to acknowledge their return to the school. The girls hustled towards Prescott Hall and their waiting beds.

Miriam reached the door first and unlocked it. She turned away from the door to say something, but Eleanor did not hear it. She was staring instead at a carved backwards E on the doorframe. It was glowing, and for a moment Eleanor simply stared at it fascination. Then the realization of what it was hit her and she grabbed for Miriam, but her roommate was already stepping through the doorway. Eleanor instinctively stepped forward to go after her, and felt the tingling of a Netherdoor ripple through her.

Over the threshold was not their dormitory room, but a small parlor with a red upholstered couch in the middle, and a row of bookshelves along the opposite wall. A fire was going in the fireplace.

Eleanor was taking this in, and Miriam's face was breaking into a confused look, when there was movement from behind the door they had just opened. From the shadows stepped a tall man with an angular face, a scar running down his cheek, and a dangerous look in his eyes. The man from Mrs. Dobbin's basement. It was him. He grabbed Miriam with one gloved hand, and slammed the door shut behind Eleanor with the other.

CHAPTER 13

AN INTERVIEW WITH MR. BULROOD

THE angular man sat them down on the couch. He said nothing, but they both understood that they were not to move. He left via a door opposite the one they had come in through. It clanked shut, but there was no sound of a lock. For several moments they said nothing. Eleanor could feel her heart pumping and her hands shaking. Miriam was quivering, just barely holding back tears.

"Wh-, What just happened?" asked Miriam, her voice breaking.

"We came through a Netherdoor," said Eleanor, looking back at the door they had entered through. There was nothing carved around the trim on this side. She wondered if that meant it only worked one way. And how had someone turned their dormitory door into a Netherdoor?

"A what?" asked Miriam.

"A Netherdoor. Madigan took me though one when he rescued Jack and me from the dwarves. They're magic. You activate the door and it opens into a different place. When we stepped through, it brought us here. Wherever here is," said Eleanor. Miriam was just barely holding herself together. Eleanor pulled her close and Miriam gave in to the sobs.

Despite being very scared, Eleanor realized she did not feel

223

panicked or about to cry. Miriam's reaction had made her realize that someone had to stay calm, and she was the only option. She could feel the panic sneaking around her, but for now she was able to let it pass by without letting it in. She hoped that would last.

There was no question in Eleanor's mind that this had to do with the *Dorian Maroon* and what the Forgotten were looking for, be it either dragon eggs or spice. Whatever it was, it had endangered her friend, and Eleanor felt responsible. It was going to be her job to keep Miriam safe.

It is me they are after, Eleanor knew. It was the information from Simon Tratford's notes that they wanted. Mr. Wellsby had the physical copy of Tratford's journal, but that was missing the relevant page. The only version of the Occlodex was inside Eleanor now, as she had spilled the remainder when she and Jack were escaping from the Forgotten in Mrs. Dobbins' basement. She was the only remaining source for the coordinates. That had to be useful, she thought. They had to keep her alive and willing to talk, for they couldn't just pluck it out of her head. She hoped.

There was no indication from the hallway that anyone was outside the room. The couch they were sitting on was very comfortable and the lamps and knick-knacks scattered about the room all gleamed. There were no windows, so they were in an interior room, and that meant a large house. Eleanor peeled Miriam off of her shoulder and stood up.

"What are you doing?" whispered Miriam.

"Having a look around," said Eleanor, trying to sound confident even though her pulse was racing.

"What if he comes back?" asked Miriam.

"Then I'll sit back down," said Eleanor. Knowing that she had the coordinates gave her some courage. It meant she had some control of the situation.

She checked the door they came in through. Behind it was a closet with nothing but a few pewter candlesticks on a shelf. There was no evidence of the reverse E indicating a Netherdoor. She moved over to the bookcases along the wall. It looked to be history books, some of which she recognized from her classes. It confirmed that this must be a wealthy household. Only someone with a lot of money could afford to buy their own copies of these books. Pacing back and forth in front she turned over what she could, or should, say when the angular man returned.

"You know, this is good," said Eleanor.

"Good? Good? Are you crazy?" said Miriam, almost screaming at her.

"Easy, Miriam," said Eleanor. "It's good because it means that the Forgotten haven't found what they are looking for. They need the information I have. Otherwise there would be no reason to capture me."

"That doesn't sound good," said Miriam, her voice calming down somewhat. "It sounds awful. What information are you supposed to have? What would they do to get the information? Have you thought about that?"

Eleanor was trying to not think about what the angular Forgotten man might do to her. She kept her focus on the fact that she had the coordinates from Tratford, and he did not. Thinking about what the man who captured her might be capable of would just send her into hysterics. She had to stay focused.

She made her way to the door the man had left through. She presumed it was locked, but there had been no sound of a key when he left. She could see that there was no keyhole at all on their side of the door. It looked like a regular interior door, with no lock. Did he leave them in here unlocked this whole time? Could they just walk out? That seemed impossible.

Grabbing the doorknob, she felt that it would not move. It was if it was stuck. There was another sensation, though, a tingling feeling. It was similar to going through a Netherdoor. Was the lock magic? Thinking about this she touched the pocket on her dress and felt her pencil case. An idea came to her, but before she could turn and say something to Miriam there were footsteps from the hallway.

Eleanor stepped back to the couch and sat down next to Miriam, who looked like she was about to cry again. The footsteps stopped outside the door, there was a pause, and then the knob turned. The angular man stepped through first, followed by a second man, shorter and less imposing. The new man looked to be about the age of her father or Uncle William, and was dressed like one of the well-to-do merchants Eleanor had seen about Flosston Moor. He had bright blue eyes that looked devious, and he wore a slick smile on his face.

"Good evening, ladies," he said, his voice smooth and measured. He pulled a chair from the corner, set it in front of them and sat himself down on it. He stayed erect in the chair, very proper. Eleanor's mother would have been proud.

Neither Eleanor nor Miriam said anything. Miriam grabbed Eleanor's hand and squeezed very hard.

"I am sorry about the abrupt way in which you were brought here," he said, pointing at the closet door. "But it was unlikely that you would have responded to a written invitation." He looked back and forth between them. "I admit, I was not expecting two of you. Which one of you is Eleanor?"

She could feel herself getting hot, but Eleanor willed herself to stay calm. "I am," she said, trying to keep her voice from shaking. "You're one of the Forgotten, aren't you?" she asked.

The man got a big smile on his face, and then laughed. It was an ugly laugh, like a cackle. "Oh, my young friend. Such an inappropriate term, as we have not forgotten anything," he said. "My name is Ravillon Bulrood. I am - " he paused, searching for a word, "for the moment, let's just stick with Forgotten. I've been asked by others in our association to take on this task."

"What does this have to do with us?" Eleanor asked, trying to sound as clueless as possible.

"I find it hard to believe a clever girl like yourself hasn't figured that out, Eleanor," said Bulrood.

Eleanor didn't say anything. It was small, but forcing Bulrood to delay himself explaining things gave her some sense of control over her situation.

"Very well," said Bulrood. "Inside of you is some information that I need. In that Occlodex is a journal from one Simon Tratford. I need to know what it says."

Eleanor could see the urgency in his eyes when he said this. He was under some pressure to get the coordinates. Perhaps that would give her some leverage, she thought.

"First you have to let Miriam go," she said, forcing herself to look Bulrood straight in the face. "She has nothing to do with this and she doesn't know anything."

Bulrood gave her an apologetic look. "I'm sorry, Eleanor, but that is not true anymore. She knows this room, and she knows my name. Perhaps she didn't have anything to do with this yesterday, but today she is as immersed in it as you are. I cannot let her go."

"So why would I tell you anything?" asked Eleanor, who found her dislike of Bulrood overcoming her fright. His detested the smug way he sat in the chair.

"Because if you don't, Lucan here is going to take - Miriam, is it? - and do something unpleasant," he said, his voice never wavering from the same indifferent tone.

A blur of motion from just out of her peripheral vision startled Eleanor, and then Lucan was standing behind the couch, a long thin blade held against Miriam's throat. Miriam stiffened and let out a tiny yelp, squeezing Eleanor's hand so hard it felt as if it might crush her fingers.

"You see, Eleanor," said Bulrood. "This is rather important, so I'm willing to take some extraordinary steps to get what I want."

228

Eleanor took a look at the knife glinting in the light at Miriam's throat. It was not only frightening but it made her seethe. Miriam was the sweetest person she had ever met, and the idea of someone hurting her gave Eleanor a surge of courage. She could play this along with Bulrood, and at least give them a chance of getting out of here. "Fine," she said, "You win. I'll give you the information."

"Very good," said Bulrood. "Now take a look at the Occlodex, and tell me what you see on page 183."

Eleanor let the journal slide into her consciousness. She could see it clearly now, her control of the Occlodex precise. She started to read through the notes on page 183, just as she had for Madigan.

She hesitated when she reached the coordinates that Simon Tratford had noted in the bottom corner of the page.

"Take your time," Bulrood said, but his fingers were tapping against his thigh. "Read it out carefully."

Eleanor's mind raced as she sat there. She still had the advantage. If it was nautical coordinates then there would be no way to confirm her story for sure. It might give her some time.

"I-, I think I have it," said Eleanor. "He wrote 4 S 92 45 E."

Bulrood gave a wicked smile. "Thank you, Eleanor. You did the right thing."

I hope he's right, she thought to herself.

Standing up, Bulrood made a motion to the angular man, and Lucan removed the knife from Miriam's neck. "Go tell them we have the information," said Bulrood, and the angular man slid out of the door and disappeared into the hallway.

"Now, girls," said Bulrood, "you'll be my guests for a while longer. I have some charts to attend to downstairs, so I'll be leaving you here to mind yourselves." He swept his arm around the room. "This room is enchanted. No one else in the house can hear you, and the lock will not open except for me. Make yourself comfortable." With that he gave them a small bow and left the room, the door clicking shut behind him.

Miriam gave a little sob, and Eleanor let herself breathe. He had taken the bogus coordinates. And Bulrood had confirmed what Eleanor suspected earlier. The lock on the room was magical.

She let Miriam recover for a moment. Then she took Miriam's face in her hands and looked her in the eye. "I need you to trust me now, Miriam," she said. "I need you to push down the tears, because we are going to have to be very careful and quiet now. Can you do that?"

Miriam nodded, sniffling a little. She took several deep breaths, and that seemed to get her past the worst of it. "What are you doing? What if they come back?"

"I gave them the wrong coordinates, Miriam," said Eleanor.

"You what? What was that all about? What coordinates? This is all about that stupid project, isn't it?" asked Miriam. "They'll kill you. They'll kill me! I just want to go back to my room." The crying almost started again.

"Please don't cry, Miriam," said Eleanor. "Right now they're checking out the coordinates I gave them. They may not be able to tell I lied, but we won't have much time if they can. We have to get out now."

"Get out? How? He said it was enchanted," said Miriam.

"With this," said Eleanor, pulling one of her Silverwood pencils from the case in her pocket. "It can absorb magic, negate it. Madigan told me about it. It's not a myth, it's true."

Miriam just stared at her in disbelief.

"If it doesn't work, we're no worse off than before," said Eleanor. "But if it does work, we'll have to sneak out of the house. We'll need to be very quiet, alright?"

Miriam nodded, and this was probably as composed as she was going to get in this situation. Eleanor went over to the door, holding the pencil in front of her. There was a vague trembling in it as she approached the lock, but she wasn't sure that was the pencil and not her hand. Madigan hadn't told her how the Silverwood worked, or if there was some magic word she had to say. Not knowing what else to do she touched the pencil to the doorknob.

She could feel pins and needles in her hand and forearm. There was a faint sound, similar to ripping paper. And then, nothing. Nothing that Eleanor could tell, at least. She pulled the pencil away from the doorknob and held it up to examine it. The pencil did not look any different, but in Eleanor's hand it felt lighter and less sturdy. She grabbed the pencil in her fist and pushed on the tip. It snapped off. Something about the Silverwood had changed. It was now nothing more than a cheap

231

pencil.

"I think it worked," she breathed, giving Miriam a hopeful look.

Eleanor put her hand on the doorknob gingerly, expecting there to be some kind of shock. Nothing happened. It just felt like a doorknob. She turned her hand on the knob and it rotated as well. Miriam was now up and standing next to Eleanor, both of them staring at the knob in fascination, as if they had never seen one before. Eleanor continued to turn and they could hear the audible click of a latch giving way.

With a faint tug Eleanor was able to open the door inward just a sliver. Nothing happened as far as they could tell. Eleanor peered out the opening, seeing only a well-decorated hallway with red carpet. Across the way were two more doors, and at the end of the hall she could make out a corner of what must be a window. It seemed like that direction was a dead end. To check to other direction she'd have to open the door more and get her head out into the hallway. Taking a deep breath she slid the door open enough to poke the top of her head around the frame. There was another door across the hall, and one just down from theirs on the same side. But beyond that she could see the hand railing at the top of a staircase.

She pulled herself back in the room. "I can see the stairs," she said.

"Could you hear anything?" asked Miriam, who seemed to have gained some confidence from the door opening.

"No," answered Eleanor. "We should go now."

"Do we have a plan?" asked Miriam.

"A plan?" said Eleanor.

"What do we do if we get out?" asked Miriam.

Eleanor hadn't thought about it. Once they were on the street they could find a Warden or someone to help them. But she realized she didn't know where they were in the city, or even if they were in Flosston Moor at all.

"Let's just get out of this house first," said Eleanor, trying to sound decisive so that Miriam wouldn't stall any more. It appeared to work and Miriam just gave a little nod that she was ready.

Eleanor cracked the door open enough to slip her shoulder and leg through. She stopped and listened, but the only thing she could hear was her own breath and the pounding of her heart. She slid the rest of her body out and pressed herself up against the wall. Miriam emerged and followed her lead. Eleanor whispered to her to pull the door shut. Miriam did and the tiny clank of the latch sounded to them like a peal of thunder. There was no noise or response from anywhere else in the house.

Shuffling sideways to stay up against the wall Eleanor made her way down the hall towards the staircase. At the top she crouched down and spent a minute listening. She thought that there was some rustling coming from downstairs, but it was muffled, as if it were in a closed room. She looked over at Miriam, who gave her an uncertain shrug.

This had to be their chance. It was too dangerous to still be here when the angular man returned and Bulrood figured out that she hadn't been truthful. She put a foot down on the top stair, being careful not to put weight on it until she was sure it wouldn't creak. The first step here held without a sound.

Slow step by slow step Eleanor led them down the stairs. As they moved downwards they could see that the staircase descended into a larger main hallway in what looked like the center of the house. Once they were halfway down they were exposed, with an open railing on one side. If someone came into the hallway now they would be seen for sure. Eleanor stopped for a moment and evaluated the hallway. At the bottom of the stairs was a large wooden door, closed. There were two more doors along the side of the hallway, one of them open. Peering over the railing, Eleanor could see a final door located at the back end of the hall, behind them. There was no obvious way out of the house.

She looked at Miriam, who pointed at the door in front of them. Eleanor nodded and was about to take a step when there was the distinct sound of a door opening. There was also a vague tinkling sound. Waving Miriam backwards they stepped back up the stairs into the shadow near the top landing. Eleanor crouched down so that she could see what might be happening downstairs.

Into view came the smug man, Bulrood. In his hand was the source of the tinkling sound, a saucer with a cup of tea on it. He walked through the open door on the right and disappeared into whatever room lay beyond.

"Now what?" whispered Miriam, "He'll see us if we walk by

234

that door."

"Maybe," said Eleanor, her voice barely audible. "We don't know what's in there."

"It's too risky," whispered Miriam.

"Just being here is risky," answered Eleanor. "We have to try. I don't want to just sit in that room until they come back."

Miriam looked torn. Eleanor took her hand and looked her in the eye. "You can do this, Miriam," she said, again gaining some courage just by noting how frightened Miriam was. "We will get out of here."

"You don't know that," breathed Miriam.

"No, but I believe it. Sometimes that's enough," said Eleanor.

Whether it was the right thing to say or not, Eleanor didn't know. But it was enough to get Miriam moving down the stairs. They went slower this time, conscious of every tiny creak or squeak. By the time they reached the bottom stair both of them were damp with sweat.

Eleanor crept across to the edge of the open door and was about to peek around into the room when Miriam put a hand on her shoulder. "Here," Miriam mouthed, and put a tiny mirror in Eleanor's palm. Eleanor forgave her for every time she had ever checked her hair.

Crouching down, Eleanor slid the mirror just an inch into the doorway and angled it up. Experimenting for a few seconds she was able to position it so that she could see the reflection of the room, and Bulrood. He was sitting at a dark brown desk, examining a large paper spread in front of him, probably a map.

He appeared absorbed, and that was good for them. He wasn't facing the door but could easily see it if he looked up.

She figured it was better if they both went at once rather than giving Bulrood a second chance at seeing them. Locking her arm in Miriam's, she put on the most confident face she could. Miriam had beads of sweat across her whole head and Eleanor could feel them dripping down her own face. Doubts started to well up inside of her, telling her all the horrible things that could and would happen. It took her several deep breaths to get them under control, reminding herself that the longer she indulged her fears, the better the chance they would get caught.

In a beat between fear and reason, without anything resembling a conscious decision, her legs were moving and she hunched over. Miriam did the same and they each took two long steps past the open doorway. It was over in a blink of an eye. They were standing next to the large wooden door at the end of the hallway. Neither of them dared breathe. Their ears strained to catch any indication of a response from Bulrood.

Nothing came. Eleanor slid to the large door and tried the handle. It opened. She started to swing the door open, again only an inch so that she could peek through. There was an umbrella stand and a hat rack. The peculiar yellow glow of lamplight from the street lit up the room. It had to be the entry. She felt a rush of adrenaline.

Forgetting to go slow, Eleanor pushed the door farther open to allow her and Miriam through. She could only wince, as there was a fantastic groaning sound from the massive wooden door.

Far more frightening, though, was the screech of a chair sliding across wood from behind them. Bulrood was moving.

"Go, run!" said Eleanor, pushing Miriam forward, stepping through herself, and then slamming the wooden door shut behind them.

Miriam was at the outer door and almost pulled it off its hinges. Whatever reserve she had maintained while they snuck downstairs was lost and she acted like a trapped animal. The door flew open and Miriam bolted down the front steps and into the street.

Eleanor could feel the thud of Bulrood against the wooden door and hear the knob turning. She leapt towards the open front door as Bulrood pushed through into the entryway. She could feel the swipe of his hand against the back of her dress as she took the stone steps after Miriam.

At first she concentrated on running. She followed Miriam, who had headed down the street to the right, passing in and out of pools of lamplight. Eleanor pumped her legs as fast as she could, catching up quickly due to her lankier frame. Behind them they could hear Bulrood shouting.

They took the first corner they came too, turning right down a narrower street. Here Eleanor managed to get a handle on her surroundings. The houses were all tall, three stories at least, and brick. The brass fixtures on the front and the decorative touches about the windows said it was one of the nicer areas of the city. And it was Flosston Moor for sure, because looming up above the roofline of the close-packed houses was the Steward's

Tower, bathed in moonlight.

If nothing else, the Tower gave Eleanor a focus. If they could get near the Tower there would be Wardens and it would be safe. She pulled at Miriam's hand, whose initial surge of energy was starting to drain. "Come on," she yelled.

They had not taken more then three or four more strides when a terrible sound reached their ears. The pounding beat of footsteps, heavy ones. Eleanor and Miriam both glanced back over their shoulders, and could see two dark shapes coming down the street after them. They were full-grown men, and would almost certainly overtake them by the end of the street.

Turning back forward, glancing at the passing houses for signs of someone being awake, Eleanor almost missed what was right in front of them. Standing in the middle of the cobbled street was another dark figure, tall and wrapped in a black cloak. He did not make any move towards them, but was blocking their way, and on the narrow street it would be impossible for both of them to get around him. They were trapped.

With only a few seconds before the pursuers would catch them, Eleanor decided what she must do. "Miriam, do your best to get away," she yelled, and ran straight ahead at the tall man in the black cloak. If she could occupy him, then perhaps Miriam could get free. It was Eleanor they wanted, and perhaps that would give Miriam enough of an opening to escape.

The tall man did not waver as she closed the remaining distance. She ran right for him, and at the last second he twisted and used one arm to push her right past him towards the side

238

of the street. Eleanor stumbled into the stairway leading up to one of the elegant houses. Looking up at him as she fell away, she was surprised to see that he didn't even glance after her.

Miriam had been just a few steps behind, and had cut to the other side of the tall man, who had ignored her as she passed by him down the street. Run! Eleanor thought, willing both herself and Miriam to get away. But Miriam seemed as perplexed by the tall man as she was. Eleanor remained leaning against the stairs, and Miriam stared behind her as the tall man began to move as the two pursuing men came upon him.

It was if someone had just let go of a top. He went from motionless to a blur of activity in a heartbeat. A wooden staff topped with metal caps on both ends and the length of Eleanor's leg appeared from under the cloak. With a wicked crack the staff made contact with the knee of one of the men, who buckled and let out a cry of excruciating pain.

The second pursuer tried to take advantage of the tall man's lack of attention and swung what looked like a long knife at him. The tall man dodged and then flicked his staff across the pursuer's forearm with a crunching sound that turned Eleanor's stomach. A second quick blow from the staff against the pursuer's head dropped him to the cobblestones like a sack of flour.

Neither Eleanor nor Miriam moved. The tall man spun in his black cloak and walked to where Eleanor lay against the stairway. In the dim lamplight she was able to make out his face. It was lean, but not all straight lines and angles like the man from the house, and there was no scar. There was a intense look in his eyes, controlled but clearly alert.

"My apologies. I had to get you out of the way quickly. You aren't hurt, are you?" he said, helping her stand up.

"No," she stammered.

"Good. We haven't much time. More men will be coming, and we need to get you both to someplace safe," he said, taking her arm and walking over to where Miriam stood. "There's a Netherdoor about a block from here that will send us on our way. Let's move."

He hustled Miriam and Eleanor before him, and out of some mix of gratitude and fear they went. Eleanor couldn't help herself, though, and turned back to face him as they veered down a small alley off the street.

"Who are you?" she asked.

"You've forgotten already?" the tall man asked in reply. Then he let his face relax for a moment, his eyes went pale and he hunched over. In that moment Eleanor knew him. It was the drunk from the dwarven prison. Hal.

"I don't believe it," she said.

"That's the point," said Hal, the menacing look returning to his face. "Now move. Just down here on the left."

Eleanor saw the backwards E for the Netherdoor carved into the frame. Hal stepped up to it, pressed his hand over the symbol, and muttered something Eleanor couldn't understand. The symbol glowed and he turned the knob. He pushed them through and slammed the door shut behind them.

CHAPTER 14

THE BOTTOM SHELF

HAL hustled Eleanor and Miriam down the dark alley they had emerged into from the Netherdoor. He did not speak, and with the numerous glances he shot back over his shoulder Eleanor guessed that they were in danger of being followed, so she kept her own mouth shut and ran as fast as she could.

The night was dark and they were in a part of the city without much lamplight. The girls were just able to keep Hal and his dark cloak in their sights as they ran on. He took them across a major road and then down another narrow alleyway littered with trash and what Eleanor thought might have been a man sleeping under a ratty blanket. At the end was a door that Hal stopped in front of. He activated the Netherdoor, and there was a faint silvery glow in the night.

"In we go," said Hal. "A little further and we'll be safe again."

Eleanor was too breathless at this point to question Hal and she stepped through the door. She found herself just off of what had to be a major thoroughfare, maybe even Norfolk Road. The lamplight was thick on the ground and there were one or two people walking up the street.

"Nice and easy, girls," said Hal. "We want to look like we're out for a nighttime stroll."

With heart pounding in complete opposition to the outward demeanor she was trying to maintain, Eleanor walked along the road with Hal and Miriam. Miriam was just holding herself together, and if anyone gave them a close look they would be able to tell something was very wrong. But the others on the street at that hour were not interested in drawing any attention either, and they were able to pass without an incident.

After two blocks Hal ducked them down a side street between a bookshop and a cobbler. The alley was neat and tidy. Numerous doors were set into the surrounding buildings, all appearing to lead upwards to apartments above. Eleanor thought she could hear Hal counting under his breath as the moved along.

Abruptly he stopped in front of a green door. On the frame Eleanor could see the backwards E and heard Hal mutter something again. He motioned them through, and Eleanor wondered if the family inside had any idea that they were using their front door to walk across the city.

On the other side it was darker again, and the buildings on the small street they emerged onto included some of the wildly painted clay ones she remembered from the Warren. Sounds of singing and yelling were coming from a pub that sat at the end of the street. Eleanor could just see the sign - it was called the Yellow Dolphin.

"We'll be staying well clear of that place," said Hal. He took them the opposite direction down the street, and just before it met up with another crossing avenue he cut down a gap between two buildings, barely wide enough to call an alley. There was a wooden stairway here that looked to have seen better days, but Hal leapt up the stairs without seeming to fear falling through. Eleanor and Miriam followed behind and met Hal on the second floor landing.

Taking off his glove, Hal reached out and grabbed the knob of the door that faced them. He held the knob for a moment and then turned it. Inside, the room beyond seemed to match the exterior, and Eleanor was sure it was not a Netherdoor.

They entered after Hal, who shut the door behind them and muttered something under his breath. There was a clicking sound, and Eleanor was reminded of when Bulrood had locked them in. A magical lock.

Inside it was well lit, with a fireplace going in the corner and several lamps burning about the room. The lamps looked similar to the ones the dwarves had carried - solid glowing orbs contained within brass cases. Eleanor was now sure those were magic as well. It was everywhere once you started looking, she thought.

"Where are we?" asked Eleanor.

"In my home," answered a voice coming down a staircase in the corner. Madigan's tall figure emerged into the light. "I see that you have come with Hal, and I fear that this implies something untoward has occurred."

"I found them escaping from Bulrood's townhouse," said Hal, dropping himself into a chair near the fire.

Madigan's eyes narrowed and Eleanor saw him in a different way than she ever had before. He looked fierce and dangerous, someone Eleanor would have feared if she did not know him already.

"Explain what happened, Eleanor," he said.

"Someone put a Netherdoor on our dormitory room," she said. If she thought Madigan had looked dangerous before, now he looked downright deadly. "Miriam and I stepped through without knowing it and we were inside Bulrood's house." After that she explained everything that had happened with Bulrood, how she had given him false coordinates, and then used the Silverwood pencil to dispel the magic in the lock.

"You did some quick thinking, Eleanor," said Madigan, some of his fierce look subsiding. "Escaping was risky, but probably the right choice. It would only have taken Bulrood a short while to realize the coordinates were incorrect. Even if you had given him the correct ones it would have been wise to get out - there is nothing at those coordinates. They're useless."

"What?" sputtered Eleanor. "It pointed to the Cinnamon Islands. There's an island there, one with a black tree that gives a magical spice. That could be what the Forgotten are after."

Madigan gave her a questioning look. "The coordinates are near the Cinnamon Islands, but at least two hundred miles too far south to actually be in the archipelago. I've consulted several cartographers, and looked at the best charts myself. There is nothing there," said Madigan. "Now what is this about a black tree?" The fearsome look on his face had changed now into one of curiosity.

"We found out about the *Dorian Maroon* from Mr. Adler,

my uncle's friend. We were at dinner at his house this evening before we were captured. He said there is a legend about the ship, and how it found a black tree on one of the Cinnamon Islands that produced a valuable spice," explained Eleanor. "It has to be what they are after, doesn't it? The Forgotten want to be rich, not burn down the city."

Madigan reached up to rub the short gray beard on his face. He stood rooted to the spot for a minute before speaking again. Miriam sat down on a low frayed couch opposite Hal, who sat in silence.

"Masalam," said Madigan. "There are ancient references to a spice by that name, I only vaguely remember reading about them. There is some truth to the story. However, it is not what the Forgotten are after. As I told you before, they want those eggs."

"But doesn't the spice make more sense?" Eleanor asked, her mind trying to fight against the fantastic ideas of dragons and magic. It was nothing compared to what must have been going on in Miriam's head. Her face flitted back and forth from shock to confusion, her mouth opening and closing as if she were about to ask a question.

"To some," said Madigan, now settling himself down into a wooden chair next to a low wooden table strewn with maps and papers. "But ask yourself what happened to that ship, the *Dorian Maroon*."

"Mr. Adler said it was nearly destroyed, as if it had been burned," said Eleanor, "Most of the crew died after they found the black spice."

"What do you think burned the ship?" said Madigan, sounding very much like a teacher trying to prod an answer out of student.

It took Eleanor only a moment to realize what he was implying. "The dragon?" she answered. It made some sense. If Tratford had violated its nest, or cave, or whatever it was that dragons had, then it may have been angry enough to try and drive the ship away.

Madigan nodded. Eleanor was still not sure that the Forgotten were after dragon eggs, but Madigan's explanation of what happened to the *Dorian Maroon* did have a logic to it.

Eleanor slumped down with Miriam on the old couch and they all sat in silence for a while. Eleanor's panic and fear were winding down from the night's events. The realization of how close they were to injury, and perhaps worse, started to sink in and she could feel herself trembling slightly. Miriam grabbed her hand.

Madigan stirred and noticed the two girls, as if for the first time. Whatever deeper thoughts about the dangers of the Forgotten that were within him seemed to disappear from his face. He looked only like a concerned old man.

"I have put you in far too much peril, Eleanor. And you, Miriam," said Madigan. "For that I apologize. I never meant for your role to go beyond help with the original code that Hal here recovered for us from Lucan."

At that Eleanor glanced over at Hal. She was able to be-

246

lieve he was the same drunk from the dwarven jail, now that he was sitting relaxed in a chair, except there was no lazy look or unsteady feel to him. His eyes were piercing and alert.

"How did you find us, Hal?" she asked.

A wicked smile appeared on his face. "Bulrood is one of the few Forgotten we know of who moves about openly. I am often in the habit of prowling around near his house. Tonight I saw you both run from the front door and cut you off in the side street. I'm glad I was there."

"Not as happy as we are," said Miriam.

"I do not like the fact that the Forgotten felt comfortable acting inside Penwick, girls," said Madigan. "We will return you to school, but I think it would be best if Hal watches you there. They may make another attempt to find out what is in your head when they find out the coordinates are useless."

"Hal's going to follow us around?" asked Eleanor.

"No," said Hal. "But I'll be there just the same. In case."

The idea that Hal would be prowling about provided some comfort after the nights events. The intrusion in their dormitory was disconcerting. Eleanor could sense that she was not going to feel comfortable going back there again. She would certainly be checking every door for the backwards E before she entered.

"Let's get you back to where you belong, then," said Madigan. "I'll remove the charm on the door. And then I believe I'm going to need to have another talk with your Headmistress to straighten things out."

247

Over the next few days Eleanor had the distinct feeling of being watched, but she only saw Hal if he alerted her to his presence. He did this occasionally, giving her a wink from another table in the Index where he sat shrouded in a robe, or as he exited the dining hall just as she was entering. It made her self-conscious about everything she did, but as the alternative was worrying that Lucan or Bulrood was going to snatch her away, she did not complain.

It was nearing the end of the term now, and a last flurry of research projects were being posed by all their teachers. She and Miriam spent every spare moment in the Index, or wandering about the Library fetching books, going over samples of different plants and bugs, or trying to figure out how use obscure astronomical tools.

The questions surrounding the *Dorian Maroon*, dragon eggs, the black spice, and Simon Tratford's useless coordinates still poked their heads above water now and then in her mind. However, she was busy enough with schoolwork that she pushed them back down when they did. The fact that Tratford's coordinates pointed nowhere was comforting, in that it meant the Forgotten were no closer to discovering where the island was located.

In the meantime, she had made no progress in choosing a Hall to join for the next year. There were interesting elements to all of them, but nothing that Eleanor could see spending the next four years studying. They didn't capture her imagination in any way. She was realizing that perhaps this was part of what Penwick taught you. Every subject will involve grinding through some boredom. There are flashes of intuition and snippets of excitement, but those are only found at the ends of long stretches of bland, hard work. This just served to depress her, and it didn't answer the question of which Hall might lead her to the most flashes and snippets along the way.

All that was pushed aside for the moment, though, as she and Miriam were trying to identify seven plants that possessed fever-reducing properties for their Botany class. They had spent the morning in the Index, and were now up on one of the upper floors of the Solarium. They were continually pulling out thin drawers containing dried examples of their candidate plants to see if they matched the drawings they had found in *Prudent Plants for Practical Apothecaries*.

They had managed to find four of the seven plants and were packing up to move on to search for the fifth.

"Where is the next one?" said Miriam wearily.

Eleanor consulted their list. The next was at 5th Sol 31 5 H, her own shorthand telling her it was on the fifth floor of the Solarium, in row 31, bin 5, shelf H. It looked similar to the other six listings on the page.

How could Tratford have stood rummaging around in all these drawers over and over again, thought Eleanor, as they made their way down a stairway. He must have spent days and days in here, she thought.

At that moment a possibility struck her so hard she almost felt herself wobble on the stairs. He was a Penwick student. He would have had his own shorthand for locating specimens and books. What if Tratford hadn't written down nautical coordinates? She stopped dead on the stairs.

"Eleanor, what are you waiting for? Let's go," said Miriam.

"Just a minute," she answered. Forcing herself to concentrate, she made the Occlodex appear again in her head. She scanned to page 183 again, and there was Tratford's code,

2 S 84 26 E.

"Come on," Eleanor said, grabbing Miriam's wrist. "Let's go." She took off down the stairs.

"Wait, you're going too far," demanded Miriam when Eleanor kept going past the fifth floor. "The Boganweed is on this floor."

"We're not looking for Boganweed, Miriam," said Eleanor, who was running down the stairs now. She could hear Miriam thumping behind her to keep up.

As they descended it was like going back in time. The lowest floors of the Solarium held the oldest specimens and were untouched except by those concerned with the most exotic plants. Like Tratford, she thought. There was dust visible on the racks, and shelves and cobwebs spanning the gaps between them.

Hitting the second floor, Eleanor swung herself into the stacks and started jogging along the rows of specimen racks. They had entered at row 54. They had thirty to go. Miriam was breathing hard behind her, yelling at her to slow down and explain herself, but Eleanor was so certain she was on the right track now that she ignored her.

81. 82. 83. 84. Here it was. Row 84 was nearly at the end of the Solarium, and the wooden racks holding the various

specimens were in bad shape. She could see several bins in which the shelves had collapsed down on those below. She hoped the one she was after was still intact. Not far now. Bin twenty-six should be about half way down. There!

Bin twenty-six was old, but not damaged that Eleanor could tell. She bent down looking for drawer E. It was at the height of her waist. With sweaty palms she grabbed the brass handles on the front and reminded herself to ease the drawer open slowly lest she break something.

In the front of the drawer were several desiccated leaves that had not survived the test of time. They were broken into bits and pieces that if put together would vaguely resemble a real plant. Each had a note next to it explaining its origin. Nothing suspicious, though.

Then at the back, a glint of light caught her eye. At the end of the drawer, set on the burlap lining were what looked like two enormous black seeds. They were each the size of a loaf of bread, just as Tratford had described in his notes. They weren't just black, either. They were the deepest ebony Eleanor had ever seen. The black on their surface was so pure that the light reflecting off of them gave them looked like someone had painted silver along their ridges. The were wrinkled like a peach pit, but the actual material of them between the ridges looked perfectly smooth.

Next to the seeds was a slip of paper newer than the others in the drawer. It said "Black fruit seeds. Unknown species (perhaps Masalam). Cinnamon Islands. S. Tratford. 1623."

251

Whatever Tratford was, he was a Penwick student to the last. He had taken the seeds with him as samples, and then brought them back here to the Solarium to be cataloged and stored. And if Madigan was right, he had probably never known what they really were - dragon eggs.

Miriam was behind her. "What are you looking for? Why are we down here, it's disgusting and dusty. Eleanor, are you listen - " She cut herself short upon seeing the two eggs. "What are those?"

Eleanor looked back at Miriam, "These are eggs that a man named Simon Tratford must have brought back with him from the Cinnamon Islands. These are what that secret project has been all about, Miriam. That Occlodex I drank had coordinates in it. It wasn't about how to find them in the Cinnamon Islands, it was a note from Tratford to himself about where he stored them in the Library. It was never nautical coordinates. The *Dorian Maroon* wasn't cursed. Tratford unwittingly stole those eggs and the dragon came after them on the ship. That's why it was burned."

She reached into the drawer and picked up one of the eggs. It was warm to the touch even though the Solarium itself was cool. The surface formed a undulating mirror and Eleanor could see a distorted version of herself reflected back.

"What are you going to do with them?" asked Miriam, peering over Eleanor's shoulder. "Isn't everyone looking for them?"

"I'll take them back to Madigan. He'll know what to do with them," she said. She slipped them both into her satchel.

252

They both sprinted back to the staircase and up the stairs to where the Solarium joined the rest of the library on the fourth floor. They sped past several confused students, and earned themselves a series of shushes from those they disturbed. Out of breath they burst out of the doors of the Entry Hall and onto the grounds of Penwick.

At this point Eleanor wished she could just whistle or signal to Hal somehow. She actually spun around in a circle, wondering if she could spot him. He could be anywhere and she wouldn't know it. She wondered if she screamed if he would come running. She considered it seriously for a moment before realizing it would just scare the students around her.

Farragut, she thought. I'll send the message myself. She dashed off towards Morgan Hall, hoping he was not in class at this time, but she turned out to not be so lucky. The first year students were in with him learning something about some agreements that ended some war or other.

Frustrated, Eleanor spun on her heels and wondered what to do. A note, she thought. I need to write the note to Madigan. She sat down right on the floor of the hallway outside Farragut's classroom and pulled out a piece of paper from her satchel. Miriam looked around furtively and then plunked down next to her. It didn't take long to write out that she had found the eggs, and then she had to wait.

She didn't move from the floor because she didn't want to risk walking away and having Mr. Farragut disappear for the day. So she and Miriam sat cross-legged outside his classroom, elbows on knees and chins in hands, counting the seconds until he finished his class.

After an eternity the door swung open and a series of perplexed first years picked their way around Eleanor and Miriam. They stood and brushed themselves off before fighting through the exodus of students to get into Mr. Farragut's room.

"Mr. Farragut, I was hoping I could ask you to send another note for me," she said, waving her letter about.

He looked up from his lectern with the same skeptical expression that Eleanor had now taken to be his natural state of being. "I was under the impression this whole thing had been put to bed," he said.

"But I've made a discovery, sir. Something that Mr. Madigan needs to know about. I found them, sir. I found the eggs," she said. Immediately she was unsure of whether she should have done so or not. Farragut's eyebrows arched up. She had no idea how much he knew about what she had found in the Occlodex, or the story behind the *Dorian Maroon*. Did Madigan keep him up to date? It was too late now to take it back, whatever the case.

"I see," said Mr. Farragut. "Well then, I suppose I can send your message." He went to the door of his office and went inside. Eleanor and Miriam followed.

"Thank you, sir," said Eleanor. "I appreciate it."

"You might consider putting this kind of focus into your *real* school work, you know," he said as he fumbled in the bottom drawer for the pebbled cup.

"I will, sir," she said. "I do, I mean."

Farragut just gave her a blank look, and took the note from her hand. Holding it over a candle on his desk it caught fire and he dropped it in the Smokespeaker. "Will that be all, Eleanor?" he asked.

"Yes, sir," she said. "Thank you." She and Miriam backed out of the office.

When they were out of his classroom, Miriam turned to Eleanor. "Now what do we do with them?" she asked. "You can't just carry them around in your satchel."

"Why not?" Eleanor responded. She had been turning this over in her mind when they were waiting for Farragut. The eggs had remained hidden for over one hundred years right here in Penwick. They could last a few hours in her satchel, couldn't they? No one knew she had found them except Farragut, and now Madigan, she hoped. She did wish Hal would make himself known. She'd feel better if he took the eggs for safekeeping.

They decided to head to the dining hall, feeling somehow safer in public than going back to the privacy of their dormitory. There were already a number of students here studying before dinner began, and the noise of people around them helped calm their nerves.

Dinner hour came without any change. No sighting of Hal or word from Madigan. They joined in the line collecting trays of warm chicken and the last of that winter's canned beans. Their table filled up with the other girls from the second year, and Eleanor and Miriam tried their best to take part in the regular

255

conversation. Eleanor kept fumbling around in her bag with the eggs, feeling them clink against each other. She ran her fingers around the ridges as if she were trying to memorize their feel.

As they were finishing eating there was a clatter at the door to the dining hall and three men came bursting in. For a moment Eleanor thought it was Madigan, but realized then that the man in front was far too old looking and frail to be the wizard. It took her a moment to recognize the pale face that belonged to Mr. Wellsby. Behind him walked two stern men wearing the red cloaks of Wardens. But these were not like the old men passing time outside the gates of Penwick. These men had a look similar to Hal when they saw him in the alley, a dangerous look.

Wellsby led the Wardens around the tables as the dining hall went dead silent. Every student followed their progress. Eleanor felt her heart sink. Wellsby had made her uncomfortable the first time she met him, and having him here gave her a dark feeling.

Pausing only to scan the crowd Wellsby made his way inexorably towards the second year table, towards her. She didn't know whether she should stand up or say something. Her legs felt like jelly, though, and her mouth had gone totally dry so she did neither. Wellsby and his henchmen were upon them.

"Miss Wigton," he said, his voice biting the air.

"Yes, sir, Mr. Wellsby," she replied in a whisper.

"Do you have them with you?" he hissed.

It was too obvious from his tone that he knew what she had found. How, Eleanor was not sure, but he knew. It was going to be no good trying to lie like she had to Bulrood.

"I do," she said.

"Bring them with you and follow me," he said.

Eleanor tried to lift herself up, but her legs were refusing to cooperate.

"Now," said Wellsby, clipping off the word.

"Yes - yes, sir," she said, and made another effort. This time she convinced her legs to help her and was able to stand up from the table. The dining hall remained silent, but Eleanor could feel every eyeball in the place turned towards her.

Wellsby turned and she followed, the Wardens falling in behind her. Did they think she was some kind of dangerous criminal? That she would run? And where was Hal? Wasn't he supposed to be there to avoid this kind of situation? What about Madigan? What if he wasn't checking for a message? How long would it take the note to reach him? Would he come?

Neither Hal nor Madigan showed their face as Wellsby marched her to Morgan Hall and into the same lounge room where she had sat with Madigan after he rescued her from the dwarves. The Headmistress and Mr. Farragut were already in the room, talking in hushed voices in front of the fireplace. Wellsby pulled out a chair at the table and waited until she took it. Then he stepped around the other side of the table, but did not sit himself.

"Put them on the table, young lady," said Wellsby, his voice high and clipped.

Eleanor did as she was told, pulling the seeds from her satchel and depositing them on the table in front of her. The sweat from her palms had left little condensation marks on the brilliant black surfaces. They looked innocuous lying there on the wide wooden table.

"All of them," said Wellsby.

She was confused. That was both of them. There were two in the drawer when she had opened it, she was sure. "Those - those are the two I found, sir," she said.

"Now is not the time to be false, Eleanor," said the Head-mistress in a quiet but frightful tone, approaching the table. "This is a far more serious business than you realize and we will have no games. Where is the third egg?"

Eleanor's head was spinning. Third? She was sure there were two. But the figures of Wellsby and the Headmistress looming over her at the table were enough to make her doubt herself. She felt back in the satchel where she had put the eggs to see if was one she was missing. "I swear, ma'am, I found only two."

"Search her," said Wellsby, and the two Wardens approached her from both sides. One pulled out the chair and took her by the shoulder to pull her up. She didn't think he was being deliberately harsh, but his grip was powerful and the fingers dug into her shoulder.

The other had taken her satchel and emptied it out upon the table. Papers, books, and the various flotsam and jetsam of her bag came floating out. Wellsby poked through it. "Pockets," he said.

The Warden holding her took his free hand and patted down the sides of her dress. He pulled out the pencil case with the one

258

remaining Silverwood pencil in it. He had switched his hands around to feel her other side when there was a loud crack from the door behind her.

"Let go of her," said Madigan as he stepped into the room. His voice bristled and he had the same terrible look of power upon him that she had glimpsed the night Hal had rescued her and Miriam. She could feel the Wardens grip weaken, but he did not release her.

"I said to unhand her, and I will not say it again," said Madigan, taking several further steps into the room. Eleanor could feel what a wave of heat, like that from a white-hot fire, wash over her from Madigan's direction. The Wardens hand let go.

"He's nothing more than an old man, you buffoon," Wellsby spat, but the Warden did not appear to share the observation. He did not put his hand back on Eleanor.

"This interview is over, Wellsby," said Madigan, his voice quiet but clear. "The girl does not concern you."

"Everything in Flosston Moor concerns me, Madigan," Wellsby replied, his eyes narrowing with anger. "I've had enough of this little game. Tell me where the third egg is."

Madigan glanced at Eleanor, ignoring Wellsby. "Are you alright?" he asked.

"I am," she said, but she was not quite sure she felt it.

"Why are you so certain there is an egg missing," asked Madigan, turning his attention back to Wellsby. "If she says there were two, there were two."

"You're not the only one with eyes and ears around the city, Madigan. I know there were three eggs hidden when Tratford returned on that cursed ship. I'll not have them loose in this city where your kind can find them," said Wellsby. He said 'your kind' with a venom that Eleanor found disturbing.

"Then I suggest you have a grand scavenger hunt for it, Wellsby. There are only two here," said Madigan. "And it would be wise if you left those with me. I don't know that you appreciate what they are capable of."

Wellsby's eyes shrunk even further, as if he meant to burn a hole in Madigan's chest with them. "I am not some ignorant school girl. They will stay with me. And in case you are thinking of arguing that point further," he said, "I have several reasons that you should reconsider." He gave a sharp whistle and there were sounds from the hallway outside. Six more Wardens, all looking as fierce as the first two, entered the room.

Madigan looked about him, and while the resolve in his eyes did not dwindle there was a subtle shift in his posture that let Eleanor know he had conceded. Wellsby saw it as well. "Very well then," said Wellsby, "I believe we are done here." He scooped up the two eggs on the table and tucked them into deep pockets inside his cloak.

He stepped around the table and stopped in front of Eleanor. "I hope for your sake that you are not lying to me, Eleanor Wigton. I can be a most unpleasant man to disappoint."

"Take what you will, Wellsby, but if you come near her again I will find you when you are not so conveniently surrounded by those braver than yourself," said Madigan, sweeping his hand around at the Wardens.

Wellsby's face grimaced and he strode from the room, his Wardens trailing after him. As the door shut Eleanor collapsed into her chair, and it felt as if her whole body was shivering.

Madigan was at her side. "Eleanor, I'm sorry for that," he said. He turned to the Headmistress and Farragut. "It should never have come to this," he said to them, his voice betraying a quiver of anger.

"You couldn't expect us to let you persist with this dangerous project of yours, could you, Lewis?" said the Headmistress. "It is not us that led Ms. Wigton into the Warren, or got her kidnapped along with another student. That is on you, Lewis, on you."

The white heat of Madigan's anger had dissipated as he knelt next to Eleanor's chair. "I have my own sins to atone for, Olivia, of that there is no doubt. But to turn over those eggs to Wellsby? Do you understand what they are, what they represent?"

"I understand enough, Lewis," said the Headmistress. "They are too dangerous for any wizard to possess. Even you."

Madigan gave a low sigh. "Let us hope you chose wisely by calling in Wellsby. I for one do not trust him to do the right thing."

"No, you trust no one to do the right thing except yourself, Lewis. It is your greatest failing," said the Headmistress as she moved towards the door, Farragut trailing behind her.

Eleanor was alone with Madigan in the lounge. He pulled

261

himself up onto a chair next to her.

"I'm so sorry sir," she said. "I didn't realize that Mr. Farragut would tell the Headmistress. I didn't know how else to contact you. I didn't know how to find Hal - "

He cut her off. "You've done nothing wrong, Eleanor. It must have been inspired thinking that led you to the eggs in the first place. Do not blame yourself for anything. Once again you've shown yourself to have remarkable instincts." He gave her a smile and look of pride. "So, how did you find them?"

"Tratford was a Penwick student," Eleanor replied. "While Miriam and I were looking for some samples I realized that his codes referred to the Library, not to a map."

Madigan gave a brief chuckle, "Brilliant."

"What did Wellsby mean about the third egg? Are there three? How did he know that?" she asked, the questions tumbling out of her.

Madigan considered her for a moment before answering. "I do not know why Wellsby is so sure there is a third egg, but while I do not trust the man I do trust his information. Tratford mentioned three. Perhaps he found some other scrap of information to confirm that Tratford brought all three back with him. But if he believes there were three, then there were three. At least Wellsby is no friend of the Forgotten, so for now those two eggs are safe."

"Do you think the Forgotten have the third one?" she asked, fearing what the answer might be.

"Perhaps, perhaps," said Madigan. "But something tells me

we'd know if they did already. No, there is some other mystery surrounding that missing egg." He pushed himself up from the chair and held out his hand to help Eleanor up. "Now, young lady, it is time for you to return to your life as a student here at Penwick. I have put you in harm's way, and I do not think Charles would approve."

The mention of her grandfather sent a quick flutter through her heart. "I promise to get back to my regular studies," she said. "More importantly, I need to figure out who I'm going to choose as an Examiner and what Hall I'll join. I have no idea what to do."

Madigan gave her mischievous smile. "I'm sure you'll think of something," he said, and led her from the room.

CHAPTER 15

_____

A NEW OLD HALL

THE days after went by quickly as Eleanor tried to finish up her last papers and prepare for exams. Sometimes whispers of Simon Tratford or the dragon eggs would drift through her mind, but they did not drill into her consciousness with the same urgency as before.

More distressing was the imperative to select an Examiner and a Hall to join for the next year. Miriam had officially joined the Numerancy Hall. The rest of her second year class had all made their selections. There were only three days to go before the end of the term and she still had no idea of what to do. She wasn't even sure what would happen if she didn't submit a Hall to the Headmistress. Could she even come back?

She was studying with a group of girls in an empty classroom when the problem kept intruding on her concentration. She excused herself to get some air. They had been studying for their Geometry exam for six hours, and no one begrudged her a moment to slip outside. The air was warm again, and the pleasant weather made being trapped inside studying doubly painful.

Walking around the grounds she could see all the Halls, and for the umpteenth time she ticked off each Hall in order. Apothecaries - too many bugs and plants. Barristers - too many arguments. Numerancy - too dull. Navigation - too many wild boys. History - too much of the Headmistress, who Eleanor was quite sure did not appreciate all the trouble that she had caused. It wasn't that there weren't interesting things to study in each, but none of the teachers in any of the Halls seemed like someone she wanted to work with for four years. None of them were like Madigan, to be honest. He had never treated her as a student, more as a partner. She liked that feeling.

Rounding back to Morgan Hall she was no further than she had been before. It was the same conversation she had had with herself a few times a day for the last two weeks. Nothing new resolved itself.

As she approached the door it opened in front of her. A man dressed in plain brown robes, probably a visiting scholar, came out and held the door for her. She thanked him and was about to enter when he gave her a wink.

"Hal?" she said.

"In the flesh," he said, dropping his hood to reveal his face.

"I haven't seen you at all for a while," she said.

"Which means that I have done my job well," he replied, smiling. "It has been quiet and Madigan feels it is safe to leave off with guarding you day and night. The Forgotten will be far more interested in Wellsby than in you at this point."

She hadn't thought much about the Forgotten for a while, but the idea that they had their eyes pointed elsewhere was comforting.

"And I apologize," said Hal, "for the business with Wellsby.

I saw him coming, but taking on eight of Wellsby's Wardens myself was folly. I warned Madigan, hopefully in time."

"You did," she said, "No apology necessary."

"Then I will wish you farewell, Eleanor. I'm not sure we'll meet again. If so, I hope it's in better circumstances that in an alley outside Bulrood's house," he said, a wicked grin catching his face. It was hard to imagine him at this point as anything like the drunk he was masquerading as in the dwarven jail.

"Me too," she replied. Hal started to move off, but Eleanor caught him as an idea surfaced in her head. "Hal, how did you end up working with Madigan?"

"Long story," he said, scratching at his brown hair. "I sort of found him. He was willing to teach me things that others would not. I was having trouble focusing, so to speak, on my regular lessons."

"Regular lessons?" she asked, surprised. "You weren't at Penwick, were you?"

Hal laughed. "Hardly," he said. "I was in a different kind of school, but a demanding one just the same. I enjoyed many parts of it, but no single part thrilled me. That's when I went searching and found Madigan. He agreed to take me on."

"So are you a wizard?" she asked, her mind now spinning.

Hal's laugh was even louder and several students walking nearby looked over. "Not at all, Eleanor. I have different talents than that. But Madigan was willing to show me all the magic that already exists around Flosston Moor and how to use it. The Netherdoors and other things."

"Interesting," she said, the idea that had surfaced now crystallizing in her head.

"Anything else I can do for you?" asked Hal.

"No, thank you," she said, smiling at him. "You've been a great help."

Hal gave her a short bow and strolled off in his brown robes towards the main gates. Eleanor turned back and entered Morgan Hall to return to her study group, but her mind was turning over all the implications of her new plan.

The next day Eleanor got up early and headed out of the dormitory, stopped for a quick bite of oatmeal in the dining hall and then made for the main gate. The Wardens there, looking very shoddy next to the ones Wellsby had brought with him, had just opened the gate for the morning and she slipped out.

It took only a few minutes for her to make it to the butcher shop. She could see Jack through the window, yawning and unwrapping a leg of something on the counter in front of him. She knocked on the window and he looked up. He was surprised but came over to open the door.

"Hello, Jack," said Eleanor.

"Well, hello to you too," he said with a sleepy voice. His hair was still messy from bed, and he started patting it down.

"I'm wondering if I could ask you for another favor," she said, smiling.

"Oh no," he said, a look of concern on his face. "Not again. I've had enough dwarves for one lifetime...Although the soup

268

was pretty good."

"Nothing like that," she said. "But it is a delivery job. I'm not sure you're familiar with those."

He gave her an indolent smile. "Very funny," he said. "What now? More books you can drink? Or is it pencils you can eat, now? Is it a great girly secret that I can't know about?"

Eleanor had armed herself to ignore his ribbing when she walked down this morning. "Nothing untoward, I promise. I have a note for someone. He lives just about a block from the Yellow Dolphin. Do you know it?"

"I do," Jack replied. "Dad even sells them a ham now and then. It's in the Warren, not far from some regular deliveries."

She explained how to find Madigan's residence from what she remembered the night Hal had taken them there from Bulrood's. It wouldn't be hard to find, she thought.

"You just have to leave the note at the door. That's it," she said.

"And I'm going to do this because?" he asked, leaving the question hanging.

"Because I went into the Warren, and you know I can and will. But I don't need to get in any trouble with my Headmistress at Penwick, and you're actually a nice fellow even though you insist on needling people," she said, some of the words pouring out faster than she might have wanted.

He gave her a smile. "Fair enough. Although I wouldn't say I was needling you. More of a prod," he said, laughing.

"Thanks, Jack," Eleanor said.

269

"Sure," he replied, "I'm at your service, lady gargoyle."

Two days later Eleanor had finished her final exam and was now pacing the hallway outside the Headmistresses office. Her uncle would be there in the morning to pick her up and take her home for the summer. Before then she still had to put herself down with an Examiner and Hall. She was pacing to stall. She didn't know what to do, and her time was running out. She kept glancing at the doors at the end of Morgan Hall, but they did not open.

The carved wooden one to the Headmistresses office did, though. Mrs. Puddlemump stuck her head out around the opening and spied Eleanor. "Ah, dearie, are you about ready? I know we said three o'clock but you can step in now. She's free."

Eleanor's heart jumped. "No, no, Mrs. Puddlemump. Thank you. I need a few more minutes to sort some things out."

"Tough decision, dearie, isn't it?" asked Mrs. Puddlemump.

"Yes," said Eleanor, glancing back at the entry doors, wishing they would open.

"You'll make the right choice, I'm sure of it. Take your time," said the plump little woman, and shut the Headmistresses door as she ducked back into the room.

Eleanor continued to pace. She was rattling back and forth between hoping that her idea of a few days ago would work out, and wishing that it didn't, so she wouldn't have to explain herself to everyone. I could always just put down Numerancy, she thought. I'm good at it. Uncle William is a fine man, and I could see doing his job some day. Maybe I could go work with him after I complete the studies. That would be the right thing to do, she thought. Her hand actually reached out for the door of the Headmistresses office when a creaking sound from the end of the hall startled her.

"Am I late?" said Madigan, coming up the stone steps towards her. Catching sight of Eleanor he looked concerned, "You seem a bit perturbed. Are you sure about this? I take no offense if you decide to change your mind."

Now that Madigan was here she was sure about her plan. It would be all right so long as he was there to help her. She could handle all the questions that would come.

"No, no," she said. "I'm just nervous about talking to the Headmistress about it."

"Oh, don't be so worried about that, Eleanor," Madigan said. "She's not as fearsome as you think she is. But she does have to be given a little nudge now and then or she gets a little stuck in her ways."

"This is going to be more like a decent shove," said Eleanor.

Madigan considered that for a moment and smiled. "It will indeed. I hope that will give us some leeway in the future."

"Alright, it's three o'clock," said Eleanor as the bells rang outside. "Time to go in."

"After you," said Madigan, who pulled open one of the massive wooden doors.

Mrs. Puddlemump greeted them, and gave Madigan a strange look but did not say anything. She showed them through the anteroom to the Headmistresses door and announced Eleanor.

"Come in, Eleanor," said the Headmistress.

There was a displeased look in the Headmistresses face when Madigan came through the door after Eleanor. She laid her pen down with a sharp thwack on her desk. "Eleanor, I thought you were coming to discuss your choice of an Examiner and Hall."

Eleanor swallowed hard. It was now or never. "I am, Headmistress. I've decided to have Mr. Madigan be my Examiner. I'd like to join the Magistry Hall."

If a pig had flown through the window at that moment Eleanor is not sure the Headmistress would have looked more surprised. She stared at both Eleanor and Madigan for a while, her mouth open, eyes wide. "Eleanor," she mustered, "you realize that the Magistry Hall has been closed - with good reason - for nearly two hundred years."

"I do," said Eleanor, now marshaling the arguments she had been rehearsing in her head for the last few days. "But the Hall still exists. I've looked in the Library, ma'am. The Magistry Hall has been empty for two hundred years because no students would take on Examiners from the Hall, but there is no rule against doing so now."

"We have no Examiners. There is no one to supervise your studies," the Headmistress said, but her eyes said she knew what was coming.

"About that, Olivia," said Madigan, who was clearly enjoying this moment. "I believe that my credentials are old, but still valid."

"You expect me to admit to the faculty a known member of the White Tower? A wizard such as yourself?" asked the Headmistress.

"There is nothing in the Penwick laws that would let you deny me a place, Olivia," said Madigan, his eyes sparkling as the Headmistresses burned. "The faculty of the various Halls determine who is eligible to teach. As I am the only member of the White Tower here at Penwick, I officially declare myself fit."

"This is preposterous, Eleanor," said the Headmistress, changing targets. "This is a lark. It is not how a serious student would spend their time."

"Serious students did spend their time this way for six hundred years, Headmistress. I have a long history before me of Magistry students," Eleanor replied. "It was a honored Hall for much of Penwick's history."

"Do your parents know about this?" asked the Headmistress.

Eleanor had thought of them as she worked on this idea. They already cared so little for her choice of Penwick that they couldn't think less of it. There was nothing to worry about there for her. "No, nor do they have a say in my Hall," she said. It wasn't entirely true, they could always refuse to let her return. However, they had never known how to deal with her, and Eleanor figured they were relieved to have a school that did.

The Headmistress opened her mouth to say something, closed it, and then opened it again before slumping back in her chair. She eyed both Madigan and Eleanor with a look of disappointment. "You'll be the death of me, you two," she said.

"Oh, don't worry, Olivia, we will make sure to do those kinds of experiments far away from your office," Madigan replied. Eleanor tried no to snicker out loud.

"Is this honestly your choice, Eleanor?" asked the Head-mistress.

"It is," she replied. "It's the one thing that excites me, ma'am."

"And are you committing to this, Lewis? No wild crusades drawing you away for years at a time?" she asked Madigan.

"My place is here, Olivia, for many reasons," he replied.

"Then you two can have each other," she said. "I can't promise anything about your accommodations. The Magistry Hall has been abandoned for years."

"I believe I can make it habitable over the summer," said Madigan. "We won't need much space to begin with."

"Fine then, off you go," the Headmistress said, waving them away. "Until next fall, Eleanor."

"Thank you ma'am," said Eleanor, her face split into a wide smile. She gave Madigan a hug. "Thank you for coming," she said to him as they left the Headmistresses office.

"It was an easy decision, Eleanor," Madigan said. "And now, to get you started I have brought along a reading list for you this summer." He pulled a sheet of parchment out from inside his cloak and handed it over. There were close to thirty books listed.

Eleanor's face must have fallen a little.

"This will not be an easy course of studies, Eleanor," said

Madigan. "I'm excited that you've chosen to have me, but I will not let that cloud my role as your Examiner. You will work."

She recovered as she read through the titles. *Barrow's History of the White Tower*, *The Veil of Illusion*, *Practical Potions*, and others. They sounded exciting, but daunting, and she couldn't wait to get started.

"I don't believe you'll have any trouble getting them from the Library," said Madigan. "I doubt anyone has read them in over a century."

"Thank you," said Eleanor, feeling like a giant weight had been lifted from her now that Madigan had agreed to be her Examiner.

"Of course," Madigan replied. "I'm honored that you thought of me. Now it's time for you to get those books and get packing. Your uncle must be arriving in the morning." He gave her a wink as she turned.

She felt light as a feather as she scurried off towards the Library to gather her reading, excited to start a new chapter in her studies.

30055463R00177

Made in the USA
Middletown, DE
12 March 2016